THE BLUFF

J.L. HYDE

Also by J.L. Hyde

Underground

Delta County

Summer of '99

Midnight in Delta County

Magnolia Court

The Grady Lake Series:

Grady Lake

Secrets of Grady

Ghosts of Grady

First paperback edition January 2025

Cover Design by Allsweet Studios and Brandon Kobs

ISBN 979-8-9871631-5-3 (Paperback)

www.jlhyde.com

 Created with Vellum

For the JAK — I don't know what I'd do without you.

Preface

*Author's Note:

Although Delta County is a real (and beautiful) place in the Upper Peninsula of Michigan, all other places and businesses mentioned in this book are fictional. Any similarities to actual locations are purely coincidental.

"The world is a dangerous place to live, not because of the people who are evil, but because of the people who don't do anything about it."

—Albert Einstein

Prologue

Everyone has guilty pleasures, and Mandy Cramer is no exception. Although her list is long, most of the pleasures are harmless. Fantasizing about killing her husband is near the top of the list, but she wouldn't dare admit that out loud.

She mostly enjoys mindless activities that allow her to disassociate, if only for a few minutes, and travel to a world much easier than her own. Whether it's catching a few episodes of *Vanderpump Rules* or scrolling through online real estate listings for houses she could never afford, she forgets about the unfortunate choices that landed her in the middle of a life that requires escaping.

On this Tuesday evening under a clear, starlit sky, she's indulging in her favorite guilty pleasure—taking her sweet little Murphy for a nighttime walk after a long shift at work and peering into the windows of total strangers. It's a small town, so technically they aren't all strangers, but they may as well be from where she's standing.

Tonight, she's walking the streets of the tiny harbor town she's called home for her entire thirty-six years. This county where she lives boasts more miles of fresh shoreline than any other in the United States, yet most of the residents rarely get to enjoy it.

Those who clock in to blue-collar jobs fifty to sixty hours a week and then come home to pray for more dollars in their accounts and hours in the day aren't the ones you'll find enjoying a leisurely afternoon at the local beach. Shops selling eight-dollar hand-scooped ice cream cones and overpriced boat shoes don't cater to the folks who were raised a few blocks off Main Street, that's for damn sure.

Every minute of Mandy's life is consumed with trying to keep up. Mop the floors. Catch up on laundry. Unload the dishwasher. Wipe down the counters. Take the dog to the vet. Make her husband's lunch. Make her husband's doctor's appointments. Remind her husband to renew his tags. Pay the bills. Hope there's enough money for next month's. Walk on eggshells because her husband had a bad day at work. Send out Christmas cards. Flinch when she receives the after-Christmas credit card bills. The thought of packing up a cooler and a good book and heading to the sand beach a mile from her house is laughable. *Who has the time?*

These nighttime walks have become her saving grace. Two to three times a week, Patrick texts her to say he's staying late at the mill to get extra hours, and her heart soars. She's free. She puts a tiny, fitted harness around Murphy's sweet little pug body and slips into her most comfortable shoes. For the next hour, maybe two, she can walk and dream and wander, and there's nobody to stop her.

Tonight, remnants from the Labor Day celebrations surround her: red, white, and blue confetti matted to the damp concrete curbs, bunting flags mounted under the railings of wraparound porches, and garbage bins pulled to the street, overflowing with empty charcoal bags and spent firework shells.

She exhales when she turns a corner and the first of her *usual suspects* comes into view. It's a blue Victorian on the corner of Second and Oak Hollow Street that was built in 1910 and has been in the same family for four generations. Although it's a full two blocks from the beach, Mandy is certain the third story must have an unobstructed view of Lake Michigan, as the top floor towers over all other homes between it and the waterfront.

It's after 9:00 p.m., so she knows she's too late to catch them at the dinner table, but she might luck out and get a clear view of whichever TV program they are watching in the family room. That's where they are most nights when Mandy walks by. She rounds the corner and squints her eyes to focus on the large flatscreen TV that illuminates the oversized den with expansive windows and blinds that are never closed. She sees the owners sitting on opposite ends of the couch and their two children on pillows on the floor in front of them. If it weren't for the Kevin Hart movie playing on the screen, it could be a scene from an old-fashioned Norman Rockwell painting.

There isn't enough action to keep Mandy's attention at 201 Oak Hollow, so she tugs gently on Murphy's leash and keeps walking. At sixteen pounds, he's no guard dog, but that would be news to him. His top priority is Mandy's safety, snarling each time they pass an unknown man on their walks. He's lukewarm to Patrick each night when he arrives home from work. She doesn't suppose she's ever seen a dog who isn't ecstatic about greeting his owner and surmises that it's possible Murphy has overheard Patrick's repeated complaints that they didn't adopt the rottweiler he so badly wanted. Mandy is a lover of all dogs but is also a realist about the time and dedication required to have such a large breed, which would be nearly impossible with the hours they work. Murphy the pug is adorable, self-sufficient, and low maintenance. He is the perfect choice for two overworked thirty-somethings, and their elderly neighbor, Georgia, is willing and able to let him out and give him extra attention if Mandy or Patrick get stuck at work too long. Mandy recoils at the thought of an oversized rottweiler greeting sweet, frail Georgia at the door.

Midway between First and Second Streets, Mandy slows at the sight of an illuminated kitchen through the window of a tan-colored craftsman. An older couple is seated at a round dinner table, leaned over a stack of papers while the husband gently rubs the wife's back. He kisses her head and then stands to retrieve a kettle from the stove a few feet away. He tops off both of their mugs, presumably of tea, and pours the rest of the water down the kitchen sink. Mandy doesn't know the couple but remembers the house because they have the most beautiful hanging flower pots on their porch each year. She doesn't know enough about flowers to identify what they are, but the overflowing stems of pink, white, and purple catch her attention each summer morning when she drives by. Oak Hollow Street isn't the quickest route to get to the gas station she manages, but it sure is the most beautiful. Unless she's running late, she always takes Oak Hollow to Lakeside to Sampson, where the vast blue water slowly disappears, and the scenic view is replaced with strip malls, auto repair shops, and payday loan buildings. That's when she knows she's been safely put in her place. This town is filled with beautiful shorelines, vast blue waters, and thick, lush woods, but those views aren't meant for her. Living in a place where others come to vacation is a complicated bag of emotions, overflowing with thoughts of resentment, exhaustion, and annoyance.

She stays a beat longer, watching the elderly couple, and sighs. Even from fifty yards away, she can feel the love between the two. The man can't take his eyes off his beloved wife while she reads whatever is sitting on the table. With one hand, he tilts her chin upward and smiles, leaning forward once more to kiss her forehead. Mandy yearns for a love like that. She can't remember the last time she caught Patrick staring at her. Maybe the summer after their senior year, when she spent ten hours' worth of wages on a black Calvin Klein swimsuit from the mall in Green Bay . . . Pat couldn't keep his hands or his eyes off her while they swam in his uncle's above-ground pool. Nearly twenty years have passed, and that's the last time she can remember her husband acting lovestruck and foolish. These days, he's just angry and tired.

As if the universe is listening to her longing, Mandy spots movement through the nearly sheer curtains of the split-level house on the corner, a few doors down from the craftsman she's standing in front of. She takes a few quiet steps toward the home, slowly making out the shapes of two people in the back bedroom. They are locked in a passionate embrace, arms desperately searching each other's bodies like an actual hunger that is manifesting in front of her eyes. She glances down at Murphy, who is oblivious to the peep show.

Mandy feels like a voyeur as she silently takes a few more steps, the toes of her shoes now on the edge of the lush green lawn in front of the home. She can't take her eyes off the display, cupping a hand over her mouth to muffle the gasp as she watches the female pull a shirt over her head in one smooth motion. The man can't get enough, his hands traveling the length of her body. She wonders if they're aware that their half-naked silhouettes are on display for anyone walking down Oak Hollow, or if they'd be mortified to know they have an audience. Their X-rated performance comes to an end when the man picks his partner up and carries her away, out of view and presumably to bed.

Once again, she longs for more. More passion, more romance, more excitement. Something, *anything* more than what she has. Her body is begging for it.

A lesson Mandy has yet to learn in life is that things aren't always what they seem from the outside looking in. She walks these streets, fixating on a momentary peek into the lives of strangers, longing for what they have. If she could travel inside the four walls of the houses she dreams of living in, she would quickly learn that looks can be deceiving.

If Mandy were a fly on the wall, she'd know that the family seemingly enjoying movie night in their stylish and cozy den isn't listening to a word of that Kevin Hart film. They spent the afternoon poring over the informational packet handed to them at the oncologist's office, explaining the diagnosis given to their youngest. The big C should be a word reserved for adults, not a child who just celebrated getting her training wheels off less than a month ago. She only knows she's sick of feeling sick, and her older brother is terrified and confused by it all. Her parents will now consider their lives in two distinct halves—before the news and after. *Would better parents have noticed the signs earlier? Is this some sort of punishment by God? What are they supposed to do now?*

When Mandy gazed longingly at the elderly couple drinking tea at their kitchen table, she couldn't see the official notice on the table they were reading for the fifth time, trying to make sense of the legal jargon. This house was supposed to be an asset they could leave to their grown children, a little bit of security for future generations long after they are gone. They fell victim to predatory investment schemes without informing their kids, who would have surely put a stop to the ideas before their names were signed to anything. Now, they aren't thinking their golden years are looking very golden at all.

The one scene Mandy caught tonight was exactly as she imagined it to be—the passionate couple caught in the midst of a lustful encounter. Although the relationship is new, they are very much in love. They never have enough time to spend together, so these stolen moments are filled with ferocious lovemaking and whispered promises of a beautiful life together. When they are dressed and saying their goodbyes, she disappears down the hall to check on her toddler son, fast asleep in his room with dinosaurs and monster truck toys littering the carpet surrounding his bed.

The man checks his reflection in the mirror and straightens the buttons on his work uniform before driving the few short blocks home to his wife and rehearsing his lies about the overtime hours he put in tonight. If he's lucky, he'll get home before Mandy so he can shower off any remaining traces of the woman he intends to leave her for.

Chapter 1

Six Months Later

"YOU NEED to learn to be self-sufficient, so you are never in the position to *need* a man," Georgia says, shaking her small gardening rake in Mandy's direction.

"I'm not arguing with you, Georgia, but I just don't feel like gardening is a necessary skill these days. I'll never have a green thumb, but I've got a gold American Express card that will buy me any vegetables I want down at Value Foods."

The woman, wry and fit for her age of nearly eighty years, drops the rake and points her finger at Mandy, who is sitting cross-legged in the brown grass on the other side of the row of soon-to-be tomato plants. "Credit card debt is another thing you don't want, Mandy Cramer! You put a pair of shoes on your charge card, and they end up costing you three times the price with all that interest you're paying."

Mandy smiles at Georgia before taking a sip of her hot

chocolate, its steam rising steadily in the chilly late March air. "Calm down, Georgia. I'm only joking with you. I don't put my groceries on my credit card."

She absolutely puts her groceries on her credit card.

Truthfully, she rotates most of life's expenses between her three charge cards and feels a great sense of accomplishment when she puts in enough hours at the gas station to pay more than the minimum payment due when the bills come in.

"Why are you tending to the garden so early, anyway? TV6 says we've got another round or two of flurries before spring thinks about sticking around."

"I'm just loosening up the soil so these plants can prepare to thrive this year. We shouldn't have any more hard freezes to worry about. This garden will provide for me until winter comes back, and maybe even for you, if you're lucky," Georgia answers with a tut at the end for good measure. She may act like she's put out by giving Mandy her excess vegetables, but the truth is that nothing gives her more satisfaction than caring for her newly single neighbor. She knows it's not her place, but she worries about Mandy. She's all alone in this world, and the least Georgia can do is make sure she's fed. A woman scorned is a force to be reckoned with, but a woman heartbroken and defeated is one who just needs a little unconditional love and kindness.

Mandy stands up and dusts the dirt and debris from the back of her jeans before patting her knee to get Murphy's attention. He's been sniffing around between the rows since they came outside to check on Georgia.

"Alright, Miss Georgia, I've got to get ready for my shift. Are you sure you're okay to check on him tonight?" Mandy asks, motioning to the pug, who is now rubbing his snout against the side of Georgia's hand for attention.

"*Check on him*? Murphy and I have plans to watch reruns of *Big Bang Theory* and tackle that thousand-piece puzzle I picked up at St. Vincent De Paul last week. If he's good, I'll give him a bite of my bologna and cheese sandwich. By the time you get home, he'll be too tuckered out to notice you were even gone."

Mandy shakes her head. "I don't know what I'd do without you. I mean that."

Georgia shoos her away and returns to her gardening, concealing a satisfied smile.

TWO HOURS into Mandy's shift and there's enough business at the Quick Stop to distract her from her own thoughts, which frankly is the best thing that can happen during a shift.

When there's a line several customers deep, she prides herself on remembering which brand of cigarettes the smokers prefer, which scratch-offs the gamblers typically want, and which old-timers are coming inside to put twenty dollars cash on pump three because they still don't trust credit cards in the year 2024. Managing the station may not be the most glamorous job, but the regulars have become like family to Mandy during the six years she's been behind the counter and her paycheck has never been late.

The title of Assistant Manager *really* only means that Mandy is trusted with inventory and ordering and makes a whopping two dollars more per hour than the other cashiers. The only true glory that comes along with the position, other than the pay increase, is wearing a smug grin when some demeaning out-of-towner demands to speak with the manager at the height of tourist season. Sometimes Mandy does a little spin before waving her hands and declaring "Here I am." There is no head manager above her, just the owner, Shorty. He only works shifts on the rare occasion that someone is out sick and Mandy can't cover it, so she's not sure why he doesn't just give her the title of General Manager. It's a promotion that he holds over her head when he needs her to hit a specific sales quota because some brand is offering an incentive that Shorty is going to keep for himself, even though Mandy and the rest of the staff did the work. Like most gas stations in America, gas is most definitely not where they earn their living. They bank on customers coming inside to use the restroom and not being able to resist a cold pop or bag of chips on their way out. They even sold a winning lottery ticket a few years back. Mandy read in the paper that Shorty received fifty grand from the Michigan State Lottery, but you can guess how much the bastard shared with his staff.

Countless people go out of their way to choose the Quick Stop over other gas stations in town for the cleanliness, friendliness, and variety of snacks and drinks. When she's not waiting on customers, the entirety of her shift is spent cleaning and stocking. Mandy is much too modest to admit it, but a lot of those customers make the trip just to see her. She's girl-next-door pretty and reminds the older men of the girls they couldn't date in high school; yet, she's from the wrong side of the tracks, so it gives them a false sense of satisfaction that they could still land a catch like her if they really wanted to. She's attractive yet accessible, which is every insecure man's dream around here.

"Let's add on one of those little bottles of Jim Beam," Paul Hayes says in a hushed tone as Mandy scans the barcodes on his frozen TV dinner and two-liter of Pepsi. She waves her hands like Vanna White between the mini bottle, quarter pint, and the half pint on the shelves behind her, showing Paul his options. He nods when her hand is over the half pint. This means his wife, Judy, is out of town. When she's at the house, he'll get the nip size and take the full shot before he's back to his car, throwing the tiny bottle in the trash can next to the gas pumps before driving off. Judy likes to brag to her bible study group that her husband hasn't had a drink in five years. Mandy's job is to mind her own business.

As Paul is leaving the store, brown bag in hand, he holds the door open for an elderly woman that Mandy recognizes but can't quite recall her name. She avoids eye contact when Mandy greets her and makes a beeline for the rotating metal rack that holds gift cards, directly to the left of the counter. Her small, aged hands are shaking as she flips through the Visa, Red Lobster, and Door Dash options before landing on a row of shiny, white Apple gift cards and plucks several hundred-dollar cards from the stack.

"I hear spring might make an appearance after we get these last two inches out of the way this weekend," Mandy says as the woman approaches the register. Weather is the universal topic to get any elderly person in this town to engage in conversation. When the woman doesn't respond, Mandy continues. "Do you have any exciting plans for the weekend?" She normally wouldn't ask this because she can't stand when people are in her business, so she gives them the same respect, but something is making alarm bells go off in Mandy's subconscious. Her hands are shaking even more dramatically now, while her fingers sort through the bills in her wallet. When the woman finally looks up to meet her gaze, Mandy involuntarily gasps at her bloodshot eyes and the red, inflamed skin surrounding them. "Ma'am, are you okay? Is there something I can do to help?"

"I'm sorry, I'm just beside myself. My grandson has gotten himself in trouble and I need to help him," she tells Mandy with pleading eyes.

"What kind of trouble?"

"I'm ashamed to admit, but he was arrested. Some gentleman from the jail just called me and said I can bail him out, but I need to buy these Apple gift cards for payment. You know, everything is electronic these days. You can't just drive down to the jail with your checkbook. As soon as I call him back with the numbers from the back of these cards, they'll release Devon and erase the charges from his permanent record, thank the good Lord. He's such a good boy; I just can't believe he got himself in some sort of trouble. He must be getting mixed up with the wrong crowd."

Without thinking twice, Mandy reaches for the woman's hands and holds them gently in hers. "Ma'am, remind me of your name."

"Eunice. Eunice Spencer."

"Eunice; that's right. Your husband was Peter from the hardware store. He was always very kind to me. My name is Mandy Cramer, but before that, I was a Smith and not the good kind, so I know a thing or two about the jail here," she says without hesitation. She quit acting embarrassed over her upbringing years ago. Some people raised by doctors and lawyers in this town, and some are raised by convicts and addicts; it doesn't mean their parents' actions have anything to do with their own. "Have you tried calling Devon?"

"No, dear. The officer told me they confiscated his phone when they booked him."

Mandy summons the patience needed to break the

news to her gently. "Eunice, I'm afraid there are some not-so-nice scam artists out there who make a living from these kinds of tricks. Why don't you try giving Devon a call, just in case?"

Eunice considers this for a moment before reaching back into her neatly organized purse and retrieving a small flip phone. She opens it and clicks a few buttons before looking up at Mandy.

"He usually calls me. It's been a while since I've placed a call myself. My daughter showed me how to get into my list of contacts, but I just can't remember."

Mandy gives a sympathetic smile. "Technology can be so confusing sometimes. Why don't you hand it to me, and I'll see if I can't pull his number up for you?"

Eunice hands it over without hesitation, and it only takes Mandy a few seconds to scroll through the ten total contacts stored in the phone. She selects *Devon - Grandson* and turns it back over to the woman. "Just push that green button in the top left-hand corner and you'll be calling Devon."

Eunice gives a skeptical look before holding the phone to her ear, as if she's fully expecting the call to go straight to voicemail because it was turned off by the arresting officers. Her eyes grow wide when a male voice sounds through the phone's speaker, which must be set at maximum volume.

"Devon? Devon, sweetie, it's Gram. Are you okay? Did they let you out?" she asks, her voice rising a few octaves from the shaky, unsure tone she had just moments ago. "Of jail, Devon. One of the officers called me an hour ago. I was just getting the gift cards ready to bail you out. Yes, the gift cards . . . What do you mean?"

As if someone stuck a pin in her balloon, her shoulders sink as she places a hand on the counter to steady herself.

"Okay, okay. I'll be back at the house in five minutes, dear. Okay, I won't. I love you, too."

She gently closes the phone and gives Mandy a look that nearly breaks her heart into pieces, right there in the middle of the Quick Stop. Eunice grew up in a world where the con artists were in plain sight, stealing your wallet or selling you a car they know won't last the week. It's a small town so the bad actors were easy to spot. They weren't nameless, faceless strangers who somehow got her telephone number and the name of her youngest grandchild so they could scam the woman out of half of her social security check this month. Why would someone choose *her* to trick with such a cruel, dishonest scheme?

She slowly tucks the cash back into her billfold and slides it into her purse before sheepishly reaching for the gift cards to put them back. Mandy gently grabs for them and tells Eunice not to worry; she was about to straighten those racks anyway and would be happy to put them back.

"What would I have done if you weren't working?" Eunice asks, placing the strap of her purse over her shoulder and pulling her keys from the pocket of her winter coat.

"Well, it would have been an expensive lesson about trusting strangers on the telephone, but luckily I *was* here, and I'm confident any of the other cashiers would have stepped in to help as well, ma'am."

That's a lie; the other cashiers would not have given a shit. They would have been too busy hurrying the transaction so they could get back to texting or scrolling or playing mindless games on their phones. Perhaps *this* is why Mandy is the manager.

"Tell me your name again, dear. I was so worked up, it slipped in one ear and right out the other, I'm afraid."

"It's Mandy," she says with a polite nod.

"Well, dear Mandy, I will be stopping here to give you my business a whole lot more going forward. Thank you for saving this old woman's day," Eunice replies before returning her nod and walking out the door to her Pontiac Bonneville.

Mandy's heart is racing. How can these assholes be targeting innocent old women, who are just trying to survive and enjoy their golden years in peace? It reminds her of a documentary she watched about romance scams. These poor, lonely retirees are spending their life savings on a partner they've never met because they believe every lie they are told, each one more ridiculous than the last. How do these jerks sleep at night?

Speaking of jerks, the next customer who walks through the glass double doors of the Quick Stop is a handsome guy, about Mandy's age, wearing a Hawthorne Bluff Club polo under a matching Patagonia jacket with the Hawthorne Bluff logo and immaculately pressed khaki pants.

"You lost?" Mandy asks, jutting her chin toward the man's outfit. She smiles to keep it lighthearted, but she's honestly curious. The Hawthorne Bluff Club, or "the Bluff" as the locals refer to it, has its own convenience store. It's rare to see someone, even a member of their live-in staff, drive down to town to buy supplies. Whatever they need, they have it behind the gates of their own little utopia.

"One of the members requested a Coors Light, and we don't . . . Um, we don't carry that particular brand at the club."

The way he enunciates *Coors Light*, as if it's a foreign language, forces a smile on Mandy's face.

"He wants a CL smoothie, does he? Must be new money. Or maybe old money who wants to see how the other half lives, eh? Slum it, just for one night?" Mandy teases.

"What's a CL— Oh, I get it. Coors Light. Um, I'm not sure where his money comes from, ma'am. I was just told to be back in ten minutes with a twelve pack, so if you wouldn't mind pointing me in the direction of the Coors Light, I'd greatly appreciate it."

This guy looks downright terrified of what would happen if he's not back behind those gates in ten minutes with a case of the silver bullet. She wonders if the member really wants Coors Light, or if he's just a rich prick who enjoys making the errand boys sweat. Either way, she's glad to be working at a place like the Quick Stop, and that's not a sentiment she feels too often.

She gestures to the oversized display of Coors Light promotional materials—a stack of cases from the floor, damn near to the ceiling.

"Right behind that display, you'll find the cold ones in the stand-up cooler. There are bottles, cans, and tall boys. Take your pick," she tells him, knowing damn well he's not going to have any say in the pick; she's sure he was sent with specific instructions.

"Twelve-ounce cans is what he asked for," he says.

"Second shelf from the top," she responds without looking.

When he brings the case up to the register to pay, Mandy leans forward with a conspiratorial grin. "So, what happens if you take longer than ten minutes?"

"I've got entirely too many student loans to even consider what would happen if I don't meet expectations."

The man takes his receipt, thanks Mandy, and hustles to the GMC Denali parked outside the front door.

What kind of wealthy maniac makes their employees fear losing their jobs if they don't drive to town and fetch their beer quickly enough? Now *those* are the kind of schmucks who deserve to get scammed out of their money, not sweet old women like Eunice.

To make the rest of her suddenly slow shift go by a little faster, Mandy does something she rarely allows herself to do at work—she takes out her phone. She doesn't text, scroll, or play games. Instead, she opens the apps on her phone one by one to note the total balances: her mortgage loan, car loan, and each of her three credit cards.

She looks at the commas and all the numbers that come before and after, while fantasizing about those balances showing big fat zeros after she acts as her own personal Robin Hood and scams the richest idiots in this county out of money they'd never even miss. She'd pay off every penny of debt she accrued when her husband left her months ago with all the bills and none of his money. She'd sue him for alimony, but lawyers also cost money. Money she doesn't have.

Mandy takes a deep breath before rejoining reality. She could never scam anyone, nor would she even know how or where to start. But damn, it sure is fun to dream.

Chapter 2

Mandy is awoken entirely too early by a strange noise. It's barely light out, and even Murphy groans when he realizes the time.

Is it my smoke alarm? When is the last time I changed the batteries? Do mine even take batteries, or are they hard wired? She'll add these questions to the long list of things she should have learned to do herself before her deadbeat of a husband decided to leave her for the charming single mother four blocks down.

When she's coherent enough to make sense of the noise, she realizes it's coming from outside. Mandy wraps a thick robe around her oversized T-shirt and skuttles down the hall toward the front of her house. Pulling back the living room curtains slightly, she sees a moving van backed up to the house next door, on the opposite side from Georgia. Tom, the old man who lived there for years, passed away last November. Mandy knew his kids would end up selling his house, but she hadn't seen any For Sale signs in the yard.

After feeding the dog and haphazardly shaking some

coffee grounds into a filter and pressing brew, Mandy throws on a pair of jeans and a sweatshirt to go outside and investigate the moving van situation. She walks out the side door, facing Georgia's house, to find the woman is already outside. She's holding an unmarked spray bottle and wiping down the two rocking chairs that sit on her covered front porch.

"Morning, Georgia. Didn't I see you clean those chairs last week?" Mandy asks.

Georgia waves a quick hand and shushes her. She points her chin toward the moving van. "What do you suppose is going on here?"

"I'm no detective, but it looks like someone is moving in next door to me," Mandy says with an obvious smile, in case Georgia is too old to understand the nuances of sarcasm.

As they stare at the van, waiting for any sort of activity that would tell them something about the new neighbors, a Ford pickup truck pulls over in front of the house and parks right up against the curb. A man hops out of the truck. They can't make out much from where they are standing, other than his build—fairly tall and relatively trim. If Mandy had to guess, he's in his thirties. Her eyes travel to the back of his truck and land on the Illinois license plate.

"Not a FIB," she whispers, referring to the vulgar acronym given to their neighbors to the south who like to snatch up affordable vacation homes in the lakeside town. One time a FIB in line at the Quick Stop asked her what it stood for after someone at the gas pump had uttered the phrase, and the local behind him replied "Friendly Illinois Buddy" before laughing at his own lie as soon as the out-of-towner left the store.

"Land of Lincoln, drive without thinkin," Georgia whispers back.

"Hi," they say sweetly in unison when they see the man walking in their direction.

"Hello, ladies. I'm Braxton," he says, reaching out a hand to shake each of theirs. Firm yet gentle handshake, understated cologne usage, and a Green Bay Packers hat; color Mandy impressed.

"I'm Mandy. Your hat is contradicting your license plate there, Braxton. Or are you just trying to fit in?"

"No, ma'am. I may have been raised in Rockford, but I've had the good sense to cheer for a winning team since I was a kid."

"Well, that's one thing you have going for you. I'm Georgia Afton. Mandy here lives in the house between us with her dog, Murphy," Georgia says, gesturing to Mandy's small single-story ranch.

"I love dogs; what breed is he?" Braxton asks.

"He's a pug, and he just turned four years old," Mandy answers.

"You're not going to believe this," Braxton tells her, holding up a finger before jogging away to his truck. Mandy and Georgia exchange curious glances. They both gasp when Braxton opens the passenger door of his truck and reaches in to retrieve a small tan pug, with a black snout, just like Murphy's.

"Oh my god!" Mandy can't help herself. They could be twins. She walks across the lawn to open her front door and Murphy comes trotting out, barking out a few yaps when he sees the stranger approaching his house.

"You've got to be kidding me; they could be brothers," Braxton says, setting the dog down in the yard. Murphy runs to him, and they sniff each other thoroughly, curly tails fluttering with excitement. "This is Max McGee."

"And named after a true Packers legend? I take back half the things I said about you when I saw your license plate."

Mandy bends down to pet Max and he hops up, propping his front paws on her thigh and sniffing her like he's performing an investigation.

"Both of you ladies will be happy to know I don't drive like I'm from Illinois," Braxton says with a wink. Mandy and Georgia both blush slightly.

Georgia is now on Mandy's front lawn, bent down next to her to pet the neighborhood's newest dog. "Just tell us you're not going to turn the house into one of those bed and breakfasts that you can rent on the internet."

"Or are you going to flip it and overcharge some poor local who can barely afford rent as it is?"

"Whoa, whoa, ladies. None of the above. I got transferred to the mill up here; this is my new home." Braxton has both palms held up in his defense and smirks when both women relax their raised shoulders at the news. "I'm not an investor. I'm a Packers fan, and I have a pug, so put down the pitchforks. I also go to bed by nine and despise loud music."

"Family?" Georgia asks, and Mandy flinches at the invasion of privacy so quickly after meeting the man.

Luckily, he smiles before answering.

"No spouse, no kids. My parents are retired and live outside of Rockford, and I have a brother in the Chicago metro area. No nieces or nephews . . . yet."

"Food allergies?" Georgia inquires, and this time Mandy laughs out loud.

"For goodness sakes Georgia, leave this poor man alone."

"You remind me a lot of my mother, and she'd ask the

same questions. You'll be pleased to know I have no aller-gies, food or otherwise, Miss Afton."

And . . . she's blushing.

"Please, call me Georgia."

"Well ladies, Max and I are going to start unpacking. It was such a pleasure to meet you both, and I'm sure I'll be seeing plenty of you once we get settled in."

Both ladies return the pleasantries, and Mandy heads for her front door to let Murphy back inside, making it to the top porch step before realizing Georgia is following closely behind her. The woman motions for her to hurry up and get inside, which makes Mandy laugh once more.

"What is your deal?" She smiles, setting Murphy down and turning back toward her neighbor.

"Now *that* is a man," Georgia says, raising her eyebrows and cocking her head toward Braxton's house, as if Mandy needs to be told which man she's referring to.

"The ink is still fresh on my divorce papers, and the last thing I need in this life is another man."

Georgia holds her hands up in defense. "I'm just saying, it might be nice to have someone around here to open jars when they're screwed on too tight. That's all I meant."

"I'm sure that's all you meant," Mandy replies, rolling her eyes in the process.

"And just because your ex-husband was a good-for-nothing cheat and scoundrel, it doesn't mean the same is true for all men," Georgia adds.

"Maybe not all of them, but I think we can agree that it's most men," Mandy offers.

"You might be right."

With that, Georgia bends down and gives Murphy a pat on the head before disappearing out the front door and across the driveway to her own house. She hasn't talked much about her late husband, but Mandy wonders if he would have fallen in the category of *most men* or if he was the exception.

Chapter 3

Mandy knows she should be doing something productive on her night off, but her body is aching to be lazy. She recently read an advice column online that said people should quit referring to it as a "lazy day" and start admitting that their bodies need the rest. This is great advice, but it doesn't stop her from feeling useless as she sits propped up against the headboard of her bed, laptop resting on her outstretched legs and reruns of *Below Deck* on the TV in front of her.

She should be searching for a higher paying job, scanning online articles for side-hustle ideas to make more money, looking around her house for things she could list online to sell and pay down a few small bills on her mountain of debt. Instead, she's staring blankly at the dashboard of her online banking account. Given her upbringing, Mandy should be happy to see a positive balance and a second line which indicates a savings account, something her parents surely never had. Instead, she's nauseated over seeing a total that was once dangerously close to five figures dwindled down to just enough to pay a month of utilities. Everyone likes to talk about how liberating it is to leave a bad marriage, but they don't talk nearly enough about what it can do to your finances.

During a late-night moment of desperation a few weeks ago, she did text Patrick asking for help. She figured it was the least he could do, and in true Patrick fashion, he read the message and didn't even give her the courtesy of a response. He's too busy playing house with Emily Myers down the block to care about the total financial ruin his ex-wife is facing. It's amazing how a man who felt like family is now essentially a stranger to Mandy. It's hard to remember now what drew her to him in the first place, but she suspects it was comfort. She'd known him since high school, and that's just what people around here do—marry their high school sweethearts, stay in town, and live the same lives as their parents and grandparents before them. The ones who get out are labeled *uppity* or *different* by those who never took the chance.

She opens her laptop and clicks on the bookmark for Reddit, where she scrolls through the newest posts on her feed. Much like looking through windows at night, it's a great way to get a glimpse into someone else's life. Selfishly, she clicks on subreddits like "Am I the Asshole?" and "Neighbors from Hell" so she can read about problems much worse than her own. Misery loves company, right?

While scrolling her feed, her eyes land on a post from a subreddit called "Scams," and she recognizes the details in the story as the "grandparent scam" that Eunice Spencer nearly fell victim to the other day at the gas station. The poster is detailing how his beloved grandmother received a call that led her to believe her grandson was being held in the local jail after getting in a car accident and blowing over the legal limit for alcohol. Although he was a thirty-something professional who would never drink and drive, his grandma didn't ask questions. She simply drove to Target and purchased a stack of Apple Gift Cards before returning home and reading the numbers off to the "chief deputy" of the jail over the phone. She sat on her couch patiently waiting for the call that he was released, a call that never came. She finally looked up the direct number for the jail only to be told that not only was her grandson never in their system, but the scam was becoming so prevalent, they were fielding two to three calls a week from distressed relatives in the same position.

"How could someone be so cruel? My grandmother has never hurt a soul, and she just drained her savings account to purchase these gift cards to 'save' me. It makes me so sick. She's a saint," the poster went on to explain. "Why can't these jerks scam someone who actually deserves it?"

Mandy's mind once again travels to the rich assholes at the Hawthorne Bluff Club. She's had several run-ins with the members over the years, when they "slum it" and leave the gated community to show their permanently tanned and surgically tightened faces in town.

It's amazing how families who live just a few miles away can have such different lives. It was no secret that Mandy's parents were not cut out for raising children. When she and her brother were growing up, the bartenders at the local dive bars were their pseudo-babysitters. They'd give the kids a rocks glass filled with maraschino cherries and a few quarters for the dented arcade game in the corner while their father lost his wages on the pool table and their mother threw herself at whichever helpless local might pay for her drinks that night.

The principal quit calling for parent teacher conferences when he realized the Smiths were never going to show. Even at eight years old, Mandy could recognize the disappointment in her teacher's eyes when she'd show up in the middle of January without a winter coat or boots. At the time, she felt shame as if *she* was the one who had done something wrong. It took years for her to understand all the ways in which her parents had failed her. The greatest failure being the night they passed out drunk in the living room of their trailer without putting out their cigarettes in one of the countless makeshift ashtrays scattered throughout their home. She'll probably never know which one dropped the ashes that ignited the mobile home's cheap shag carpet because her father died in the fire, and she hasn't spoken to her mother since she was sentenced to life in prison under the three strikes law. It took two days in the hospital before her brother, Jeff, succumbed to the effects of smoke inhalation, but she only knows that from reading the court documents. The entire ordeal is a blur for Mandy, including the makeshift memorial service at *South Town Sally's* and the two miserable weeks spent living with her Uncle Peter before the authorities realized he was another Smith that wasn't fit for raising children and placed her in the custody of the state.

Her first Christmas in foster care was also her first experience with Bluff residents that she can recall. At ten years old, she was forced to pose with a stack of Christmas presents generously donated to her by the family of Chandler Hawthorne Jr., President of the Hawthorne Bluff Club and son of its founder, Chandler Hawthorne Sr. Her awkward smile and messy hair were in full display on the cover of the *Daily Press*, with the Hawthornes standing on each side of her, careful not to touch the child, for they may catch the crippling disease of poverty.

When the Hawthorne family left immediately after the photo op, Mandy's foster mother allowed her to open the gifts. None of the clothes were even close to being her size, the dolls were antique and terrifying, and the books were for children much younger than her. The woman gave Mandy a sympathetic smile as she finished opening gifts and stared at the pile in front of her. Mandy knew enough to show gratitude, even though none of the presents particularly excited her. Later that night, she overheard her foster mom talking to a friend on the phone about how out of touch the Hawthorne family was and how they just wanted "good PR to overshadow all the bullshit they are hiding up there at the Bluff." She couldn't hear the friend's part of the conversation, but she'll never forget her foster mom saying, "A few gifts for underprivileged kids can't erase the fact that people *died*, Sharon; how is this still being kept out of the news? How many people have they paid off? Those women had families."

Chapter 4

Mandy learned early that when you're in the working class, you don't have the luxury of not being a morning person. You work when you can get the hours because the bills aren't going to pay themselves while you hold out for a position with better hours.

Today she's working the early-bird shift at the Quick Stop, her least favorite of the three possible shifts—seven to three, three to eleven, eleven to seven. Just like the Kenny Chesney song. If she had kids, she'd be relieved to be off by three to be home when they get out of school, but since she doesn't, the early shift means getting to work before her body is even ready for coffee, dealing with all the morning regulars who talk too much (that talk often bordering on sexual harassment), and having to single handedly put up all the product deliveries as they arrive.

The midday shift is her favorite because she can sleep in, enjoy most of her afternoon before going in, and still have enough energy to do a late-night walk with Murphy when she gets off. Overnight shifts are rare since she's a supervisor, but she doesn't mind them. Armed robbery isn't exactly common in the Upper Peninsula of Michigan, so the nights are typically uneventful.

She did once have an incredibly drunk customer attempt to bring a horse inside the store. A Michigan State Police officer was inside getting coffee when the man stumbled through the front door, coaxing his horse in behind him. The officer never stopped blowing on his steaming mug as he calmly lifted one finger, shook it, and then motioned for the man to turn back around. Luckily, he listened, and the officer threw a few bills on the counter in Mandy's direction and walked out without a word. She still wonders if the whole thing was some sort of fever dream.

"Steve, how the hell are ya?" one of her regulars shouts before engaging in an interaction that feels like an SNL sketch about Midwestern dads.

"Oh, just on my way to Menards. The wife saw these oversized planters in the weekly flyer and apparently, she just can't live without them," Steve tells the man with a smile.

"I thought these broads were going to let us relax once we retired!" he shouts with a jovial chuckle at the end for good measure.

Fifteen minutes into the shift and Mandy's already over it.

Around eight thirty, she gets a short break in business and goes outside for some fresh air. Just as she perches herself on the edge of the wooden bench outside the front door, the Butch's Meat truck pulls in for their weekly delivery. It'll be an easy load; a few cases of beef sticks, cheddar brats, and cheese snack packs is all she ordered this week. They are her three top sellers in the refrigerated foods section, and she does her best to keep a backstock, so they don't run out on her off days.

She smiles when the door of the truck cab opens and

two boots hop down onto the concrete, boots belonging to Luke, a guy she's known her whole life. That smile fades when she sees his downturned mouth and thick eyebrows, which are pulled together in a scowl.

"Luke, what's up?"

He slams the door shut without a word and stomps around to the back of the truck, where he unlocks it and lifts the rolling door. Mandy's not sure she's ever seen Luke with a temper, and she also can't imagine what could be so upsetting before 9:00 a.m. in the meat and cheese delivery business.

"Hello, earth to Luke," she adds, taking a few steps toward her old friend.

"I'm done, I'm fucking done," he mutters so aggressively, tiny beads of spit fly from his tight lips.

"Hey, hey now. Whatever it is, we'll work it out. Talk to me," she offers.

"Those fucking rich-ass motherfuckers don't give a shit about any of us. I'm done," he says, gesturing vaguely to his right, in the direction of the towering bluff that overlooks the town. She doesn't need to ask for clarification. She knows he means the Hawthorne Bluff Club.

"What did they do?"

"They've got too much money and too much time on their hands, so they like to play games with our fucking lives, Mandy. This is my job. This is my livelihood. It's how I feed my family. They want to put that in jeopardy because they're bored and need some poor blue collar to pick on? Fuck that, man. Fuck that."

At this point, Luke's hands are shaking so Mandy takes a few tentative steps in his direction and grabs her order from his hands. He doesn't resist, but he also doesn't even seem to register that she took the boxes at all.

"Luke . . . what did they do? Talk to me."

"They are crazy up there about being on time. Their prime rib delivery on Saturdays has to be there at eight o'clock on the dot so the chef can slow cook them all day for dinner service. I get there five minutes early, every week, so I can watch the clock and pull into the dining hall right at eight, just like they ask."

Now Luke is pacing, his eyes a wild shade of gray that Mandy's never seen before. She can't help but feel like she's witnessing a mental breakdown stampeding right before her eyes, and she's not equipped to slow it down. The best she can do is stay calm and continue to listen.

"I pull up to their bullshit security booth, which is usually staffed with the same assholes we knew in high school. They're pricks, but basically harmless. Today, it's some guy I've never seen before in his rent-a-cop outfit and these dark ass sunglasses, even though the booth is in the shade. He starts fucking with me the minute I pull in. Asking for my ID, proof that the club even made an order, insisting on calling the chef to make sure I'm in the right place. He's taking his time, and I'm watching the minutes tick by, sweating because I know Hawthorne will have my ass if I'm not on time."

"He held you there past eight?" she asks.

"All of a sudden, his eyes dart behind my truck and he smiles. It's this devious ass smirk so I know something's up. I look in my rearview mirror, and there are two of the younger members, the "new generation" they call themselves. One of them opens my passenger door, reaches over and turns the truck off. Before I can even realize what's happening, he's got my keys. Kyle one and Kyle two because I don't know their fucking names. Well, they start playing catch with my keys. That's when I lose it."

"What did you do?" Mandy asks, setting the load she's holding down on the bench outside the store. Her hands were beginning to feel numb from the weight of the cold boxes.

"I told them to quit fucking around and give me my keys back, I have a delivery to make. They decide to keep acting like idiots for another five minutes, until the rent-a-cop says it's time. I look at my dash and it's 8:05. I'm fucked. 'Good luck with your delivery,' Kyle two says as he tosses my keys back through the window and on the floorboard in front of the passenger seat. I couldn't believe it; it was like some eighties movie villain type shit."

"Did anyone notice you were late?"

"Notice? Fuck, Mandy. Chandler Hawthorne himself was standing outside the dining hall with his arms crossed, like he was waiting for me. Ed, the chef, was behind him and shaking his head. Not at me, but because he knew exactly what they did to me and there wasn't a damn thing he could do about it either. He's a good guy, but I imagine they pay him well enough to keep his mouth shut."

"So, Chandler tried to write you up for being late or something?"

"Worse. He told me that showing up late was blatant disrespect for his time, which is *very* valuable, he reminded me. He told me to call my boss and explain why he was getting a twenty percent discount on today's delivery. Twenty percent is a lot of money when we are talking about that much meat."

"Did you tell him what those idiots did to you at the guard station?"

"He knew what they did, Mandy. Don't you see? It's a game to them. And there's nothing rich people love more than getting something for free, especially when it's on the backs of people like us. He could have cost me my job today, but he wouldn't have lost a minute of sleep over hearing that I was in the unemployment line, I guarantee you that."

"What did your boss say?"

"He cussed a lot, but it wasn't directed at me. He's lived in this town long enough to know how those people are. The Bluff might as well be a different planet; they're not like us, Mandy."

He closes the rolling door and hands Mandy a clipboard to sign. She doesn't even bother opening the boxes to inventory the order; he's never shorted her, and she wants to send him on his way so he can cool down.

"I am so sorry, Luke. I swear every new story I hear about those pricks is worse than the last."

"Just promise me, Mandy. Promise me you'll never become one of them, that you'll never marry one of them."

"I won't ever be getting married again, that's a promise. And I think you know me better than to think I have it in me to become anything like those assholes. Now go finish your deliveries so you can go home to Pam and the kids."

Luke smiles at the mention of his family. "You're right. I've gotta focus on what matters. Thanks for talking me off the ledge Mandy. I owe you one."

She may have talked him off the ledge, but now her thoughts are filled with rage and revenge. Luke is right—these rich bastards can't keep treating the rest of the town like their own personal toilet, but what the hell can she do about it? Mandy's always been a helper and prides herself on solving everyone else's problems. It pains her to watch those inconsiderate jerks continue to come out on top, knowing there's not a damn thing she can do to stop them.

Chapter 5

By Tuesday, Mandy finds herself cracking open a cold one in the middle of the day without remorse.

It's 3:30 now, and she's home from a god-awful shift filled with difficult customers and shitty texts from her boss about things that were completely out of her control. If it weren't for the unseasonably warm temperatures, she'd be curled up in her bed in a post-work depression nap. Unfortunately for her, it's a crime in Michigan to stay indoors on a day like this. She feels like a true Smith as she raises her Busch Light can to wave at the school bus driver while she drops off a few of the neighbor kids in front of Mandy's house. The woman shakes her head in disapproval before closing the door to the bus and driving off.

"Blow me, Margo," she mumbles. "I didn't even like you when we were kids."

"Whoa, somebody got a case of the Mondays?"

The voice nearly makes her jump out of her Dollar General chair. Mandy's head spins to her right to catch her new neighbor, Braxton, heading her way with his own chair tucked under his arm.

"It's Tuesday," she says, correcting him.

"You can have a case of the Mondays any damn day of the week, ma'am. Mind if I join you? I could use a break from the unpacking."

She gestures limply at the empty spot in the lawn next to her, reaching on the opposite side of her chair to offer him a beer from the cooler. He looks at the can, at his watch, back at her, and shrugs. "Why not?"

"Neighborhood watch meeting?"

They both turn to see Georgia walking over from the side of her house, also with a lawn chair in tow.

"It's sixty degrees in March; that's worthy of a lawn meeting."

Georgia nods in agreement. "So, what's the scoop?"

"Mandy's having a no-good, very bad day," Braxton offers.

Mandy shakes her head at him, not because he's wrong but because she doesn't make it a habit of telling people her business, specifically someone she just met.

"Rough day at the station?" Georgia asks.

"Station? Are you a cop?" Braxton basically yells.

"Calm down, it's just a gas station. I manage the Quick Stop."

"Ahh, the one with the red roof right off the highway?" he asks.

"That's the one," Mandy confirms. "I think it's possible I've developed a disdain for anyone with money. My boss just sits on his fat ass all day, spending his inheritance and thinking of new things to bitch about. And I can't tell you how many times in the last month I've heard stories about the assholes at the Bluff . . . I think it's all starting to get to me. One of my favorite delivery drivers got harassed by them on Saturday. Right before I left today, Randy Johns said he was trout fishing in the river and one of their pretend officers chased him down and threatened him for getting too close to their property. What the hell is their motive behind trying to make our lives harder? Don't they have it good enough up there?"

Georgia leans back in her chair and shakes her head. "It's a game to them, Mandy. It's all a game. A game they have gotten quite used to winning."

"Sorry to interrupt here, but the Bluff? Like the hill at the edge of town?" Braxton asks, motioning in the direction of the towering edge of the bluff, sitting just a mile behind their houses. "Everyone who lives up there is a jerk or something?"

Mandy and Georgia exchange glances as if to ask, *Who is going to explain it to this poor bastard from Illinois?* Mandy juts her chin, deferring to Georgia.

"In short, there's this private club—"

"The Hawthorne Bluff Club," Mandy interrupts, unable to contain her rage. "It's a gated community, founded by an old rich guy named Chandler Hawthorne, and now it's run by his grandson, Chandler Hawthorne III. I shouldn't even call it a gated community; it's more like a cult."

Braxton's head slightly jerks in disbelief. "A cult? In the Upper Peninsula of Michigan? C'mon. What goes on there?"

"Hardly anyone is allowed beyond the gates and when they come out, they sure as hell aren't talking about it. The club was founded almost a hundred years ago, has tens of thousands of acres of land, guards stationed at a booth in the front and scattered around the property, and they have enough resources to never have to leave. It's like their own little city, filled with rich white people. All we hear are rumors, but if you can believe them, the Bluff has every kind of business you'd need, several lakes and rivers, even a doctor's office. Unless they need major surgery, there's no reason to ever leave the gates."

"It's not a doctor's office, it's just a doctor who operates out of a wing in his home when needed," Georgia says, a sheepish look on her face.

"Who told you that?" Mandy asks.

"I saw it with my own eyes . . . when I worked there."

Braxton, who just met Georgia the week before and learned of the Bluff Club's existence five minutes prior, gasps just as loudly as Mandy, who nearly drops her now-empty aluminum can of beer.

"You *worked* there?" Mandy manages to get out. "How could you not have told me this?"

"We've never really discussed the club before, and I didn't find it relevant to any other conversations we've had," Georgia replies with a shrug.

"Didn't find it *relevant*? Georgia, you better tell us every-thing," Mandy demands. "Were they all horrible?"

Georgia stares across the street for a moment, contem-plating how to answer the question.

"Most of them, yes. They were born with silver spoons in their mouths and taught to judge anyone who wasn't. The world is their oyster, or more accurately tens of thou-sands of acres of pristine land all to themselves."

"What did you do there?" Braxton asks.

"I worked in the kitchen. I had recently lost my husband and was close to retirement age. I needed a job that would consume my time and energy so I could keep my mind off missing him. Grief counselors weren't exactly in vogue in those days. You just did what you could to survive it."

"I'm so sorry to hear that, Georgia," Braxton says in all sincerity. Mandy squeezes Georgia's forearm gently to convey the same.

"Did you work there before or after the fire? That was in the nineties, right?" Mandy asks.

"During. It was the last year I worked for the club, 1998."

"No way," Mandy says, eyes growing wide.

"What fire?" Braxton asks.

"A fire burned down several structures inside the club's grounds. The details have become local lore because several people died, and it somehow stayed out of the news. Rumor is, a few of the bodies were never found. Is that true?"

The minute the words are out of Mandy's mouth, she regrets them. Several of the dead were employees of the club, so Georgia most likely knew them.

"I'm sorry, Georgia. I shouldn't pry. I just haven't met anyone with Bluff connections before, and I never dreamed I'd get to talk to someone who was there during the fire."

"It's okay, sweetheart. Well, I wasn't on property because it was my night off, but it's true that several people perished in the fire. It's also true that a cause was never determined, the case was closed, and the bodies of Mr. and Mrs. Hawthorne were never recovered. The going theory is that the remains were incinerated to dust because the fire department took so long to respond, but I think it's more likely that the department wasn't called immediately because they needed time to leave town, or maybe they were forced out of town against their will."

Braxton interjects. "Mr. and Mrs. Hawthorne—the parents of the guy who currently runs the place? They supposedly died in the fire?"

"No, the couple who reportedly perished were Jack and Tilly Hawthorne, Chandler's aunt and uncle. Jack was the other son of Chandler Hawthorne the first, who founded the club. They didn't have any children that I knew of."

"What happened to Chandler's parents after the fire? I actually remember meeting them when I was a kid. They brought some disappointing Christmas presents to my foster home. Even as a ten-year-old, I knew they weren't doing it to help a poor kid. They were doing it so the town would see they helped a poor kid, if you know what I mean," Mandy adds.

Georgia coughs out an irritated laugh.

"Well, that certainly checks out. Money could keep their names out of the newspapers and avoid an official police investigation, but they could never control the rumblings of the folks down here in town. They all knew something was amiss, and Chandler and Leslie Hawthorne thought they could buy their way back into everyone's good graces. They retreated behind the gates for a few more years and then retired in South Florida. Unfortunately, they were both killed in a car accident that *did* make the news in the early two thousands—they were both three sheets to the wind after a country club dinner and drove headfirst into a tree. Thank goodness they didn't kill anyone else in the process."

"Excuse my silly question, but why did the people down here in town care so much? So a few of the elite may or may not have died in a fire . . . If everyone in town hated the Hawthorne Family so much, why did they care?" Braxton asks.

Mandy waits a beat before answering, in case Georgia wants to take this one. When she doesn't speak, Mandy answers solemnly.

"Because the other structure that caught fire was a cabin that housed employees. Two of them died that night, and they were both townies. They were just like us—overworked and just trying to earn a decent living for their families. I can't imagine how their loved ones handled it when there wasn't an investigation."

"I imagine they didn't handle it very well at all," Georgia adds with an ominous tone.

"Were any of them your friends?" Mandy asks.

"One of them was a coworker, very nice gal. The other . . . well, she was one of my dearest friends. It was a senseless tragedy and I never set foot behind the gates of the Hawthorne Bluff Club again."

Chapter 6

Mandy can't get her mind to stray from the conversation with Georgia today. She would have never in a million years guessed that the sweet old woman next door had momentarily sold her soul to work for the Bluff. Mandy replays every word out of Georgia's mouth that after-noon—the pain she felt losing her husband followed by the pain of working for rich soulless pricks and ending with even more pain, that of losing her best friend in a tragic fire. No wonder Georgia rarely leaves the house. She's experienced more loss than Mandy could ever imagine. Maybe they have more in common than she thought.

She's not sure if Georgia is familiar with the trailer fire that killed half of Mandy's family back when she was ten, but she can't imagine how she *couldn't* have heard about it —it had been front page news in a small town that has nothing better to talk about. How could a fire that took the lives of an underprivileged, drug-addicted family from the wrong side of the tracks make headlines and yet a larger fire with five possible victims, including two millionaires, get swept under the rug, when they occurred the same year?

Mandy pulls up a quick internet search of the fire from 1998 and essentially comes up empty-handed. A few chat forums discussing the various conspiracies, a memorial for one of the blue-collar victims (posted by a family member fifteen years after her death), and a link to the Hawthorne Bluff Club's website with information about its rich history.

She clicks on the link for the Bluff website to see a timeline of notable events in the club's history, beginning with its creation in 1926. In 1965, the House Minority Leader (and future President of the United States) was granted membership to the club. 1970 is the year Jack Hawthorne is voted in as President after the death of his father. In 1977, ten thousand additional acres are purchased by the collective members. In 1986, a new species of trout is discovered on the property, and researchers from the Department of Natural Resources are allowed on the grounds to confirm and study the fish. In 1998, Chandler Hawthorne, Jr. is sworn in as president and serves for four years before his life is tragically cut short in an automobile accident. In the summer of 2002, Chandler Hawthorne III becomes the fourth and youngest Hawthorne to serve as President of the Hawthorne Bluff Club, a position he still holds.

Mandy scans over the smaller tick marks that denote less significant events in the club's history, such as the construction of the new dining lodge, bowling alley, and installation of an inground pool in 2004. Other than stating that Jack Hawthorne served as President until 1998, there is not a single word about his death or the fire that killed two employees. She clicks on the navigation bar for the site, hoping that maybe there's an entire page dedicated to the fire. Nothing. Not only is any mention of the fire missing, but the site itself doesn't have a crumb of useful information, other than a link to apply for a summer job, a document detailing their code of ethics and whistle-blower policy (an odd choice when your site only has five pages), and a contact form. That's it. The page itself looks like it was designed by cheap build-your-own-website software from the early aughts; you'd never guess this was an organization made up of the wealthiest men and women in the state of Michigan.

Mandy wonders why a lawsuit against the club was never filed by the victims' families, but the two most likely scenarios are that they were quietly paid off or they didn't have the money to retain a lawyer in the first place. Both options are equally infuriating. All these years later, and they are still getting away with whatever they want.

She navigates away from the Bluff's webpage and back to Reddit, when Murphy barks in disapproval.

"What, Murphs? It helps me unwind. Don't you want to read about other people's problems? There are far worse vices I could have. Be thankful it's not drugs."

He sighs and lays his head back down on his front paws. Mandy reaches for the wine glass on her nightstand, only to find it empty. "I've got a solution to this problem," she tells Murphy before reaching further to retrieve the half-empty bottle. She remembers the two beers she had earlier while pouring herself a third glass of wine. She swore she would never drink like her mother, but she also didn't expect to be broke and divorced in her mid-thirties, working for a deadbeat creep at a gas station. She just needs to feel sorry for herself for another month or two and then she'll get her life in order, and that plan will not include drinking all day, that's for sure. In fact, once she's finished with the half-case of beer and two bottles of wine left in her house, she'll be done drinking. Yes, that's the plan.

She sips the cheap bottle of red while scrolling and as is often true, her boldness grows with her level of intoxication. Just as she reaches that sweet level of buzz (the very level where she should quit so she doesn't have a headache tomorrow), she lands on a subreddit called "Upper Peninsula of Michigan Lore" and immediately clicks the link.

The Upper Peninsula is the heavily wooded section of Michigan that makes up around thirty percent of the state's land mass but only three percent of its population. Because the U.P. is so secluded from the rest of the country, there is no end to the list of urban legends told around the campfire or, more recently, around the internet. Bigfoot hunters gather yearly, paranormal reality show crews are a fixture in the historic bars and hotels, and every small town in the area boasts of once being home to Al Capone. Mandy's heard it all, but tonight she's searching for a different type of lore, that of the Hawthorne Bluff Club's deadly fires.

She types the key words into the search bar for the group and is shocked to see only two results pop up. The first is an over-eager conspiracy theorist wanting to discuss the rumor of the Bluff Club's members sacrificing children and drinking their blood to stay young but is quickly shut down by several commenters telling him to get lost with that nonsense. The second post catches Mandy's attention when she sees the word *arson*. She clicks on the post to expand it.

WHAT ABOUT THE HAWTHORNE BLUFF CLUB IN DELTA COUNTY? MY AUNT USED TO WORK THERE IN THE SEVENTIES AND SHE'S SO TRAUMATIZED, SHE WON'T EVEN TALK

ABOUT IT. A GROUP WEALTHY AND POWERFUL ENOUGH TO CONCEAL ARSON AND POSSIBLE MURDER IS A GROUP I WOULD NEVER MESS WITH. I CAN'T IMAGINE WHAT GOES ON BEHIND THOSE GATES. ANYONE HAVE STORIES?

SEVERAL OF THE responses are from commenters in other areas of the U.P. who obviously aren't familiar with the rumors, and Mandy realizes most of them probably weren't even born in 1998. They all have questions, they all want more details, and several are voicing frustration over the lack of information via Google search.

THERE'S NO WAY THIS HAPPENED AND THERE'S NOTHING ON THE INTERNET ABOUT IT. C'MON DUDE, IT'S A STRETCH. PROBABLY JUST A RUMOR SOMEONE STARTED BECAUSE THEY WERE BORED. HOUSES BURN DOWN ALL THE TIME IN THE U.P. WITH EVERYONE USING PROPANE STOVES AND SPACE HEATERS.

MANDY RECALLS the sadness in Georgia's eyes when she confirmed that one of the fire's victims was a good friend. A life that ended in vain because the fire was swept under the rug, never to be investigated.

She stops scrolling when she lands on the next comment.

NOT A RUMOR. YOU WOULDN'T BELIEVE WHAT GOES ON THERE. ONE DAY THOSE ASSHOLES WILL GET WHAT'S COMING TO THEM.

. . .

THE COMMENT WAS from someone with the username DANNYBOY06. Mandy clicks on the name to view his profile, which typically shows any posts made by the user, as well as any comments they have made on other posts. She clicks around a few times, thinking there must be some sort of mistake—that is the only comment on the profile. She checks their info; the account was created two years ago. Two years of lurking and only one comment. *How odd*, she thinks.

Fueled by liquid courage, she sends DANNYBOY06 a private message.

"Sorry to bother you, but I've developed a bit of an obsession with the Hawthorne Bluff Club lately. Care to share what you know about it?"

Mandy stares at the screen, as if this random user is sitting at his computer that very moment, waiting for her message and preparing a response. He's made one public comment in the last two years; he obviously isn't of the "chronically online" generation. Regardless of what common sense is telling her, she waits a few more minutes, refreshing the page in case DANNYBOY06 decides to answer her. Mandy navigates to her own page to see what visitors to her profile are greeted with. Oddly enough, her username also ends in 06: MCramer06, for her married name and the year she graduated high school. Probably time to change that username, although she has yet to retake her maiden name because losing the scarlet letter of Smith on her driver's license was the best thing about her marriage.

Apparently DANNYBOY06 isn't taking the bait tonight, so Mandy closes her laptop and lets Murphy out one more time before she calls it a night. After both doors are locked and her sound machine is turned on, she drifts into a peaceful slumber until that peace is interrupted by the most disturbing nightmare she's had in years.

She's fighting for her life in a large body of water inside the gates of the Bluff. Every time she starts to gain traction on the shore, she slips back in and begins to float away. On the lawn in front of her stands a group of well-dressed adults, who she somehow knows are all members. First, they laugh at her and then they turn their backs, carrying on conversation without any regard for the fact that a stranger is drowning in their lake. Suddenly, the water dries up and Mandy is free falling through the air, grasping for something or someone to save her.

She wakes with a start and it's already morning, the spring sun shining brightly through her bedroom window. She grabs her phone to check the time. 8:48. That's the latest she's slept in years. Luckily, she has the midday-shift today, so she's in no hurry. She swipes to open her phone and sees a notification on her Reddit app. Her heart flutters as she clicks on the icon and opens her inbox. DANNYBOY06 has responded.

"Yeah, I get the fascination. You must be a townie? Maybe you should apply to work there for the summer. Trust me . . . you have to see this shit to believe it."

Chapter 7

"A *townie*? So, you must be one of *them*?" Mandy types aggressively. She hasn't been referred to as a townie in years, because they are the only people she surrounds herself with.

Much to her surprise, DANNYBOY06 replies almost immediately.

"LOL, nah. I'm somewhere in between. Sorry, didn't mean to offend."

She contemplates what to even respond to that. Somewhere in between? The only group she could imagine being in between would be someone who lives by the beach. They aren't all assholes, but they still have nice homes and don't associate much with *townies*.

"Thanks so much for the suggestion, but I have a job. I was just curious about the place, that's all. Have a great day."

There. She's done with that conversation. She's not sure why she even messaged him in the first place, but then she notices the red ring of dried liquid on her nightstand,

and it all comes back to her. The ping of a new message catches her off guard and she nearly drops her phone.

"If you change your mind, let me know. I have a 'certain set of skills' and I just checked out their employment portal; it would be easy to hack and guarantee you an interview. It looks like they have a nearly full schedule of applicants for the next week or so, and they are starting at twenty-five dollars an hour for summer help. Not bad for this area."

That's five dollars more per hour than she's making now. She begins to wonder about the hours and the benefits before mentally scolding herself for even considering the idea.

"That is good money. Why don't you work there?" she asks.

"I've experienced enough of that place, trust me."

Ugh. Why does he have to be so vague and ominous?

"I'm happy with my job, but thanks for the offer. Maybe one day I'll find out what they're hiding up there, but it's not going to be because I'm one of their employees. I heard that hasn't ended well for some people in the past." She throws in a fire emoji and a ghost emoji before realizing how insensitive that is to a stranger who may not share in her admiration for dark humor. Luck appears to be on her side.

"LOL. You're not wrong. Let me know if you change your mind; it's just a few keystrokes on my end and you're in."

"If you're that good at hacking, why don't you log into one of their bank accounts and transfer me enough to pay my mortgage?" This time she adds an angel emoji, in case he is somehow actually capable of doing this.

"Hacking a basic employment website and online calendar is a completely different task than hacking into a mobile banking system, but I like where your head's at. Steal from the rich and give to the poor; I could be Delta County's own online Robin Hood."

She flinches at being referred to as poor. Poor was the broken-down trailer she was raised in, the one that had the utilities turned on only about seventy percent of the time and never once saw a full pantry. Sure, she may be stressed about bills now, but she has a clean, two-bedroom house on a quiet street with a semi-full fridge and a fenced in backyard for her little dog. By Smith standards, she's living high on the hog.

"You'd be this *townie's* hero," she quips.

"I'm at your disposal," he replies with a winking emoji.

Mandy logs off and goes through her morning routine, noticing Georgia once again in her backyard garden as she opens the door to let Murphy outside. He runs up against the fence and barks at his friend before Mandy follows behind and opens the small gate to reunite them. He bunny hops over to Georgia, leaping into her arms like the end credits in an after-school special.

"My little Murphs!" she cries. "How did you get so handsome? You must be getting your beauty sleep!"

He appears to understand her as his little tongue licks the side of her face and his tail wags so aggressively, his entire rear end shakes.

"You're too good to him, Georgia. He's going to get a big head with all those compliments," Mandy tells her. She's now outside her fence and at the edge of her neighbor's garden, where she takes a seat on a small concrete bench and takes a sip from the steaming cup of coffee in her hand. "It sure is chilly out here; want me to grab you some coffee?"

Georgia bats away the idea with one swoop of her

gloved hand. "I've got half my day in, dear. I had coffee hours ago."

Her knees are propped on top of a padded board made for gardeners. She's using a small rake to level out an area of fresh soil where there was grass the day before.

"You're expanding the garden again? You need to slow down, or Martha Stewart is going to be calling you for tips," Mandy says. She has a hint of playfulness in her tone, but the truth is she's genuinely impressed. Georgia's garden belongs on the cover of a magazine. She can't wait to see what it looks like by mid-July when everything around here is in full bloom.

"Martha Stewart probably hasn't tended to her own garden in decades. That woman has enough money for an entire staff to keep it up. I value the work I put into these plants entirely too much to allow someone else's grubby hands all over them. When my health starts to fail, I'll teach you everything you need to know to keep it healthy when I'm gone. I'm trusting you not to let anyone else touch my precious babies."

Mandy lets out a quick laugh before realizing that Georgia isn't joking at all.

"Georgia, whoever inherits your house is going to have to tend to the garden. Sure, I'll be here to help, but I'm not going to overstep my boundaries with your relatives, especially while they are in mourning."

"Family? My parents and husband are long gone. I never had children, and my siblings are the most useless bunch you've ever seen. My estate is going to you, Mandy. There may not be much, but it will be all yours when I leave this earth."

Mandy doesn't know how to respond to this; she's not equipped to deal with kindness and generosity on this level. There obviously wasn't an estate when her father died and her mother went to prison; only debt. Her paternal grand-parents died before she was born and her maternal grand-parents have wanted nothing to do with her since the day she was born, from what she's been told. The last she heard they were somewhere in Arizona. Nobody has given Mandy a handout like this.

"Georgia . . . I don't know what to say. I just . . ."

"There's nothing to say, Mandy. Just don't go killing me over a single-story ranch; it's not worth the prison time," Georgia replies with a wink.

She sure is a wild card. Just when Mandy thinks she has her neighbor figured out, she drops these bombs on her, like the fact that she worked for the Hawthorne Bluff Club or that she's leaving all of her earthly belong-ings to Mandy. What else does this woman have up her sleeve?

"We can talk more about this another time. You're healthy enough to be on your knees with your hands in the dirt for hours; I don't think death is knocking at your door anytime soon. I need to hop in the shower and run some errands before my shift. Are you okay to check on Murphy? I suppose I could start asking Braxton, as well, since he has a pug, too. He might appreciate them running each other's energy off."

"Oh, nonsense," Georgia insists. "I enjoy my quality time with Murphy. If his little dog would like to join us sometime, that would be fine. But I'm not giving up my babysitting duties anytime soon."

Mandy smiles. Georgia favors Murphy like he's her grandson and it's precious. She refers to their new neigh-bor's pet as *his little dog*, despite absolutely knowing his name is Max.

"Great, I'll mention it to Braxton next time I see him and maybe we can have a playdate. You could even start charging us when you check in on the dogs; it could be your retirement side hustle," Mandy suggests.

"I'm not sure what a side hustle is, but I have a feeling I've already got one and it's called gardening."

Mandy stands and pats her thigh for Murphy to join her. He positions himself up on his hind legs to sniff Georgia one more time before climbing down and returning to his owner.

"Call me if there are any issues. I'm off at eleven tonight," Mandy calls out as she closes the gate behind her.

"There won't be any issues, dear. There never are."

Chapter 8

As Mandy pulls into the Quick Stop, the sight of Shorty's car takes the wind out of her sails before the shift has even begun. She can't recall the last time one of his visits ended well.

True to his nickname, Mandy's boss is five foot seven on a good day, carrying around a seven-foot-tall attitude for no reason at all. He inherited the store from his father, the beloved John Massey Sr., but doesn't seem to have inherited any of his decency. He's crude, lazy, and cheap. He's the perfect example of being born on third base and going through life like he hit a triple. The business' saving grace is that Mandy is the face of the Quick Stop while Shorty is off doing God-knows-what. The people of this town don't want to be reminded that their hard-earned dollars are lining that man's pockets.

When Mandy walks in through the suspiciously unlocked door of the back employee entrance, she's startled by the sight of Shorty and the morning cashier, Jaymie, in the storage room. He is leaned with his forehead close to hers, his arm stretched and leaning against the wall behind her. Her arms are crossed and her eyes, first fixated on the floor, dart up to meet Mandy's when the light from the opened steel door casts an illuminating glow on the unlikely pair.

"Hey Mandy, you're early," Shorty says, a tinge of annoyance in his tone.

"My shift starts in five minutes," Mandy reminds him. "Are you good, Jaym?"

Without words, Mandy understands everything the girl is conveying with her pleading eyes.

"Of course she's good. We were just talking about the schedule."

"What about the schedule?" Mandy asks. The schedule *she* makes, which only has three possible shifts and six employees to fill those shifts. She could make the schedule in her sleep.

"Well, Tina's out. She quit without notice, the ungrateful bitch," Shorty spits out.

Mandy instinctively pulls her phone out of her purse to check for missed messages. Tina is one of her favorite employees, and she can't imagine the woman would quit without talking to her first. She sure as hell wouldn't inform Shorty of her resignation before telling Mandy. No way.

"*Tina*? When?"

"Right before her shift ended, around six thirty this morning. I had to stay here and work the last thirty minutes to cover until Jaymie here showed up. *You're welcome.*"

Mandy would love nothing more than to knock that smug grin off his face.

"Did she say why she was quitting? She just asked me for more hours last week and I gave them to her. She bought a used Honda off crooked-ass Bruce Shanahan and has been stressed about the payments. I can't believe she'd just quit," Mandy says, not even trying to disguise the mistrust in her voice.

"Nah, she just walked out. There's nothing more to it," Shorty says with a shrug.

Jaymie pushes him lightly and practically leaps in Mandy's direction.

"That's not true, Mandy. Tina texted me and said Shorty tried to hook up with her in the storage room when nobody was in the store. She was terrified until a trucker came in and interrupted them and she grabbed her bag and ran out."

Mandy stretches an arm out in front of petite Jaymie, in case Shorty gets any ideas. His hands are balled into tight fists and Mandy can see a vein throbbing from the side of his neck.

"And what was he discussing with you when I came in, Jaymie?" Mandy asks, keeping her eyes fixed on Shorty, who is now fidgeting and preparing his defense.

"He said that if I took Tina's shifts, he'd make me General Manager," Jaymie says, barely above a whisper.

Mandy laughs out loud. Of course he offered the promotion he'd been holding over her head for years to a younger, more attractive, and less qualified employee.

"You have to be fucking kidding me," Mandy says, her first time ever showing a hint of disrespect to the man who hasn't done anything to earn her respect in the last six years.

"I think you misunderstood," Shorty says with his palms raised, attention focused on Jaymie.

"I don't think she misunderstood a fucking word," Mandy fires back.

A cheery tone rings out, signifying the front door to the business opening. Mandy pulls Jaymie closer and whispers in her ear, asking if she's ready to quit. Jaymie nods. Her body is shaking. Mandy's would be as well if she wasn't running on pure adrenaline.

"You're going to have to handle that customer yourself, Shorty. We're done," Mandy says, not allowing herself to think of the repercussions of not having a job during this season of her life.

"Done? You're going to quit your job because you believe the lies of two little girls?" He practically spits as he spews the words at Mandy.

What begins as pure rage smolders into acceptance in her throat before the words come out.

"Yes, I believe these two *women*. I also believe that you will mail our final checks, as I'm sure you don't want word getting around a small town that you don't pay your employees after you sexually harass them. Best of luck, Shorty."

The women can hear his muffled rants as they walk out the back door and let it slam behind them.

"You good?" Mandy asks her now former employee.

"Honestly, my uncle has been begging me to work at his feed store because they're short-handed. I just didn't want to let you down. I bet I can start tomorrow," Jaymie says, before adding, "Will you be okay?"

"I'll be just fine," Mandy lies. It's the same lie she told everyone after half of her family died in the fire. When foster families explained why they could only keep her temporarily. When the grants and loans weren't enough to cover college tuition, so she decided against going at all. When her husband left her alone and broke, after abusing her for years. Mandy's entire life has been a series of convincing the people around her that she'll be fine.

Chapter 9

"You know, there's no award for suffering," Georgia says, throwing back the thick comforter to expose Mandy's body, clothed in the same faded pajamas she's been wearing for three days.

"What does that even mean?" she moans, yanking the blanket back from her neighbor.

It's strange to have Georgia in her bedroom. They normally stay in the kitchen or on the front porch while they have coffee, and she typically uses Mandy's spare key to retrieve Murphy and take him back to her place when she dog sits—a kind gesture that Mandy no longer requires because she doesn't have a job. Having this sweet woman in her bedroom, running a gentle hand along her scalp and replenishing the water on her nightstand makes Mandy wonder if this is what it would have been like to have a mother who cared about her. What an amazing childhood that would have been.

"It means that nothing good is going to come of you staying in bed all day and feeling sorry for yourself. Also, I think it would be beneficial for you to shower today."

Mandy can't help but laugh. What a polite way to tell someone they stink. The worst part is—she's right. Mandy hasn't showered in three days, since she quit her job in a fit of rage. Because of her unstable childhood, she is not a person who makes rash decisions very often. Walking out on a job she's had for six years could not be more uncharacteristic of her. She is ashamed to admit how amazing it felt.

"Want to go to the Rail and drink a Bloody Mary with me?" Mandy asks, a renewed optimism sparkling in her eyes. A stiff drink and a game of darts would surely take her mind off this mess.

Georgia tuts.

"No, dear, I don't want to patronize a dive bar in the middle of a Monday afternoon with you to use alcohol as a coping mechanism for your issues. I want you to get off your heinie, dust yourself off, and find another job."

"You're zero fun, Georgia."

Mandy has never met a homebody quite like her neighbor. *It's where my peace is. You'll understand when you get older.* That's what Georgia told her last month when she refused to go watch a movie with Mandy in Escanaba, the nearest town with a theater.

"Do you have friends you could call to help get you out of this funk? I fear I'm not equipped to give you what you need. The best I can do is hassle you to get out of bed," Georgia offers.

"I have two friends in this life and they both went off to college and got married to stupid men who didn't want to live in the U.P., so I'm going to have to figure this out on my own."

When Mandy's two best friends, Laura and Becky, left for college, they did something Mandy never dreamed would happen—they made new friends. It's a strange,

strange feeling when the two girls you've known your entire life suddenly spend time with people you know nothing about. They had inside jokes of their own and took spring break trips without her, posting the pictures on social media for all to see. Mandy wasn't emotionally mature enough to admit how much it hurt her, so she just slowly drifted backward, away from the pain. She quit checking in, she quit visiting them on campus, she simply quit the friendships. At thirty-six years old, she's just now admitting that she's at fault and worries it's too late to repair what she has broken. Now they are both married with kids of their own, and she's not entirely sure they'd even be interested in rekindling a bond they probably wouldn't even have the time for.

"Look, I'm going to go make a fresh batch of lemonade and some of those ginger snap cookies you like so much. I'm taking Murphy with me because he doesn't deserve to witness such despair. When we come back, you better be showered and ready to face the day," Georgia tells her before bending down to pick Murphy up in her arms. She lifts his little paw to mimic a wave goodbye and turns to leave.

Mandy groans and taps the screen of her phone to check the time. It's nearly one in the afternoon. She'd laugh if she wasn't so sad.

Moments later, the sound of raised voices steals her attention. She slides her bare feet into the slippers beside her bed and tiptoes to the guest room, in the direction of the noises she's hearing outside. She gently pulls down one of the slats in the window blinds to steal a peek, surprised to see Georgia stomping away toward her own house. Left standing on her lawn is Braxton. He is rubbing his eyebrow with one hand, the other resting on his hip. What in the world could they possibly be arguing about?

Strange, she thinks, before heading to the bathroom to turn the shower on before she can talk herself out of it. When Georgia brings Murphy back, she'll get the rundown on how the old woman managed to piss off the new neighbor so quickly. She could use a good laugh.

It's amazing what a hot shower after days spent drowning in a depression haze can do for a woman. Fifteen minutes after stepping into her bathroom and out of her dirty pajamas, Mandy is wrapped in a clean, fluffy robe with her fully charged laptop in front of her, ready to change her life. She can do this. She was a manager at a damn gas station, not the President of the United States. It can't be that much of a challenge to find a similar position with similar pay. She has valuable skills, a resume that shows steady employment, and open availability. She'll have a new job by the end of the day.

She logs on and scans all of the usual job listing sites—the local online bulletin boards, the national job postings, and openings on the Michigan statewide jobs database. Thanks to her time spent obsessing over online scams as of late, she easily weeds out the con artists. Rule of thumb: If it sounds too good to be true, it probably is.

Next, she eliminates positions that would involve working for or alongside people she grew up with and has no desire to see again in life, let alone work next to them for forty hours per week. Considering the town has a population of less than five thousand, this eliminates half the postings. She scrolls past the out-of-town listings, the minimum wage posts, and the countless insurance sales positions. She nearly falls for a few job descriptions before clicking the links to realize they are MLM schemes disguised as sales positions.

She laughs out loud when she lands on an ad for the Hawthorne Bluff Club. Just as DANNYBOY06 told her online, they are looking for seasonable help and starting at twenty-five dollars an hour, based on experience. She's been a manager for over ten years now—six at the gas station, three at Taco Bell, and two at the shoe store in the mall. Does that mean she would be qualified to make *more* than twenty-five? She can't imagine. The day she got a raise and started making twenty, she came home and cried in the kitchen. The first in her line of Smiths to make a decent living, she felt like she was breaking a multi-generational curse. Patrick mocked her for being so excited about it. He mocked her about a lot of things. Mandy would never settle for a man like Patrick again.

She stares at the Hawthorne job posting, scrolling with her fingers up and down the listing until she knows it by heart.

SEVERAL POSITIONS AVAILABLE IN FOOD SERVICE, GROUND MAINTENANCE, AND FAMILY WORK.

SCENIC WORK LOCATION WITH FREE HEALTHFUL RECREATION AND ON-SITE HOUSING AVAILABLE IF NEEDED.

POSSIBILITY TO STAY ON AFTER THE SEASON IS OVER.

BE PART OF A TRADITION, DATING BACK NEARLY A CENTURY.

Intrigued, she clicks on *Family Work* and hovers over the position of "keeper" before the curiosity gets the best of her and she follows the link to learn more. It doesn't say nanny or babysitter or tutor; it says "keeper." *What a strange title*, she thinks.

KEEPER IS RESPONSIBLE FOR THE CHILDREN OF MEMBERS AND THEIR APPROVED GUESTS. MOST KEEPERS WILL HAVE AN INDIVIDUAL CHILD TO OVERSEE. KEEPERS ARE DIRECT EMPLOYEES OF THE MEMBER/FAMILY AND NOT EMPLOYEES OF THE CLUB. SCHEDULE AND COMPENSATION TO BE NEGOTIATED WITH THE FAMILY DIRECTLY.

Mandy hesitates on the word *negotiated*. Although her

childhood has given her, as her friends used to say, "balls of steel," Mandy has never had the gumption required to negotiate a salary. She simply accepted what was offered to her during a job interview and subsequently during promotions. She cannot fathom sitting in front of an affluent family and *negotiating* what they will pay her to keep an eye on their spoiled little child a few hours a day.

Fuck it. Mandy clicks on the link to apply. What's the worst that can happen; they don't call her for an interview? Maybe she could hit up that mysterious user from Reddit to hack in and get her an interview as a final resort. This is the only job listing that even remotely interests her, so she's going for it. Maybe being around these rich pricks will humanize them, and Mandy will realize she's been exaggerating their villainous behavior.

Mandy doesn't have children of her own, but she received a lifetime of education in childcare each time she was placed in a less-than-stellar foster home and forced to "keep an eye" on the younger kids. That somehow developed into getting them up for school, fed, helping with homework, and knowing their bedtime routine like the back of her hand. She had a mild annoyance over the responsibilities, but it wasn't until many years later that it dawned on her what was really going on. Mandy is incredibly appreciative of the foster care system that looked after her for years, but she also thinks there are some families that simply don't need to be approved for the role. Growing up, she often heard people saying the foster families were just "in it for the money," but Mandy couldn't imagine the money was that good.

An email pops up immediately, confirming receipt of Mandy's application and informing her that a representative will contact her to schedule an interview if her experience is a good fit for their needs. She scoots her chair back from the kitchen table and crosses her arms in satisfaction. *There, done. First step to my new life is complete.*

She can't really explain why she thinks to do this next, but she scoots herself back up to the table, reopens her laptop, logs in to Reddit, and sends DANNYBOY06 a message.

"Job circumstances changed. I ended up applying at the Bluff. Thanks for the heads up about pay; I could really use that kind of money right now. Fingers crossed I won't need your hacking skills to land an interview. Double fingers crossed I can handle the jerks if I do get the job."

She inserts a winking emoji before deciding that it seems flirtatious, so she backspaces and presses send. She eyes a half empty bottle of wine on the counter and decides that 3:00 p.m. is socially acceptable to pour a glass. She's sniffing the liquid to determine if it's been sitting in the opened bottle too long to consume when a *ping* sounds from her computer. DANNYBOY06 has responded.

"Best of luck to you on the interview, but remember what I said when we discussed you working there in the first place: these people are nuts and they *cannot* be trusted. Make that bank, but don't let your guard down."

Chapter 10

Mandy is applauding herself for leaving her house early for her interview at the Bluff when the dreaded gas warning light pops up on her dashboard. Her eyes dart over to the fuel gauge and sure enough, she's on empty. The only gas station between her house and the Hawthorne Bluff Club is the Quick Stop, and she sure as hell won't be stopping there. She got a text from Tina letting her know that the rest of the staff quit the second they heard what happened, so part of her wants to swing in to see Shorty fighting for his life and trying to figure out the register, but she doesn't have time for games right now. She's about to interview for a job that could change her life.

Reluctantly, she drives three miles out of the way to choose another station to fill up, but her shoulders relax when she checks the time and sees she's still ahead of schedule, even with the detour. She remembered Luke, the Butch's Meat driver, talking about what a stickler for punctuality Chandler Hawthorne is, so she left the house with plenty of time for unexpected mishaps, such as forgetting about her empty gas tank.

She couldn't believe her luck when she woke up to an email from a representative at the club, asking if she was free for an interview this afternoon. Then her jaw nearly hit the floor when she was told it was for a position working directly for the Hawthorne family. There wasn't even time to tell Georgia about her good news, as she'd spent the last four hours obsessing over her hair, skin, and clothes for the interview. Sure, she wanted to look nice and presentable, but she also didn't want to dress so nicely that they think she's afraid to get dirty playing with their child or, even worse, that she doesn't need the money. After flipping through every garment in her closet, she realized that she doesn't even own an outfit that would make her look like she doesn't need the money. She settled on a pressed pair of khakis, a baby-blue button-down shirt, and brown penny loafers. Her hair is combed neatly back into a bun at the nape of her neck, and her makeup is understated yet flattering. She matched it with a set of faux pearl earrings she found on the clearance rack at Marshall's last winter.

"Looking like a hot-ass Mary Poppins," she'd told herself in the mirror before saying goodbye to Murphy on her way out.

Focusing intently on the numbers on the gas pump display so she can do her best to stop the nozzle at twenty dollars, Mandy is caught off guard by someone yelling her name from a few cars over. *Great, just what I need*, she thinks to herself as she recognizes the rusted car as belonging to her ex-sister-in-law, Dee.

When Mandy married Patrick after high school, she was excited to gain a sister. She envisioned shopping trips and girls' lunches, maybe even a couples' trip or two with their husbands. What she got was a cold, judgmental bitch who didn't believe anyone would be good enough for her brother, especially not Mandy Smith.

"What exactly do you gain by telling him not to answer our calls?" she practically shouts as she approaches Mandy. The distraction makes her lose track of her gas total, which is over thirty dollars before she shuts it off and cusses under her breath.

"What are you going on about? I haven't talked to your brother in months, Dee. He obviously doesn't care what I have to say about whose calls he should be answering. Why don't you ask Emily?"

Dee spits on the ground next to her. What a lady. Mandy wonders if she'll crush an empty beer can on her forehead as an encore.

"Don't play games with me, Mandy. She told us what you did," Dee snarls.

It wasn't long ago that Dee intimidated Mandy enough to bow to the pressure and tell her whatever she wanted to know. These days, she's got nothing to lose. The divorce is final. Mandy barks out a sarcastic laugh, the exact one she's been wanting to use in response to her evil sister-in-law's bullshit for years.

"*What I did*? I got cheated on while I worked full-time and cooked your brother dinner every night and made sure his work uniform was clean. He slept with Emily while I cleaned his house, remembered all your birthdays, packed his lunch, and made sure our bills were paid. Don't get me started on how many times that man laid his hands on me after a bad day at work. I didn't say a damn word when he told me he was leaving me. I just signed the papers. What do you want from me?"

"She told us he went back to you," Dee says, and she barely gets the words out before Mandy erupts with laughter. She props an arm up on the back of her car to steady herself before responding.

"Well, looks like he moved on to someone else, Dee. I'm not sure who he left her for, but it sure as hell wasn't me. Now, if you'll excuse me, I've got somewhere to be," Mandy says before tearing off her gas receipt and retreating to her car.

God, Mandy can't believe how good it feels to no longer tiptoe around that miserable cow. It was just the confidence boost she needed before facing the richest family in town to ask for a job. She hopes that when Patrick finally returns Dee's calls, she mentions how good Mandy looked when she ran into her. She doesn't need to know it was for a job interview; let her think Mandy dresses like this all the time for her new life. The one that most certainly will never include Dee's brother again.

When Mandy is pulling up to the famous (well, small-town famous) gates of the Hawthorne Bluff Club, she realizes she wasted the entire drive replaying her conversation with Dee. Maybe she's not as tough as she convinced herself during the confrontation, because now she's just overthinking every word and wondering how Dee could still harbor all this hostility toward her. She's done nothing wrong to the woman. She took care of her brother for nearly twenty years and didn't cause any sort of drama when he decided he wanted someone else. What could she possibly still have to be mad about? She also momentarily wonders who the new girlfriend is and what Emily did to lose his interest so quickly, but she gathers enough willpower to stop those thoughts in their tracks. Patrick Cramer is someone else's problem now; she mustn't concern herself with thoughts of him anymore.

She has mixed feelings when she sees that the guard inside the small, wooden building isn't someone she's familiar with. She would have liked the comfort of seeing a familiar face in so-called enemy territory, but she also didn't want to face someone she graduated with while on her way to apply for a glorified nanny job at the ripe age of thirty-six. She leans over to retrieve the wallet out of her purse on the passenger side and flips it open to show the man her driver's license.

"No need, Miss Cramer. I know what you look like," he says, holding up a clipboard with a printed photo from one of Mandy's social media accounts. She hasn't checked the privacy settings in years and her mind instantly travels to the highly inappropriate posts she's made, lusting over Glen Powell in recent weeks. Mandy blushes, and the guard nods as if he's reading her mind. Those posts were just supposed to be for her internet friends . . . who all enthusiastically agreed, for what it's worth.

"Keep going down this drive until you see the main dining hall. There are a few guest parking spots to the left of the building. Someone will be waiting there to escort you," he tells her, leaning an inch or two out of the small window of his command post to gesture with two fingers in the general direction of her destination. Come to think of it, he somewhat resembles Glen Powell. It's also a good possibility that Mandy hasn't been with a man in over six months and her judgment is clouded. She goes with the second option and politely thanks him before coasting down the winding drive to the Hawthorne Bluff Club.

The road is nearly half a mile long, and it's completely paved. She notices small dashes on each side of her car, and she comes to a near-stop to get a better look before realizing that they are small lights installed in the concrete to illuminate the drive at night. She couldn't begin to imagine what a project like this would cost.

The words *someone will be there waiting to escort you* play in her mind. Who is *someone* and where will they be escorting her? It all sounds so official, like she's visiting a military base or a secured government building.

Her thoughts are interrupted by the gasp that escapes her mouth as she nears the end of the drive and the woods open to the most beautiful view she has seen, possibly in her entire life.

When the man told her to drive to the dining hall, she pictured a large, boring, barn-like structure, one you would see at a summer camp. Instead, she's met with a grand two-story lodge made of red cedar, with a wraparound porch overlooking a quaint lake, it's water the stillest she's ever seen. There are picnic tables scattered throughout the grass (which is somehow already green, despite spring barely making its arrival) between the lodge and the lake, with countless strands of bulbed lights strung throughout the trees above the tables. At golden hour, she's certain the view must be majestic.

A laugh escapes her lips as she puts her car in park and opens the door to birds singing a song so sweet, it belongs in a Disney movie. She's never heard birds like this and wonders if they somehow shipped them in to entertain the wealthy. She's less than five miles from home, but the air feels lighter and smells fresher. Is it simply her mind playing tricks on her?

Speaking of tricks, surely she's seeing things as her attention diverts to the man approaching her car, presumably the one assigned to be her escort on the property. She could swear it's Wesley Rudden, a man she's known her entire life.

At just twelve years old, he woke from a deep sleep in the mobile home next door to the smell of flames coming from the direction of her family's trailer. He ran out the door barefoot and sprinted directly to Mandy's window, where he climbed in, woke her, and pulled her outside to safety. Once on the grass, gasping for breath, she watched him run back in and pull her mother from the living room and onto the redwood deck. They barely made it to safety when something exploded inside, making it impossible for anyone to reenter and save her father or her brother.

Wesley Rudden saved her life. He's the only one who knows and understands where Mandy came from, because he suffered a similar tragic childhood. He may not have lost his house and half his family to a fire, but he experienced just as much neglect.

Mandy was never sure if she loved Wes because of what he did that night or if she was meant to love him anyway, but she spent years pining for him. He checked on her in every foster home placement and carried her backpack to the bus after school five days a week until his senior year. The harder she tried to communicate her true feelings for him, the more he pulled away. She was too young to understand the complexities of their relationship, and just foolish enough to let heartbreak be her guiding emotion. She loved Wes, and he didn't love her back; is there a worse pain for a sixteen-year-old to experience? That's the same year Patrick Cramer bumped into her while he was leaving wood shop and asked her if she'd like a ride home. The rest is history.

All these years, she'd allow herself to wonder what happened to Wes for a few minutes before she forced her brain to redirect. He was a ghost—no social media, no class reunions, no updates on where he's been. Could it be possible that he has been at the Bluff all these years, just miles from her?

As he gets closer, Mandy's knees nearly give out and her hands are shaking so intensely, she drops her keys in the gravel next to her car. When she bends to retrieve them, she stands upright and is met with Wesley Rudden's face, just as handsome as when they were teenagers, with the addition of sporadic gray stubble in his tightly trimmed beard and sideburns. His warm brown eyes meet hers, and he doesn't seem at all surprised that she's there.

"Hello, Mandy. I've been expecting you."

Chapter 11

"Wes," she whispers. The beautiful name that hasn't touched her lips in years feels so good, she can't help but smile. "You work here?"

She has to actively fight the instinct to grab him into a tight embrace when she remembers it's a job interview. God knows who is watching. She needs to remain professional, no matter how hard it may be.

"I do work here. I just happen to live on property, as well," he replies.

On property. What is this, a resort?

"What, um . . . What do you do?" she asks. His attire doesn't give away much; he's simply wearing a Hawthorne polo and khakis, like the dozens of other employees she's encountered in town over the years.

"Well, after high school I started here in the kitchen. I've worked my way up over the years; I'm pretty sure I've worked in every position at the club. Now I'm the Director of Member Affairs."

"What does that mean?" she asks before she can allow herself time to feel foolish.

He leans forward, and the intoxicating scent of his wooded, masculine cologne nearly sends her to her knees once more. "I keep the rich people happy and keep my mouth shut," he whispers. The corner of his lips turn upward in a casual smirk and she sees it—the boy she loved for so long. He's still in there.

"I've missed you," she says, barely above a whisper this time. She knows she shouldn't have said it, yet she doesn't exactly regret it.

He stares at her for a few seconds, and she sees the recognition set in. She watches the memories dance behind his eyes, the confirmation that he's standing in front of the girl who once knew him better than anyone. He doesn't return the words, but he nods, and that's all she needs for confirmation.

"Have you talked to your mom lately?" Wes asks.

"Not once. The prison called me a few years back when she was having surgery, but everything must have went well because I haven't been asked to pick up her remains. Have you talked to yours?"

His smile doesn't quite make it to his eyes, which are the same sad eyes she gazed into each time they met in the woods behind the trailer park to play foolish games of make believe because real life was too hard to stomach.

"Not in over a decade. She's still somehow married to my dad and living off the state, last I heard."

They both nod and stare at the ground for a moment. It's a wonder they both made it out alive and physically unscathed. Mentally; now that's another story.

"How are you feeling about the interview?" he asks.

"Honestly, they just emailed me this morning to schedule it, so I haven't had time to worry about it yet. I'm not sure what to expect."

She kicks a few pieces of gravel around before adding,

barely above a whisper, "I haven't heard the greatest things about these people, Wes. I'm not sure I should even be trying to work here."

He looks off in the distance, presumably toward the house he's about to escort her to, before looking back at her. Static sounds from a small radio he has clipped to his belt, startling them both. A man's voice booms from the speaker, telling Wes that he's ready for his next interview. He's not exactly rude, but there's certainly no kindness in his tone. Wes tells him they're on their way and is sure to end the message with a strong "sir" before signing off. Mandy barely catches it, but a hint of unease washes over Wes's eyes for a moment before he regains a look of indifference.

"Listen, Mandy. These people have wealth like you've never seen, and they also will behave unlike anyone you've ever been around. If you decide that you want this job, you need to act like it doesn't affect you. Act like you're around extravagance all the time and you harbor absolutely no hostile feelings over the unfairness of it all. Be polite and decisive, but never speak out of turn. If you decide to mention your upbringing, just know that they will treat you like a charity case. They will mention to their friends that their new help was in the foster system. The recipients of their charity aren't allowed any dignity; remember that. The charity is never about the person it benefits; it's only to make themselves look better for the others. If Mrs. Hawthorne asks for your opinion on anything, always compliment her. Today is probably the only day Mr. Hawthorne will even acknowledge you. He works a lot. You'll mainly be dealing with Mrs. Hawthorne and the kids."

Mandy struggles to take it all in. "Kids? There are multiple? How old are they?"

"Frankie is seven, and she's going to adore you. She's precious. There's still hope for her. Remy is a good kid, but he stays in his room as often as possible. They usually force him to come out for family dinner, but he's a gamer, and that's all he cares about. He's about to turn eighteen."

"Remy and Frankie . . . Okay, I can remember that. Pretty progressive names for old money, eh?"

Wes laughs; the first time she's heard that beautiful laugh in years.

"Remington and Frances, and trust me—Chandler Hawthorne is no fan of nicknames, but enough people use them with his kids, he had no choice but to allow it."

Mandy considers this as they walk along a wooded path toward the Hawthorne home. *No choice but to allow it.*

The woods open to what is unsurprisingly the most impressive home Mandy has ever seen. It rivals the mansions on the cliffs of Mackinac Island, a tourist destination in Michigan that she visited once for a school trip.

"Firm handshake, but not so firm that you're trying to seem dominant. Cross your legs at the ankle when you sit. If you accept a beverage from their housekeeper, use a coaster before you set it down. Be confident but polite. Don't speak ill of any former employers." Wes speaks so quickly, Mandy can barely keep up.

She hopes they don't ask about Shorty because she can't fathom coming up with anything positive to say about the creep.

"Are you nervous for me?" Mandy asks, elbowing Wes lightly.

He stops and looks at her directly.

"I know how capable and special you are, Mandy. I just want to make sure these people see it, too."

She nods, fighting back tears. Other than sweet Georgia, she can't remember the last time someone said something so kind to her. She forgot what it feels like to have someone else on her team.

"I can handle it. Don't worry," she assures him.

They walk the last few feet in silence, Mandy mentally preparing for her introduction. Wes catches her off guard when they walk across the front porch, between the white pillars, and he opens the front door after two light knocks. She can't imagine someone being comfortable enough with the Hawthornes to just walk into their home without waiting for someone to answer the door.

"Wes, my man," Chandler Hawthorne greets him as they walk into the grand foyer. He looks like the stereotypical wealthy white dad from a nineties movie—a stack of mail in his hands and expensive reading glasses perched at the end of his nose. He removes the glasses and sets them with the mail on an expansive entryway table before meeting Wes with what can best be described as a fumbled handshake and awkward hug from a man who is trying to seem much younger and cooler than he is.

"You must be . . ." He turns to Mandy, holding out his hand but quickly glancing to Wes for assistance.

"Mandy Cramer. She's interviewing for the keeper position."

Mandy nearly laughs before remembering that keeper is the actual position she applied for. She can't imagine introducing herself to her new coworkers: "Hi, I'm Mandy. I'm the Hawthorne family's new keeper." It's all so ridiculous.

"Mr. Hawthorne, it's a pleasure," she says, before stepping forward to give him a firm yet respectable handshake.

He looks at Wes and pulls a face that says *Wow, this girl knows her manners. I'm impressed.* It takes everything Mandy has not to turn around and walk back out the door. *Twenty-five dollars an hour*, she keeps reminding herself.

"Mandy, if you'll follow me to the library, Mrs. Hawthorne and I would love to ask you a few questions to get to know you a little better. Wes, thank you for showing this young lady around. If you'll come back in an hour, she should be ready to be escorted back to her vehicle."

There's so much about these words that make Mandy's head spin, she doesn't even know where to begin. It's also so insanely weird to her when people refer to their spouses as Mister or Missus. And why does she have to be escorted again? She knows how to get back to her car. Do they think she's going to steal something and make a run for it? Will Wes be instructed to search her purse for gold plated flatware before she can leave the property? It's all too much.

She follows Mr. Hawthorne to the library and is disheartened to see that most of the floor to ceiling mahogany shelves appear to be stocked with decorative books, chosen for their aesthetic, rather than their contents. An avid murder mystery reader, Mandy had high hopes that she'd see some Agatha Christie first editions in with a stack of other well-read classics. Maybe she'd even see some of her favorites on the shelf so she could strike up a conversation about common interests. Instead, she's entered a library that she's certain was designed for drinking scotch and smoking expensive cigars, rather than spending a perfect rainy day reading worn paperbacks.

He motions for her to sit on a leather couch in the center of the room. It's weathered in an expensive kind of way, not like the secondhand couch she had growing up with scattered spaghetti sauce stains and torn stitching, her butt nearly sinking to the floor each time she sat down. This couch's chicly battered cushions barely give as she sits toward the edge, remembering at the last minute to cross her legs as Wes suggested. The moment she finds a comfortable position that still makes her feel presentable,

Mrs. Hawthorne makes her entrance, and Mandy jumps to her feet.

"You must be Mandy," she says, extending a hand to her. Mandy attempts a firm handshake but softens her grip when the woman places a second hand on top. It catches her off guard to receive such a warm gesture from someone she has anticipated detesting. Equally perplexing is the kindness radiating from her smile.

"Mrs. Hawthorne, it's such a pleasure to meet you."

"Please, call me Allison."

Mandy wonders if she means it and decides she will instead use the neutral term of "ma'am" whenever possible. She retakes her seat on the couch but struggles to find the right position on the second try. She is seated too far forward and knows it must look as uncomfortable as it feels, but it's too late to scoot back now. She didn't expect to be this nervous. There are two matching leather chairs across from the couch, and the couple each takes their seats, facing Mandy.

"Tell us a little about yourself. Are you from the area?" Allison Hawthorne asks. While Mandy is quickly organizing her thoughts for a response, Chandler Hawthorne pulls out his phone and appears to respond to a text. Allison gives him the briefest glance of annoyance before plastering on a smile and returning her focus to the prospective employee sitting across from her.

"Yes, born and raised in town. I graduated from GHS in 2006 and have worked full-time ever since. I rarely get sick and don't have any obligations that would affect my schedule. Well, I have Murphy. He's my pug. That's my only obligation, but I have a neighbor who is kind enough to help with him when I work long hours."

Allison nods sweetly.

"And you applied for the job of keeper, which basically

means you're helping with our children, who are seven and seventeen. Obviously, you'd be focusing your attention on Frankie, our seven-year-old, as our son, Remy is fairly self-sufficient. I didn't see any childcare positions on your resume; do you have any experience with kids?"

A slight hesitation causes Chandler to glance up from his phone. There's a strange look on his face, almost as if he's amused already with whatever this unpoised imposter is going to come up with. Mandy remembers the warning from Wes—*if you mention your foster home background, prepare to be a charity case.* Mandy makes a split-second decision to keep it as vague as possible.

"Yes, ma'am. I was the oldest in a home with an over-worked mother, so I most certainly have experienced caring for multiple children at once. Only having two in my care would seem like a walk in the park," Mandy explains, adding a lighthearted laugh at the end to display just how easy it would be for her to do the job. Allison seems to buy it, nudging her husband's elbow with a smile.

"Availability?" he asks, briefly looking up at Mandy before returning attention to his phone.

"Chandler, dear, she just told us that she doesn't have any major obligations."

"She said something about a child," Chandler mumbles.

"A dog, darling. She has a dog. His name is Murphy, correct?" Allison asks, and Mandy can see the tension in her jaw, the clenched teeth—exactly what she used to do when she was trying not to upset Patrick during their marriage. She wants to grab this woman by the shoulders and tell her life doesn't have to be this way.

"Yes, Murphy is my pug. And although I love him and want to be the best pet parent possible, I also have my neighbor who helps when needed. Murphy wouldn't affect my availability whatsoever."

Chandler places his phone back into his pocket and shoots daggers at his wife. She pretends not to notice. Mandy decides to throw a Hail Mary.

"Is that a TAG Heuer? It is stunning," she says, pointing to the gray-blue steel watch on Allison's dainty wrist. Wes was right about the compliments. Her face lights up.

"Why, yes it is! Good eye. Chandler bought it for me for my birthday in March."

March birthday . . . Mandy assumes that she must be a Pisces, judging by her patience and the kindness in her tone. Surely not an Aries, like Patrick. They tend to be impulsive and short-tempered. The only fondness she currently has for her ex-husband is due to his wealthy Aunt Terri, who taught Mandy about luxury watch brands on Thanksgiving a few years ago. Apparently, three hot toddies equaled the perfect amount of alcohol to inspire the woman to brag about her collection of three-thousand-dollar watches to her nephew's wife, who had known nothing but poverty since the day she was born.

Chandler excuses himself, giving Mandy a curt nod, and has his phone glued to his ear before the door is even closed behind him.

"Sorry, he's a workaholic, as I'm sure you can tell. He doesn't mean to be rude . . . He was just born into a long generation of men with a similar demeanor. It's a genetic curse, I'm afraid." Allison gives her a conspiratorial wink, but Mandy doesn't let her guard down yet. Sure, it feels like they're on the same page and sharing a wink-wink-nudge inside joke about how exhausting men can be, but she's been warned enough about the members of this club to be wary.

The women spend the next thirty minutes getting to know each other, which is really just Mandy answering questions in the most pleasant, evasive manner possible while ensuring Allison that she's up to the challenge of keeping her children alive. When she asks if Mandy has any questions for her, she doesn't think Allison was really prepared to answer any about herself.

"What is your favorite part of living inside these gates?" Mandy asks, plastering a smile on her face so the woman won't take the question the wrong way.

Allison has the demeanor of a small-town pageant queen, preparing her best lie for the judges. She briefly tugs at the bottom of her knee-length tweed skirt before smoothing her thin blond hair down over her collarbones. After a quick nod, she answers.

"The bluff is a beautiful place to live. So much nature and undisturbed beauty. You could take a walk every single morning for a year and see something new every day. A lot of people would kill for this kind of solitude."

"And the people?"

A look passes between the two women and, for the first time, Mandy wonders if it could be possible that Allison Hawthorne wasn't always a member of the upper class. There's an air of understanding in her eyes.

"I may be biased, but my children are fantastic. Frankie is wise beyond her years, but not in an arrogant way. She is a charming, old soul who is permanently content. She's been like that since she was a baby. We were very lucky. Remy can be awkward, but he's so smart and he'd give anyone the shirt off his back. He didn't inherit all the Hawthorne genes."

Mandy smirks. There is undoubtably a connection with Allison. A connection she never dreamed of having.

"Mandy, I'd like to officially offer you this position, if

you're interested. I can pay you thirty dollars per hour and would need you forty to forty-five hours per week. It would mostly be Monday through Friday, with the very occasional weekend day. This is all contingent on you meeting my children and all parties agreeing that it's a good fit. What do you think—would you like to meet them?"

Chapter 12

"Do you like Taylor Swift?" The little girl asks, brown eyes stricken with anticipation.

Her room is exactly what you'd expect a seven-year-old millionaire's daughter to be—a king-sized bed that could swallow her whole, a floor-to-ceiling bookshelf of children's books and American Girl dolls, pale pink walls, and expansive windows overlooking the property, with a slightly obstructed view of the lake that is less than two hundred yards away. Frankie is petite for her age, but what she lacks in height she makes up for with charm. She's preciously good looking with bouncing brunette curls and smooth almond skin like her father.

"Like her? I love her!" Mandy replies with as much enthusiasm as a casual Taylor Swift listener can muster whilst trying to impress a child. She's caught off guard when Frankie squeals and takes her by the hand, pulling her toward the walk-in closet. Mandy is thirty-six years old and has never had a closet big enough to house her wardrobe for more than one season at a time. This closet is bigger than Mandy's first apartment.

"You have to see this," the girl tells her, holding a tiny finger to her lips. "It's my secret room."

She leads Mandy through a vast array of pink and purple outfits and more shoes than she's seen in her life, before they reach a small white door at the back of the closet.

"You have to tap on it three times before you open it; that's the rule," she explains. Three light raps on the door by her miniature fist and she raises her eyebrows in Mandy's direction, letting her know the secret code worked and they can open the door.

Frankie easily walks through the entryway and Mandy only has to bend slightly. Once they are inside the room, a motion-sensor light kicks on to reveal a six-foot ceiling, so Mandy is once again able to stand upright. There's so much to look at, her eyes don't know what to focus on first. A life-size cardboard cutout of Ms. Swift looms in the corner, countless signed records are framed and hung, several hands made of plaster are mounted on the wall and covered with friendship bracelets, and—most surprisingly for a seven-year-old—a record player. Normally, Mandy would be slightly annoyed by such an obvious display of wealth and privilege, but after watching Frankie bounce around the room, excitedly showing off all her memorabilia, she can't help but smile. It's not the behavior of a spoiled little rich brat; it's the joyous presentation of this sweet girl's favorite possessions.

"Have you ever been to a concert?" Mandy asks her.

"I've been to three!" Frankie shouts. "I know how lucky I am," she adds, obviously something her parents have taught her.

"Lucky, indeed. That is very cool, Frankie. She's lucky to have a fan like you."

Frankie considers this, a foreign thought. Taylor Swift is lucky to have *her*. She likes that idea.

"Are you going to be hanging out here this summer, with me?" she asks.

"Well, I need to talk to your mom about it a little more, but I sure hope so."

Frankie once again surprises Mandy by leaping forward and hugging her neck. Maybe it's just an emotional time of the month, but she finds herself quickly wiping a tear away before the young girl can see it.

They reenter the room to find Allison standing in the middle of the carpet, arms crossed and wearing a smirk.

"Frances Hawthorne, I know you didn't make your new friend bend down and crawl into your secret room."

"Mom, she loved it!" Frankie exclaims.

"I loved it," Mandy confirms with a discreet wink.

"I need to steal Miss Mandy so she can go meet your brother," Allison tells her.

"Yuck, good luck. His room stinks so bad."

"Frances," Allison says with a stern look.

"I had a brother, too. They do kind of stink some-times," Mandy says to Frankie, pinning her nose and waving off an invisible stench. Frankie giggles, and Allison can't help but smile. I *had* a brother, not *I have* a brother; she's glad Allison didn't notice the slip.

Mandy follows Allison down a walkway that overlooks one of the living areas below. Chandler is below them, still on a phone call that appears to have gotten heated. She can't make out the words, but his voice is slightly raised and he's pacing around the couch. Allison glances briefly down at him before looking back to Mandy and shrugging.

"There are two rooms on this end of the wing—Remy's bedroom and a guest room that doesn't get used very often. Guests prefer the small cottage we have on the property, but I keep the linens clean in this one, in case we have overflow."

Mandy's certain that Allison isn't the one keeping the bedding clean; they must have staff for that. She wonders if the woman even knows which floor the washer and dryer are located on.

"Remy's a good kid, but he spends a lot of time in his bedroom. He's at that age."

This is the third time it's been mentioned that this kid spends a lot of time in his room. Mandy knows the type—gamer, most likely a pot smoker, can't wait to move out of the house and go off to college just so he can spend all his time locked in a bedroom there, too. Allison leans forward and hesitates before giving the door two loud knocks.

"Remy, sweetheart. There's someone I'd like you to meet," Allison calls out. Mandy's not sure what the kid looks like, but she's preparing for acne, body odor, and an energy drink firmly gripped in one hand with an Xbox controller in the other. When the door finally swings open, Mandy nearly gasps before catching herself.

Remington Hawthorne is incredibly handsome, with piercing eyes that widen faintly at the sight of Mandy. His brown hair falls forward into his eyes slightly before he absentmindedly brushes it out of the way. Despite his ridiculously handsome face, Mandy could never find herself attracted to the soon-to-be eighteen-year-old. Not just because of their age difference or the fact that she's on the verge of being his glorified nanny, but because she's known Remy for years, since the day he got his driver's license and came down to the Quick Stop for a Monster Energy Drink.

Since that first day, he's stopped at the station two to three days a week, to grab a beverage and talk to Mandy. His name is Chandy. From the very first day he introduced himself, they joked about their names rhyming. He'd complain about school and homework, and she'd complain about the customers who drove her nuts. She even confided in him when Patrick left her. She remembers feeling a pang of jealousy as she listened to him detail how much he loves his parents and how highly he thinks of them.

"Remy?" she asks with furrowed brows.

"Remington Chandler Hawthorne. My family calls me Remy. You must be our new keeper?" he asks before widening his eyes slightly and reaching forward to shake her hand. Ahh, Remington Chandler . . . Chandy. She's not quite sure why visiting a gas station for non-alcoholic beverages should be a dirty secret he'd keep from his parents, but she'll play along.

"Yes, Remy. My name is Mandy, and I'm interviewing for a position with your family. It's such a pleasure to meet you."

"Oh, let's skip past the formalities. She's got the job. Your sister adores her," Allison says, placing a hand on Mandy's back before thinking better of it and moving it back down to her side.

He smiles and Mandy feels like she's looking into the eyes of a stranger. "Well, I guess that's that. Welcome to the family, Mandy."

Chapter 13

"Wes, would you mind escorting Mandy back to her vehicle and showing her where the employee parking lot is? She'll be starting on Monday," Allison says with a smile, once again raising her arm to put around Mandy's shoulder but stopping before she touches her. Mandy pretends not to notice.

"Of course, Mrs. Hawthorne," Wes responds with a genuine smile. Allison cocks her head and shoots a flirtatious smirk in his direction. She has undoubtably told him to call her Allison and thinks this formality is meant to be playful. Mandy's sure Wes is oblivious and simply being polite to his employer.

She spent the last twenty minutes filling out new hire paperwork with Allison while mentally replaying her introduction to "Remy" and trying to figure out what the hell he is up to. Is he not supposed to leave the gates of the club? Is that it? When he comes into the Quick Stop, he's always polite, well-mannered, and has never so much as hinted at trying to purchase alcohol or tobacco. She cannot imagine what aspect of these visits would make it necessary to lie to his mother.

She makes a split-second decision *not* to discuss the Remy situation with Wes as they leave the Hawthorne home. Sure, he was once the person she knew better than anyone, but it's also true that she hasn't known him that well in nearly two decades. Everything about a person can change in twenty years.

"Well, it sounds like they adored you, just like I knew they would," Wes says as they enter the wooded path back to the dining lodge.

"I'm not so sure Chandler adored me, or even noticed I was there during the interview, but Allison and I seemed to hit it off."

Wes shakes his head while focusing on the path before him. He's worked for the club for a long time; he's certainly aware of Chandler Hawthorne's indifference to anyone he deems to be below his social class, but how can he say that to Mandy without offending her? *Sorry, my friend, but you're applying to work for Chandler, which means you're the help and don't even qualify as being worthy of a conversation with him.*

"Yeah, he's a workaholic for sure. But Allison is cool to work for; I think you'll really like her. Did you meet the kids?"

Mandy nods. "That Frankie is a little sweetheart, eh? I can't imagine how many girls would dream of having a bedroom like that."

Wes laughs. His eyes crinkle at the edges and he looks like a proud uncle. "She sure is. I think there's still hope for her."

"What's that supposed to mean?" Mandy asks.

"Children of the rich are usually a little less ambitious,

less generous, less kind. I guess they've just never had anything to strive for; it's all been given to them. I've worked for a lot of different families here, and it's been a pretty consistent truth. But those two kids, I somehow think they'll turn out alright. They've got good heads on their shoulders and they're kind. They obviously take after their mother."

"Speaking of their mother, does Allison come from money? She seems pretty down to earth."

"She's fiercely private when it comes to her upbringing. I know she grew up in Colorado and that's about it. I don't even know her maiden name."

Mandy finds it odd that Wes has worked for the club since high school and doesn't know anything about the president's wife, but she also has never known Wes to be a gossip. He most likely does his job every day, clocks out, and goes home. Well, home apparently *is* the club now.

"And you said you're living here?" Mandy asks, gesturing vaguely to their surroundings.

"Well, I'm not living here in the same sense that the Hawthornes are. I live in one of the employee cabins. They are over on the west side of the property. I used to have a roommate, but when I got my last promotion, it came with my own residence, so that's been nice."

"So . . . no wife, no kids?"

Wes smiles. "Haven't had the time. How's ol' Patrick doing?"

Mandy returns his smile. "I wouldn't know; we're divorced."

He tries his best not to look pleased, but it's no secret that he's despised Patrick Cramer since they were teenagers. "I'm sorry to hear that."

"No, you're not," she says, elbowing him in his side.

They arrive back at the massive dining lodge just as the sky begins to darken and thunder sounds off in the distance. They both look in the direction of the incoming storm just as the gray clouds grow thicker and lightning strikes a little too close for comfort.

"When you pull in on Monday morning, the guard at the gate will have an employee ID for you. You'll take a right when you come into the clearing after the entryway drive instead of coming straight to the dining lodge. You'll see signs for the employee parking; it's not far. I'll meet you there a few minutes before nine; sound good?"

"Sounds great," Mandy says, quieting the flutter in her stomach that arises when Wes opens her car door for her.

"I'm really looking forward to working with you. You know, catching up, hearing what you've been up to for the last eighteen years . . ."

"I'm really looking forward to that, too," she replies, and for the first time in a long time, things are looking up.

Chapter 14

Although the drive is only a few miles, the skies have turned to dark by the time Mandy pulls back into her driveway.

Nothing better than a spring storm, she thinks to herself and then laughs out loud because she can't remember the last time she was filled with such optimism. Not only did she just accept a position making more money than she has in her life, but she also seems to have found the only kind and reasonable member of the Bluff to be her employer. Allison Hawthorne is a unicorn millionaire. So long as she sticks close to the Hawthorne house and away from the other rich assholes, surely she can survive the season.

As she's turning her ignition off, Mandy notices a light on in Georgia's kitchen and is surprised to see two figures sitting at the small table by the window. Georgia and a man, sitting together and drinking from steaming mugs while the storm approaches. His back is to Mandy, but it appears to be their new neighbor, Braxton. They must have gotten over whatever disagreement they were having the other day, which is good. It's about to be summer, and

Mandy has high hopes of grilling out and letting the dogs play together.

She swallows hard with the realization that she's going to have to tell Georgia about the job. There's no way she can keep it from her. She's going to be working full time at the club where a tragic fire broke out and Georgia's friend was killed. She already knows her neighbor doesn't have a great impression of the Bluff, but a lot has changed since the nineties. She even said it herself; the couple who were in charge at the time died in a car accident decades ago. The third Chandler Hawthorne is in charge now and, for all she knows, things could be a lot better. She pushes back the memory of Luke, the delivery driver, and his experience with Chandler; maybe he was just having a bad day. She's not going to let it ruin her joy today; joy that is long overdue.

Mandy gives Georgia's side entrance door a few light knocks before opening it; the same ritual they both perform at each other's homes since her divorce. When Patrick lived with her, he would have thrown an absolute fit if their neighbor didn't wait on the porch for him to answer the door before entering. Mandy loves her new, close relationship with the woman Patrick always deemed "strange" and "overbearing."

Both Georgia and Braxton seem caught off guard by Mandy's arrival, and she is about to apologize when a loud, thundering boom sounds and the skies open into a downpour.

"Thank goodness you made it inside in time," Georgia exclaims. She reaches in the cupboard for a mug and chooses a tea bag from her collection—honey lavender, Mandy's favorite. "Have a seat."

"Hi, Braxton, how are you settling in?" Mandy asks

with enough self-awareness to know she's being entirely too formal.

"Oh, I still have to hang things on the walls and put away the last of the boxes before it really feels like home, but I'm in no rush. Max has enough room to roam around, so he's happy."

Georgia leans forward, setting a mug in front of Mandy and carefully pours from the steaming kettle. She then retrieves a few packets of sweetener and sets them next to the mug. Mandy tries not to display her emotions when Georgia does things like this because she knows it's second nature to the woman, but it's just so foreign to Mandy. She had a few foster parents who were generally kind, but never like this.

"Speaking of Max, anytime you want to get him together with Murphy, we would love that. It's been too cold to bring him to the dog park, so he could sure use a little exercise."

"Well, you have your nightly walks, right? You're a good dog mom. But yes, of course we'd like to get together soon. I have to work tonight, but I'm off all weekend," Braxton replies. Luckily, he was focused on his mug and not at Mandy's reaction when he commented on her nightly walks. How does he know she walks Murphy every night—does he stand by the window and wait? Did he install cameras on the front of his house? She hasn't seen him open his blinds once since moving in; not that she's been keeping track.

Georgia retakes her seat at the table and smiles sweetly at Mandy. "It sure is nice to see you up and around, kiddo."

Mandy blushes, remembering Georgia's visit to her house the day before, which now seems like a lifetime ago. Getting out of bed seemed like an impossible goal and now here she is, a day later, newly employed and on top of the world.

"Well, I actually have some good news for you," Mandy begins, forcing an enthusiastic smile and hoping it will influence Georgia to be excited for her.

"Did you find a job? Oh, I just knew you would!" Georgia claps her pale, weathered hands together.

"I did, Georgia. I don't mean to be ill mannered and discuss money, but it's more than I've ever made in my life. Also, she said I'd hardly ever have to work weekends. And no nights. I can help you in your garden all summer long!"

"Mandy, that's fantastic news. Who is *she*? Where is this job located?"

Braxton's attention shifts between the two women, taking in every word.

"I know you might have some reservations about this decision, but I've accepted a job working at the Bluff," Mandy says with conviction. She *will* convince Georgia that this is a good idea, no matter how hard that may be.

As soon as the words are out of Mandy's mouth, she catches Georgia shooting a blink-and-you'll-miss-it glance at Braxton. Braxton, who just learned of the Hawthorne Bluff Club's existence days ago.

"What position did you apply for?" she asks.

"It's called keeper, but it's basically a glorified nanny. The kids are seven and almost eighteen. Their parents are Allison and Chandler Hawthorne."

This time the reaction is too obvious to hide. Braxton flinches.

"What? What was that for?" Mandy asks, with a slight smile.

"It's just that . . . didn't you ladies just tell me that Chandler Hawthorne is the man who runs the entire club? The club that has his family name? Surely that's not going to be a very easy job. I don't mean to overstep; I just didn't think you were too fond of the Bluff people."

"The Bluff people—you make them sound like a different species," Georgia adds with a laugh, no doubt attempting to lighten the mood.

"You're right. But the money is really good and the woman I interviewed with, Allison, seems like an exception. She was lovely. The kids seem great. Georgia is the only person I know who has worked at the club, and that was nearly thirty years ago, so I'm thinking a lot has changed since then. Worst-case scenario is that I hate it and I quit."

Georgia is staring at Mandy now, not in an unsettling way, more in a loving, caring, *hoping this girl has enough sense to actually quit when it gets bad* way.

"You're not mad at me, are you, Georgia?"

"Heavens, no. I'm so proud of you for securing a better paying job. And you're right; I haven't been to the Bluff in decades. I'm sure a lot has changed."

"Well, here's to Mandy and her fancy new job," Braxton says, raising his mug.

The two women lift theirs and clumsily tap them together as the rain begins to hit the window a little harder.

"To Mandy's new job," Georgia echoes.

Chapter 15

Thirty dollars an hour. Forty hours a week. Paid weekly. That's twelve hundred dollars a week before taxes—even more if she gets overtime. The official season at the Bluff is April first through November first. That's roughly thirty-one weeks. She'd be making just shy of forty thousand dollars a year for working eight months. It is entirely possible, if she budgets, that she could take the winters off.

With that realization, Mandy free-falls backward onto her bed, kicking her legs in the air like a teenager. Murphy uses his doggie steps to climb in next to her, and she picks his round little body up, holding him in the air like a scene from *the Lion King*.

"Do you understand what that means, Murph? Time off together. We've never had that much free time. This is too good to be true."

He makes a brief hacking sound and Mandy nearly throws him back onto the bed.

"Too much excitement; I agree."

Mandy is on such a high from today's events, she decides to take a risk and text both of her childhood friends, Laura and Becky. They've been in the back of her mind since she mentioned them to Georgia the day before, and she sincerely regrets letting the friendships go over her insecurities and feelings of being left behind. She creates a group text with both Laura and Becky and presses send before she can think better of it.

HEY GUYS – LONG TIME, NO TALK. I'VE BEEN THINKING A LOT ABOUT ALL THE GREAT MEMORIES WE HAVE AND I'M SO SORRY I'VE LET US FALL OUT OF TOUCH. I'D LOVE TO CATCH UP WITH YOU BOTH AND HEAR ABOUT YOUR FAMILIES AND WHAT'S NEW IN YOUR LIFE. I LOVE YOU BOTH.

BEING the bigger person and admitting fault feels amazing. She wishes she had been capable of it sooner. As she's mindlessly scrolling through her phone, a notification from her Reddit app catches her eye. It's a message from DANNYBOY06.

"Well . . . did you get the position?" he asks.

"I did! I start Monday. Ready or not," she replies, smiling. DANNYBOY06 is beginning to feel like a friend.

"Congrats! You're going to be the best keeper they've ever seen. Let me know how it goes and remember: KEEP YOUR GUARD UP."

Mandy smiles and shakes her head. She won't be letting her guard down anytime soon. She's going to make a living from these people, but that doesn't mean she's going to trust them.

She begins to type a response, when a nagging thought at the back of her mind distracts her enough to stop. She scrolls up to their earlier conversations, beginning with the first message she ever sent DANNYBOY06, when she was asking if he had any information on the club. Mandy reads through each of the messages they've sent each other in the last week, and it hits her when she makes it down to the bottom—she never told this person what position she was applying for. How did they know she was hired as keeper?

"I didn't tell you what I applied for . . ."

Moments later, a new reply appears.

"LOL you didn't need to; I hacked into their employment portal the minute you told me you had applied. It looks like they had already talked to six candidates before you, so congrats on getting the job."

It feels so invasive. Also, how does this person have so much time on their hands? An idea pops into her head, and she quickly types a message.

"How far back do their employee records go on the portal?"

This time, they take nearly ten minutes before responding.

"Looks like the early nineties. They must have kept paper records before then. Why do you ask?"

"Would you mind looking up an employee named Georgia Afton for me?"

She feels guilty the second she presses send. She's betraying her friend. Georgia's time at the Bluff has been weighing heavily on Mandy's mind since the minute she told her about it. She has lived next to her for years, and not only did the woman keep it a secret all this time, but now she's also purposely vague about her employment. Since she had never mentioned a job to her before, Mandy has always assumed that Georgia was a housewife.

"Looks like she worked in the kitchen, first as a pastry chef and then as a private chef for Jack and Tilly Hawthorne. She worked there for three years, and her last day was October 30th, 1998. Who is she?"

Mandy ignores the question.

"She worked for Jack and Tilly Hawthorne, and her last day was the same day as the fire that killed them both?"

"I didn't realize the date. I guess you're right. She must have been grief stricken over the death of her employers, maybe? Also, are you going to answer me about how you know this woman?"

She briefly hesitates before deciding on an easy lie.

"She used to be a customer of mine. She'd mentioned a time or two about working at the club, so I thought I'd check if she was bullshitting me or not."

"Ahh, I see," DANNYBOY06 replies.

"Well, I better go enjoy my free time. Come Monday, my ass belongs to the Hawthorne Bluff Club," Mandy says.

"Godspeed," they reply with the prayer-hands emoji.

In that moment, Mandy decides she'll keep up the friendship with the Reddit user. If things go south at the Bluff, having a hacker friend may just come in handy.

Chapter 16

A few light knocks steal Mandy's attention from her makeup application, but when Murphy runs down the hall and doesn't bark, she knows it must be her neighbor.

"Hey, Georgia!" she yells. "I'll be right out."

Mandy forgot to ask about a uniform, but she wasn't given one or instructed to dress a certain way, so she used her best judgement and went with a salmon-colored cardigan over a plain white shirt and khakis. She tied her shoulder length hair back into a loose bun, in case she was asked to prepare any food for the kids. She's scheduled to work until five today, just like a banker. Although she prefers having more time in the morning, she'll gladly give it up for weekends off.

When she walks into her small kitchen, Georgia is bent over in front of Mandy's open refrigerator, placing several Tupperware containers on the shelves.

"What in the world are you doing?"

She's caught by surprise and stands straight up, spinning to face Mandy.

"Good morning, my dear. I was up early this morning,

thinking about how mentally taxing the first day at a new job can be. You're not going to want to be doing any cooking tonight, so I made a little chicken alfredo plate for you to heat up later. I set some of the chicken aside without seasoning and chopped it up for little Murphy."

Mandy's eyes travel to the round table in the center of the kitchen.

"And this?"

Georgia blushes slightly.

"Some muffins for breakfast and a protein drink for the road."

It starts as an itch in the back of her throat before a single tear escapes from her right eye. Trying to hold in the emotions only makes the sob that escapes her lips even louder.

"Oh, dear," Georgia says, rushing across the kitchen to hold Mandy in a tight embrace. "It's okay, it's just a little food," she whispers in her ear. "Everything is going to be okay."

Mandy didn't cry when Patrick left her, nor did she cry when she quit the Quick Stop. She's not a crier; it's not in her nature. She can't believe that a sweet old woman making her homemade alfredo would be the event that finally did her in.

"Thank you for looking out for me," Mandy says, furiously wiping the tears from her face and cussing when she realizes she'll have to reapply her makeup before she leaves.

"You really didn't have anyone in your corner growing up, did you?" Georgia asks, running her hand gently down the side of Mandy's head, smoothing the hair that was ruffled from their hug.

"My brother always looked out for me. After he was gone, my neighbor Wes became my protector for a while, but never a mother figure," Mandy replies with a shrug. "Oh, I almost forgot to tell you, Wes works at the Bluff. I saw him for the first time since high school at my interview."

"Let me guess—you two grew apart when you married Patrick?" Georgia presumes.

"More like when I started dating Patrick, but yes. That's when we lost touch. That's when I essentially was on my own. God knows Patrick never really looked out for my best interests."

"Do you have any recollection of your mother before she was an addict? Any pleasant childhood memories?"

Mandy's thoughts travel back to the very first memories of her mom. Wes, who is two years older, insists that he remembers Skylar bringing them, along with Mandy's brother Jeff, to Green Bay to visit Chuck E. Cheese. He said she was sober, happy, and let them play games for so long that they all fell asleep on the car ride home. She always assumed he was making up the story so Mandy could have something positive to think about her mother, but there were moments where the memory felt real to her. Quick mental snapshots appear in her mind of the animatronic mascots dancing on the stage and of crying when Wes and Jeff wouldn't let her hold the giant mallet and whack the characters that popped up through dark holes in the center of the machine.

"I do have a few hazy memories of her coming in my room to tuck me in at night before she started drinking. I remember that she would wake up before us and cook breakfast. I can't remember what she cooked or if it was any good, but those memories stick out in my mind because the rest of my childhood, she slept in while we got ourselves ready for school."

The words take the air out of Georgia's lungs, and she

puts a hand over her chest, fidgeting with her gold chain when she realizes how much she caught Mandy off guard with her reaction.

"Mandy, I am so sorry you and your brother had to experience that. Sometimes it's so hard to understand how life can be so easy and beautiful for some and so devastating and unfair for others. You were just children, and you deserved so much better."

Mandy reaches for Georgia's hand.

"I could spend the rest of my life making bad decisions and blaming it on my childhood, or I can break the cycle by working hard and making something of myself. It's just nice to have someone who cares. I wish everyone had someone like you; this world would be a different place."

Georgia gives a sympathetic smile and squeezes Mandy's hand.

"I'm happy to be the one to care for you. It's been one of the great joys of my life since I moved in next door," Georgia replies, bending over to pet Murphy's head as she turns to leave. After opening the outside door, she turns back around. "Hey, I believe one of my old coworkers still works at the Bluff. If you get a chance to peek into the kitchen of the dining lodge, look for a woman about my age but not nearly as good looking," Georgia says with a laugh. "Her name is Amelia Crain."

"Amelia Crain, lovely older woman in the kitchen. I'll be sure to send her your best."

After a moment of hesitation, Georgia adds, "Don't let anyone else hear you talk to her. I don't need everyone knowing my business."

Chapter 17

Mandy is about to put her car in reverse when she hears her phone vibrate from deep inside her purse. She reaches over to see a text from the group she created last night.

"Hey girl – we were JUST talking about you! We miss you so much and would love to reconnect. Laura has a new number; I'll text it to you separately."

Sure enough, seconds later, a text comes through from Becky with Laura's new number. She also tells Mandy that they both will be in town for Memorial Day weekend and would love to get together. Mandy lets her know that she's starting a new job but will find out as soon as possible if she's working that weekend. She doesn't mention where she's working; that's a conversation to have in person.

"Congratulations on the new job! Just let us know when you find out your schedule and we can work around it. Can't wait!"

A smile slowly spreads across Mandy's face as she stares at her phone, reading the messages over again. She allowed herself to create this narrative in her mind that distancing herself from them meant they must hate her now. Just because you've grown apart from someone doesn't mean there is any ill intent; sometimes friendships just run their course. Now that they are on the back end of their thirties, there's a great chance they can find enough common ground to be casual friends who check in on each other and visit a few times a year. The thought of it makes Mandy smile again.

WHEN SHE PULLS UP to the guard's building outside the gates of the club, the same man who was working when she came for her interview steps out, a genuine smile on his face.

"Good morning, Miss Cramer. Congratulations, and welcome to the Hawthorne Bluff Club family. This is your ID; you'll need it any time you enter the gates, and it would be a good idea to carry it with you inside the gates for the first week or two, until the other guards get to know you," he says, leaning down to hand her the laminated card, which hangs from a maroon lanyard, the Hawthorne logo printed along the side. The same picture he had the other day, the one from her social media profile, is printed on the card, along with her name and title.

MANDY CRAMER, KEEPER
EMPLOYEE SINCE 2024

She glances up at the badge pinned to his front pocket. Tanner Harris, Security. Employee since 2023.

"Has anyone showed you where to park?"

"Yes, Wes showed me last week. I think he's going to meet me there and escort me to the Hawthorne house," Mandy replies, again wondering why it is that she needs an escort.

"He's already there, ma'am. Enjoy your first day."

He tips his hat, the gesture of a gentleman much older

than him, but she smiles nonetheless. He looks a little less like Glenn Powell today, but she still wouldn't kick him out of bed for eating crackers.

The short drive to the employee parking lot is even more breathtaking than she remembers from last week. The trees that tower over her seem to connect, forming a tunnel of beautiful pink blossoms. She was entirely too nervous for her interview to notice other details, such as the small white signs posted to her left as she coasts down the main entryway. Each has a separate phrase:

Today is a beautiful day.

But every day is beautiful . . .

Every evening is tranquil . . .

Every morning is heaven . . .

When you're at the Bluff.

Welcome Home.

She wonders when the last time any of the Bluff members had a bad day or even an inconvenience that wasn't immediately remedied by someone else and quickly scolds herself for the thought. She promised she'd try her best not to detest these people simply for being wealthy. Allison Hawthorne was the prime example of why Mandy knew she had to change her behavior. Going forward, she'd only judge those who did something to deserve it. Lord knows enough people have judged her simply for being born a Smith.

As she veers to the right to enter the employee parking lot, Mandy's not sure if she should be excited or ashamed that all cars are nicer than hers. There are over a dozen vehicles, and they are all mid- to high-range SUVs, with a luxury sedan or two sprinkled in. Hiring employees at entry level for twenty-five dollars per hour may not seem like much for the rest of the country, but in a small town like this, it can provide a comfortable living. She imagines most of the employees receive pay increases the longer they stay, so most of the staff is probably doing quite well for themselves. She can't imagine what Wes makes after twenty years on the payroll.

Speaking of Wes, he is standing next to an empty bench with his phone to his ear. One hand is holding the phone, and the other arm is crossed over his chest. Mandy detects the stress on his face from ten yards away as she pulls into a spot and shifts into park. She knows that look well because he wore it often when they were growing up. The unlucky occasions where both sets of their parents went on benders were the worst. Wes and Mandy's brother, Jeff, would act as pseudo-parents to her since she was the youngest. They'd pack her lunch, usually a stale packet of crackers and some fruit snacks, and make sure her socks and shoes matched before they walked together to the bus stop. The moment Wes would realize their parents weren't waking up in time—or worse, weren't coming home at all —he'd wear the same expression he has now.

Mandy gives him a weak smile, not because she's pleased that Wes is stressed, but because some things never change. Very little in Mandy's life seems familiar anymore, so she's oddly thankful for this one glimmer of nostalgia.

Wes hangs up the phone when Mandy shuts her car door, and he waves to get her attention, as if she hadn't already seen him. Now he's wearing another expression Mandy remembers from their youth, a smile to hide how he really feels.

"You always were right on time, Mandy Smith," he says, and the mention of her maiden name makes her flinch. She shakes it off because it sounds so sweet coming from his lips.

"Except for when you burnt the toast," she replies, and the memory makes Wes throw his head back in laughter.

Instantly, he's a child in her eyes. Always smiling, always laughing, always trying to convince Mandy that everything is going to be okay.

During one of the "bad" weeks, when none of the four parents between the two trailers could be accounted for, Wes assigned himself as breakfast chef. His parents had just received their food stamps for the month the day before and stocked up on bread, cheese, milk, bacon, and eggs. Mandy and Jeff couldn't believe their luck when Wes told them to come over before school for a breakfast "fit for kings," and "okay, for a queen, too" when Mandy looked insulted.

The eggs were runny, the milk spilled over their glasses, and they were too scared to cook the bacon because the package didn't have specific instructions. Wes threw two pieces of bread into the toaster and got distracted cleaning up the milk. The toaster malfunctioned and didn't spring up when the bread was fully toasted; it simply held them hostage until they began to smoke. The kids didn't think to unplug the toaster; they simply flipped it upside down and banged on it until the charred remains popped out. By then, the damage had been done—the entire home was filled with smoke so thick they could hardly breathe. They spent the next hour cleaning up their mess and opening all the windows in thirty-degree weather to air out the stench. They all knew what the consequence would be if Wes' parents came home to such a scene. The trailer was always a mess, but it was *their* mess. Any disturbance caused by their child was unacceptable, even if it happened while they left him home alone at the age of ten.

"That was the first and only time I ever let you miss the bus. We ran to school and begged Mr. Degrand not to tell our parents about it," Wes recalls. "Do you think he ever did?"

"I think every adult at that school learned not to call our parents because nothing good would have come of it," Mandy replies, forcing a tight-lipped smile. What a fucking childhood they had.

"You're probably right. Well, on a better note, are you ready for your grand tour?"

Mandy looks at the time on her phone.

"Um, Mrs. Hawthorne said that I should start at nine today. Should I check in with her first?" she asks.

Wes shakes his head.

"No need; the kids have a tutor until eleven, so she told me to show you the ropes, and we'll meet at the house for lunch."

A tutor. It never even occurred to Mandy that it was early April and the kids in Michigan still had nearly two months of school left.

"So they are home schooled by a tutor?" Mandy asks.

"Their school in South Florida caters to families . . . like the Hawthornes. The kids attend school from September to March, and they're given take-home lesson plans for the last two months. Apparently, a lot of the families have multiple homes, so the flexible schedule isn't uncommon."

A look passes between them and they both smile. It's all so ridiculous. Who would have thought that two kids from River Ridge Estates Mobile Home Park would end up at the Bluff?

"Alright, let's start on this path. I'll show you Dr. Ingalls's home. He's the resident physician and lives here year-round. Hopefully you won't need him, but it's good to know where to find help in case you do."

She remembers the conversation with Georgia when Mandy mistakenly said there was a doctor's office inside the gates. *Actually, it's just a doctor who operates out of his home.*

It's amazing how much better fifty-five degrees feels in April than it does in October. It's been a long winter, and the sun on Mandy's skin feels like all the medicine she could ever need. It's intoxicating.

As they round a corner, Wes points toward a large, white Victorian-style home, with a matching white picket fence surrounding the property, which is only three feet high at best, with two-inch spaces between each slat. Who in the world is that fence designed to keep out? It sure isn't offering any privacy. An older gentleman, presumably Dr. Ingalls, is in the side yard with a pair of gardening shears in his hand. He's wearing an old-school Ascot cap and tweed jacket. Between the house, the fence, and the perfectly trimmed bushes, it looks like a scene from the 1950s.

"Wesley, good morning!"

"It is a beautiful morning, sir. I'd like you to meet Mandy Cramer; she's the Hawthorne family's new keeper."

The man briskly walks to meet the pair at the miniature white fence, and Mandy reaches out a hand to shake his. He takes her hand with both of his and makes such intense eye contact, she's borderline uncomfortable.

"Mandy, what a beautiful name that is. I once had an Irish Setter named Mandy. Hell of a dog. Welcome to the Bluff. You're going to love it here."

She doesn't quite know the correct response, so she just gives the man a polite smile and tells him how lovely it is to meet him and she's sure she will love it here, too.

As they are walking away, Dr. Ingalls yells, "Wesley, be sure to show her where the good candy is at the commissary!"

"Now, Dr. Ingalls, that's not very healthy advice, but of course I'll show her where we keep the good stuff,"

Wes shouts back, before muttering "Christ" under his breath.

"The commissary?" Mandy asks.

"It's our convenience store. I'm not sure why they insist on naming everything here like it's a summer camp or military base."

They walk a few more paces before Mandy asks Wes what he likes to do in his free time, when he clocks out.

"Honestly, I stick around here a lot. I don't have a relationship with my parents, and there isn't much in town that we don't already have here, so I do a lot of reading, fishing, snowmobiling in the winter. There's a lot to do at the club."

"What made you decide to live on-site when you took the job?" Mandy asks.

"What was the alternative?" Wes quickly answers.

The alternative for Mandy was getting married immediately after high school and sharing a one-bedroom apartment with Patrick for years, owned by a slumlord who sexually harassed her each time he did a "surprise" inspection to verify they weren't breaking their lease in any way. Patrick always told her she was overreacting and that maybe if she flirted a little more, they'd catch a break on their late fees. Wes made the right decision by moving to the Bluff when given the chance.

As they walk along one of the main roads in the club, Mandy is amazed by the mansions on either side of them and streetlamps on every corner. Although the houses are all built in different styles, each home has an identical mailbox—large and white with the Hawthorne logo and the resident's last name printed on the side. There are ten houses in view, five on each side, and Mandy doesn't see a single vehicle.

"Where are all the cars?"

Wes takes a deep breath. Explaining these things to Mandy isn't like any other new hire he's taking for a welcome tour. She knows him. In fact, there was a time that she knew him better than anyone. He can't bullshit her.

"Most of the members aren't here yet because they come from Memorial Day to Labor Day, or Halloween if it stays nice like it did last year. But when they are here, it's actually a club violation to park in the driveway unless you're having an approved gathering and expecting guests."

It takes a good five seconds for Mandy to realize he isn't kidding. She lightly grabs his forearm and searches his eyes for any indication that he hasn't lost his mind. She gasps when he leans forward to hug her, the first hug they've had in decades. She's trying to make sense of it when he puts his mouth up against her ear and whispers so quickly, it sends chills down her spine.

"They have cameras everywhere. Watch what you do and say when you're inside the gates. I know it's ridiculous, but we can talk about that somewhere else. Nod if you understand."

Reluctantly, Mandy nods.

Chapter 18

Mandy's thoughts are racing when they near the end of the residential street and *Hawthorne Commissary* comes into view.

The building is the size of a small grocery store, but the exterior looks like a movie set with its lush topiaries and hanging plants. There is a small parking lot and a bike rack, two of the slots taken with old school pedal bikes with large white baskets on the front. A Golden Retriever is tied to a lamppost outside, and he's sitting at attention, waiting for his owner to exit the store.

To the right of the commissary is a movie theater and bowling alley, and to the left is a supper club with an over-sized sign in old-fashioned cursive that reads THE NIGHTIN-GALE SUPPER CLUB. There is a park across the street with brand-new playground equipment, ample benches, and a fenced-in area for dogs. The entirety of the park is adorned with string lights, just like outside the dining lodge.

"What in the Stepford . . ." Mandy mutters under her breath.

Wes shoots her a look and she holds up her hands in defense.

"Okay, okay. Wow, this is very beautiful, Wes. Would you please do me the honor of showing me inside the commissary? Maybe if I'm good, you'll show me where the special candy is."

He shoots her a worse look and she smiles sweetly. She knows deep down he wants to return that smile.

He opens the door to the commissary for Mandy, and she's hit with the sweet smell of cherry blossoms and freshly baked apple pie. The man working the meat counter to her left is wearing an old school butcher's getup, complete with the white hat and apron. He's smiling at a woman as he hands her a package of wrapped meat and pats it twice before saying, "Now, remember to let that rest before you throw it on the grill, Diane. Give Ken my best."

Two women are behind the bakery counter; one is talking to a customer, and the other is decorating a cake that sits on the spinning perch in front of her. They are both smiling, even the one who is alone and decorating the cake. Mandy does a three-sixty spin . . . Everyone is smiling. The cashier at the checkout, the man stocking the shelves, the three customers Mandy can see from her vantage point—all of them are at the very least smirking, and one is even whistling to himself.

Mandy scans the shelves surrounding her; she's never heard of half the brands in the store. Eight dollars for a box of crackers? Twenty-nine dollars for olive oil? She nearly passes out when she leans over the refrigerated cheese display and glances at the prices.

Her attention goes back to the cashier up front, who bags a woman's groceries and says, "Enjoy your Monday, Mrs. Hammersmith. I hear the weather is supposed to be gorgeous."

"It sure is, Benjamin. I hope you get off in time to enjoy it," she responds before turning to leave with her left arm wrapped around a brown paper sack with—you guessed it—the Hawthorne logo.

Mandy realizes that the woman never took out her wallet to pay and the cashier didn't hand her a receipt.

"Did she not pay?" Mandy asks Wes.

"All groceries are charged to the household's account, and they're billed monthly."

"She didn't even get a receipt; what if they dispute the charges?"

Wes subtly points to the ceiling, where Mandy sees three separate security cameras with an overhead shot of the checkout lane. There are two more facing the entry and exit doors to the building.

"Those are the highest quality cameras on the market. There's no disputing the footage of what groceries went into your bag," he says.

"And the employees just know what household every shopper belongs to?" she asks, this entire concept being too much for her Quick Stop manager brain to grasp.

"They don't get to work the checkout lane unless they are *very* familiar with all the households and who lives in them."

"How many households are there?"

"Fifty," he answers quickly. "It's in the founding covenants that there will never be more than fifty residences in the club."

They are interrupted by the man working the cashier counter, who nearly shouts to greet them. "Hi, Wes; who is your new friend?"

"Lewis, this is Mandy. She is the Hawthorne family's new keeper. Today is her first day."

Lewis, a freckled man with fire-red hair and a space

between his two front teeth, comes around the counter to shake Mandy's hand. She's startled when she realizes he's the third person in this club to grasp her hand with both of theirs—first Allison Hawthorne, then Dr. Ingalls, and now Lewis. He holds her hand like it's a precious gift and makes direct eye contact, just like the doctor.

"Mandy, that is such a lovely name. Dr. Ingalls used to have a beautiful dog named Mandy. Welcome to the club. You're just going to love it here."

"Lewis, it's such a pleasure to meet you," she says and takes her free hand to place on top of both of his. Now all four of their hands are joined in an awkward embrace. *Checkmate*, Mandy thinks. *You want to be weird? I can be weird right along with you, buddy.*

"I feel like I'm on another planet," Mandy mumbles as they walk away.

"You'll be surprised how quickly you get used to it, Ch — Mandy."

She gasps.

"You almost called me Chubbs," she speaks just loud enough for him to hear.

The nickname stemming from her overweight baby photos isn't quite as endearing now that she's a grown woman, but it still stirs something in her when it comes from his lips.

"Old habits die hard. Now let's move on to Easy Street," he says, placing a friendly hand on her back and moving her toward the exit.

"I thought we were on it," she responds with a wink.

"Very funny, but try to keep up. You'll need to know these grounds like the back of your hand by the time season is in full swing next month."

She glances to her left and right. Other than the handful of people in the store and the few she's seen out walking their dogs, the club does appear to be fairly empty. She wonders what it will be like when all the residents arrive from their winter homes.

"So, what's on Easy Street?" she asks as they pass the park and a small diner on the far side of the property. A couple is leaving the restaurant with to-go boxes in their hands. The man pats his stomach and smiles, waving to Wes as they pass.

"Easy Street is where all the on-site employees live. It's where you can find me when I'm not on duty. We also have a small store if you need anything, and you can just charge it to your house account, and they'll take it out of your paycheck. Well, with you working directly for the Hawthornes, I'm not sure that's true . . . but I'll find out."

"That's okay, Wes. I'm not ready to sell my soul to the company store yet."

Wes scrunches his nose. "Huh?"

Mandy snorts out a quick laugh. "Never mind."

A little less than a quarter mile down the road, the pavement ends and is replaced by dirt. Small cabins come into view in neat rows on either side of the drive. They aren't decrepit or in disrepair, but they are small. There are no parking spots or driveways for their cars, so Mandy assumes they must all park in the same lot she did. *That's quite a walk in the winter*, she thinks. A few of the cabins have small covered front porches. She sees a woman, probably a few years younger than her, sitting on a folding chair with her feet kicked up and a book in her hand. A few cabins down, there are two young men playing cards outside with a small radio playing next to their table.

"Which one is yours?" she asks. Wes points to the only cabin that is set back off the main road. It's visibly a bit larger than the others and has two windows on the front instead of the one that the other cabins feature. His truck is parked directly next to the door.

"Oh, so you *are* a big shot, eh?"

His skin flushes slightly.

"I've been here a long time, and I've worked really hard."

"Hey, I'm only joking, Wes. I can't imagine the work you've put in here. You deserve it all."

He catches Mandy by surprise when he wraps an arm around her shoulder and squeezes, resting his head against hers.

"It's really great to have you back, Chubbs."

Her skin tingles, but in a good way. She cannot believe how much has changed in her life over the last six months. She still has her reservations about working at the Bluff, yet she has an overwhelming feeling that she's exactly where she's supposed to be.

A thought prickles in her mind, and she spins to take in her surroundings. The dozen or so cabins, along with the small employee store located at the end of the row, are completely secluded from the rest of the club. The area is surrounded by lush woods.

"Wait, you heard about the fire that happened here when we were kids, right?"

Wes stiffens and nods.

"I was told that Jack and Tilly Hawthorne's house burned down and an employee cabin, where those two workers died. There's no way the Hawthorne house was back here with the employee housing, right? How did the fire spread this far?"

He doesn't make eye contact when he answers.

"We were kids, so I'm just going off the things I've been told, but . . . it wasn't one fire; it was two. Both houses just happened to burn down on the same night. It was tragic."

Chapter 19

Two hours after Wes concludes his tour, Mandy is helping Frankie with an art project but can't focus on glue and popsicle sticks when all she can think about is the night of the fires. Two fires in two homes on opposite ends of the club, two confirmed deaths, two others presumed dead, and zero mention of it in the news. In a county where nothing ever happens, *everything* is newsworthy.

"A girl at my school in Florida said that you used to be able to eat glue. Is that true?"

Mandy flinches, the young girl's words snapping her out of a daze.

"Well, not that I recall. Your friend was probably misinformed."

Frankie shakes her head, curls slapping her face in the process. "She's not my friend. My friends don't eat glue."

Mandy laughs harder than she intended, which makes Frankie smile. Mandy remembers that age—she'd do anything for validation. An adult so much as smiling in response to something she said would improve her mood for the rest of the day.

"What's so funny down here?" Remy asks, entering the den where Mandy and Frankie are sitting cross-legged on the floor, their work spread out on the coffee table in front of them.

Mandy's pulse quickens at the sight of Chandy, or *Remy* as she needs to make a habit of calling him. She still hasn't been alone with him to ask any questions.

"Miss Mandy is helping me with my art project so Miss Kelsey will get off my case," Frankie responds, with a touch of sass.

"Whoa, whoa, whoa—Miss Mandy is helping you because she likes to help you. Miss Kelsey can be on your case all she wants; that's not my department," Mandy says. The last thing she needs is workplace drama with another member of the household's hired help.

"Can I help?" Remy asks, walking across the room and taking a seat next to Frankie without waiting for a response. "What's the plan here?"

Frankie launches into an explanation of how the assignment is to choose an animal and replicate their natural habitat in a shoe box, and she chose a house cat, so her model is going to be of a little girl's bedroom, where the cat spends most of its time.

"Do you have a cat?" Mandy asks, not seeing any of the telltale signs that an animal lives in the house.

"No," Frankie says, crossing her arms over her chest with a loud huff. "Dad's allergic. He's allergic to all animals, so we can't have anything. Not even a fish."

Mandy's never heard of someone being allergic to a fish tank, so she keeps her suspicions to herself. It might be a similar situation to her childhood, when her mother told her the ice cream truck only played music when they were sold out of ice cream. There will come a day where Frankie learns how rare it would be to have allergic reactions to *every* animal, with or without fur. Mandy would like to keep her job, so that day will not be today.

The three begin to work on the project together, with Frankie adorably giving instructions while Remy and Mandy dutifully comply.

"So, Mandy, where did you work before you got this job?" Remy asks. Mandy isn't sure what game he's trying to play.

"Well, Remy," she begins, putting emphasis on his given name. "I actually managed a gas station and store downtown called the Quick Stop. That's what I've been doing for the last six years."

Without missing a beat, Remy asks, "Are you married?"

This man . . . or rather this *boy*, since he is not yet eighteen, knows damn well she's divorced. In fact, Remy was in the store the morning after Mandy found out about her husband and Emily Myers. He showed great concern when she could barely ring up his morning Red Bull because her hands were shaking so furiously.

"Nope," she responds with a tight smirk. Short and sweet.

"I'm never getting married," Frankie says, eyes laser focused on the miniature replica of her bed she's assembling. "Boys are disgusting."

"You're not wrong," Mandy says, handing her another popsicle stick.

"Never too young to teach them to fuck the patriarchy, right?" Remy says, and Frankie gasps before slapping a hand over her mouth and giggling.

"Five dollars for the swear tax, and if you don't pay me, I'm telling Dad."

Remy rolls his eyes and suppresses a smile, reaching in his back pocket for his wallet. Frankie takes the five-dollar bill with a content grin and hands it to Mandy, asking her to hold it until they can go back to her room and add it to her secret swear tax fund.

When Frankie is satisfied with their house cat habitat project, she leads Mandy over to the desktop computer in the corner of the room. This space is made up of items the house already has, much like several other rooms Mandy has seen this morning. There's a computer and desk, although Chandler has his own office. There is a seating area, although there's another living room just past the foyer. There's a fireplace, a piano, and a wet bar—all extras in this extravagant home. She can't imagine sitting at the dinner table with her millionaire husband and discussing which wet bar they planned to use that evening for their after-dinner cocktails.

"I need to write a one-page report explaining the habitat for Miss Kelsey," Frankie explains, taking a seat in the office chair in front of the computer and reaching down to pump the lever a few times, raising her small body enough to reach the keyboard.

"Okay, how can I help? Do you need me to open a Word document for you?"

Frankie laughs, but not in a smug manner. More like she's amused by Mandy's lack of faith in her.

"No, Mandy. I know which one is Word, but I can't type yet, so I'll tell you the words and you type them."

Frankie points to an ottoman in front of the love seat for Mandy to pull up. So, she's doing all the work and Frankie gets the office chair. It's not the worst misjustice she could imagine when she took the job, so she dutifully pulls it up and takes a seat.

Although her arms are so short that she has to kneel in the chair to reach the mouse and navigate the icons, she quickly finds Word and opens a blank document. At that age, Mandy only knew how to play Oregon Trail, and the librarian had to set it up for her. She could barely sound out the words displayed on the screen, and before she knew it, she and her entire convoy had died of dysentery. A snot-faced kid in her class named Benji Olsen was kind enough to explain what dysentery was. She didn't sleep for a week.

Frankie rattles off the description of Josh, her fictional cat, and his habitat. Mandy is careful to type exactly what Frankie is saying so it can be in her own voice. Fifteen minutes later, Frankie claps her hands together once and nods. "Done. Put 'the end' so Miss Kelsey knows it's done, please."

The printer next to the screen comes to life and spits out a single sheet, perfectly spaced, with a bold heading on top that says, "A House Cat's Habitat." Frankie beams with pride.

After following Frankie to her room and placing her hands over her eyes while the young girl accessed her *extra super-secret hiding spot* for Remy's cuss-word fund, she checks her watch and sees it's nearly five o'clock. This day has flown by. Eight hours, thirty dollars per hour, equals two hundred and forty dollars. Mandy smiles.

The front door slams shut loudly enough for Mandy and Frankie to hear across the house. Frankie's shoulders tense, and she stares at her bedroom doorway for a few beats until footsteps retreat in the opposite direction and another door slams, presumably that of Chandler's office. Moments later, the front door closes again, this time much gentler but still audible.

"That's Mom," Frankie whispers, hopping to her socked feet and scrambling out the door toward the foyer. Mandy's not sure if she should follow but takes a few steps in that direction anyway. She doesn't want Allison Hawthorne to think she would let Frankie go anywhere without being a few steps behind; it's her job.

She slowly descends the stairs, but not before she catches a glimpse of Allison crouched down in front of Frankie, speaking in a low tone with both hands on the girl's shoulders. Mandy doesn't think it's possible for Allison to ever look unkempt, but this may be as close as she can get. Her makeup is splotchy, necklace is slightly off-center, and several strands of hair have tumbled out of her chignon. She attempts to regain her composure when she notices Mandy halfway down the steps.

Like the flip of a switch, her eyes light up and her hands clasp in front of her chest.

"And how was your first day with Mandy? Did you two have so much fun?"

Frankie nods. "We finished the cat habitat, and I made my report for Miss Kelsey. Regina made me a chicken Caesar salad."

Mandy still can't believe she watched a young child willingly consume a chicken Caeser, with a full-size knife and fork, no less. The family chef, Regina, prepared it from scratch, and at thirty-six years old, Mandy learned the truth about the ingredients in Caeser dressing. Until today, she thought anchovies were just a funny ingredient people joked about ordering on their pizzas in old movies.

"You finished the entire project? Way to go, kiddo," Allison says, giving Frankie a high-five. "Since you worked so hard, I think you and Mandy should have a fun day tomorrow. She can either take you bowling or on a nature walk. You can think about it and decide in the morning which option you'd prefer." Allison glances up at Mandy and winks.

Mandy can't imagine having a childhood with choices. She was raised on the policy of *you get what you get, and you don't throw a fit*. Being asked what she wanted in life would have been an absolute luxury.

After two light taps, the front door swings open and Wes glides in. Once again, Mandy wonders just how many years he worked for the Bluff before he felt comfortable just appearing in the Hawthorne family's foyer.

"Hey, Mandy, I just realized I never gave you a tour of the dining lodge or the waterfront, so I thought I'd swing by and grab you so we can check them out on your way back to your car," he says, hands clasped behind his back like the dutiful employee he is. Frankie leaps in his direction and climbs his leg like a tree, making Wes break his stance and grab her around the waist, maneuvering her up to a sitting position on his shoulders.

"Put me down!" she squeals, laughing and kicking her legs against his chest.

"No ma'am, you started this. Now I need you to change all the light bulbs in the chandelier for me," Wes replies, dancing foolishly under the towering light fixture overhead.

"No way!"

In one swift move, he grabs her under the arms and flips her forward, setting her gently on her feet on the tile below. Mandy and Allison are beaming while watching the two. They have the appearance of a sibling duo, no doubt the relationship Remy and Frankie's mother wishes *they* had.

"You got out of it this time, but next time I'm in this house, we're putting you to work. You need to earn your keep, just like everyone else," Wes teases, much to Frankie's pleasure. She shrieks again before sprinting upstairs to her room while the three adults watch in pleased silence.

"So, how did your first day go? Any issues?" Allison asks, her voice lowered slightly so the kids don't hear.

Internally, Mandy thinks *Yes, except for the small issue of your son acting like he doesn't know me*, but verbally she only confirms it was a good day.

"Honestly, I had a lot of fun helping Frankie with her project. It was almost therapeutic to just sit in silence and focus on it with her. She's such a good kid," Mandy tells Allison, and it's not just a rouse; she means it. "Remy even helped us for a few minutes before he was sanctioned by the swear committee."

Allison laughs, and Wes shakes his head. "I told him to watch his language around her. Not only is it a bad influence, but she's going to have more money than any of us by the end of the summer if he keeps it up."

The two women confirm plans for Tuesday as Mandy gathers her bag and keys. Mandy will arrive shortly after nine and go over Frankie's homework with the tutor, Miss Kelsey. Allison even refers to her as Miss Kelsey, which Mandy thinks is strange, but a lot of things around here are strange so she goes along with it. The forecast is looking good, so Allison assumes Frankie will want to go on a nature walk, but they'll see in the morning. Frankie will decide how she wants to spend her afternoon after she decides what she would like to eat for lunch . . . This is a level of privilege Mandy didn't know existed. An even sadder thought occurs to her. What if this is how childhood should be, and the life Mandy lived is the abnormal one?

Mandy and Wes leave together, so he can take her for a tour of the waterfront on their way to the dining lodge. As expected, it's peaceful and breathtaking. Mandy stops for a moment to take it all in. She doesn't bother taking out her phone because a picture would never do it justice. A few ducks are gliding along the surface of the lake, and several turtles are sunning themselves on a log against the water's edge. A pedal boat is chugging across the lake with a young couple in the seats, the woman smiling as she reaches over the ledge to allow her fingertips to move through the calm waters.

"How has this place been just miles away from us our entire lives? I didn't know beauty like this existed. The entire place looks like a computer background. It's ridiculous." Wes searches across the water with his eyes and inhales deeply.

"No children should have to grow up the way we did, Mandy."

"How do you spend every day with these people and not resent them?" she asks. It's not an accusation; she realized earlier in the day that she would genuinely like to be a part of this world, but she can't shake the anger she feels toward the members of the club.

"It's a hard pill to swallow, but you've gotta accept the fact that them being rich isn't the reason we were poor. Them spending time with their kids isn't the reason our parents were absent. Sure, some of them are assholes. In fact, some of them are the worst people I've ever met in my life. But the rest of them are surprisingly decent. You'll see," Wes says to her while she watches his eyes for any hint of dishonesty. She sees none. She also swallows her pride enough to admit he has a point.

"What about being watched all the time? Don't the cameras get to you?"

This time, Wes smiles.

"Look, I've gotten to know the guys who work the security booth. I don't think they're paying much attention to the cameras. I'm not even sure the recordings are even logged anywhere. I think they were just installed to make the members feel safer. Nevertheless, I mind my p's and q's around them, just in case."

"Safer? Safer than this club? Has there ever been a crime here?" Mandy asks.

He looks at her without saying a word. The fires. The one crime nobody wants to talk about.

"You see that house?" Wes asks, pointing across the lake at a mansion, a fortress built of gray bricks and white pillars. Mandy nods. "The owner isn't here much, but the rumor is he makes his money as a hacker."

"What? Why isn't he in jail if it's a well-known fact that's where his money comes from?" Mandy asks.

"Because he launders the money through legitimate businesses. I think he has a laundromat and some rental properties. Most of these guys are smart and don't have much evidence tying them to the crimes. My point is, you'll meet some great people here, but there are also some shady ones, just like anywhere you go. Keep your guard up."

Chapter 20

After finishing the tour of the dining lodge, Mandy is thankful that it's not the area she applied to work in. She never knew there could be so many kinds of forks or methods to serve a bottle of wine. They walked in on one of the more seasoned servers training a new hire and she looked like a deer in headlights, trying her best to take it all in.

"What is the difference between the dining lodge and the other restaurants on property?" Mandy asks and screams internally when she catches herself using the term *on property* after less than twenty-four hours at the Bluff.

"The restaurants here are just like anywhere else; you get a menu and order what you'd like. At the dining lodge, an email is sent out each week with the scheduled meals. There's usually a meat option and a vegetarian option. The dining lodge dinner is included with their membership dues, and they serve Monday through Friday. On the weekends, members can reserve the lodge for private events."

"And how much are membership dues, if I may ask?"

Wes shrugs. "They're on a sliding scale; I'm assuming

based on the size of the lot they own here. I'm not sure what each family pays, but I know they take in about two million dollars from the fifty families who own property here."

If Mandy had a drink, she would have spit it out.

"Every single year? For what—a few meals and a security guard when you already live in one of the safest places in the world?"

"Members have meals five nights a week from professional chefs, access to two lakes and three rivers on property, countless miles of hiking trails, and thousands of acres of undeveloped wilderness. There are a lot of other benefits, but I'd have to—"

"Reference the brochure you were just quoting from?" Mandy interrupts. "You sound like a walking advertisement for the millionaires of northern Michigan. When they start selling spots on one of Elon's spaceships for after the apocalypse, they should hire you as a salesman."

"Hilarious," he says as his walkie-talkie radio crackles and a man's voice comes through.

"Wes, can you meet us at the commissary? Small issue."

Mandy's head cocks, but Wes doesn't give any indication what the small issue could be.

"You can make it back to the lot from here?" he asks.

She glances at the employee parking lot, where she can clearly see her vehicle from where they are standing.

"It's a dangerous voyage, but I'll stay strong."

"See you tomorrow, Chubbs," he says, turning to walk away in the direction of the commissary. Within a few feet, that walk turns into a jog.

Mandy remembers the urgency of the employee who came down to the Quick Stop for Coors Light a few weeks back. She hasn't worked here long, but from what she has witnessed, the only ones in a hurry seem to be members of the staff.

As she's walking to her car and thinking of Georgia's chicken alfredo in her fridge, Mandy is startled by a door closing from the car next to hers. She politely smiles at the older woman walking toward her when she notices the name embroidered on her gray chef's coat: Amelia.

"Amelia Crain?" Mandy asks.

The woman stops in her tracks.

"Do I know you?"

She looks to be in her sixties or early seventies, with white hair tied back into a neat braid and orthopedic shoes with Velcro closures on her tiny feet. Her smile is warm, yet curious.

"I'm a friend of Georgia Afton's. She told me to look for you when I got a job here. I'm working as a nanny for Chandler and Allison Hawthorne. Well, a keeper I guess is what it's called. I still have to get used to that," Mandy says with a self-deprecating laugh. The woman's face has gone pale.

"Did you say Georgia Afton?"

"Yes, she's my neighbor. She also watches my dog. She said you used to work together?"

"How long have you been neighbors?"

"Oh gosh . . . My ex-husband and I bought the house a couple years ago, and she moved in shortly after. Maybe a year and a half?"

"Who does she live with?"

"Well, she lives alone. Her husband died, but I think she told me that happened before she got the job here, right?"

The woman's expression turns from shock to amusement.

"That's right. I just didn't know if maybe she found love again."

"Nope, she just tends to her garden and fusses over me most days. That seems to keep her busy enough," Mandy says, her polite laugh dying quickly when she sees Amelia isn't sharing in it. The woman is staring at Mandy, wide-eyed, taking in this information.

"What did you say your name was?" Amelia asks.

"Mandy. Mandy Cramer. Well, that was my married name. I would take back my maiden name of Smith, but I'm trying to distance myself from that name in Delta County, if you know what I mean."

She's rambling, which she often does when she's uncomfortable.

"Mandy Smith?"

"Yes, ma'am. That's my maiden name."

"Were you related to a Skylar Smith?"

Mandy's cheeks redden slightly.

"That would be reason number one that I don't like to use my maiden name. Yes, Skylar was my mother. Or, is my mother. I haven't talked to her in years, but I'm assuming she's still alive. Did you know her?"

The woman nods while continuing to assess Mandy, deciding how much she'd like to reveal to this stranger.

"Yes, yes I did. When I knew her, she wasn't so bad. She was a hard worker."

Mandy doesn't mean to, but she laughs. Amelia isn't pleased.

"I'm sorry, I've just never heard Skylar Smith described as a hard worker. You must have known her before I was in the picture. Did you bowl together or something?" Mandy asks, listing the only hobby she's ever known her mom to have other than drinking or shooting up.

Alas, Amelia smiles.

"Good guess; that's exactly where I knew her from. We were on a team at Bowl-A-Roo together. We were sponsored by Gibby's Bar."

Mandy returns her smile, imagining a time where her mom was sober and responsible enough to show up for a weekly obligation like bowling.

"I remember seeing the shirt in her closet; it was green with white stripes on the sleeves."

Amelia nods. "That's right."

"Well, it's such a pleasure to meet you. Hopefully I'll be seeing more of you around," Mandy says, raising her hand in an awkward wave goodbye because shaking the woman's hand seems excessive.

"Nice to meet you, too. Would you mind giving Georgia a message for me, when you see her?"

"Of course; I'll probably stop over there when I get home."

"Great. Tell her I didn't realize she was back in town and that things haven't changed much around here since she's been gone. It would be really great to see her again; she's due for a visit."

Chapter 21

Something catches Mandy's eye in the distance, to the right of her car as she pulls into the driveway from work. A smile spreads across her face when she sees it's Murphy doing bunny hops through Georgia's garden while she tends to it. Her neighbor is so smitten with that dog; Mandy wonders why she doesn't adopt one herself.

"Well, how was your first day?" Georgia says, climbing to her feet and dusting the soil from the front of her slacks.

"Pretty uneventful, to be honest. I helped Frankie, the little girl I'm watching, with a school project. The teenager kept to himself for most of the day. Oh, I did run into your friend Amelia when I was getting into my car to come home," Mandy says, while watching for Georgia's response. The woman's eyes are a perfect mix of surprise and curiosity.

"How is the old bat?"

"She looked good. She said to tell you that things haven't changed at all and you're overdue for a visit."

Georgia nods slowly when Mandy tells her this, as if

she needs to decide on the logistics for a visit right this moment.

"She also said she didn't know you were back in town. Did you live somewhere else after you worked at the Bluff?" Mandy asks. Georgia's not exactly an open book when it comes to her personal business, but Mandy is still surprised she never mentioned living outside of Delta County.

"Oh, we just did what every other aging Yooper does and went to Florida for a while. I decided those summers just weren't for me, so I came back. I'd rather have a few months of snow than that miserable heat any day. If I ever talk about moving back south, slap some sense into me. You have my permission."

"We?"

This would have been after the death of Georgia's husband. She doesn't have any children. Who in the world did she go to Florida with?

"What's that?" Georgia asks, caught off guard.

"You said 'we' when you were talking about moving to Florida."

Georgia searches the ground with her eyes, replaying the words in her mind before shaking her head.

"Oh, several of us didn't go back to work at the Bluff after the fire. We were close enough to retirement age, we figured Florida would be a good idea."

Mandy finds it incredibly sad that Georgia doesn't seem to keep in touch with any of her old coworkers from the Hawthorne Bluff Club. In fact, she doesn't seem to keep in touch with many people at all from her past.

"So, how is the Hawthorne family? Chandler III and Allison were newlyweds last time I saw them," Georgia says, after a few seconds too long of uncomfortable silence.

Mandy can barely picture the couple as young and

smitten. All she's witnessed is Chandler's loving relationship with his cell phone. Mandy decides to tread lightly with her response. Georgia still hasn't come clean about working directly for Jack and Tilly Hawthorne at the end of her time working at the Bluff, and Mandy has decided she's going to remain patient and let the woman tell her when she's comfortable talking about it.

"Pretty much what you'd expect. Chandler is always working, and Allison is the more present parent, but she was still gone most of the day today. The daughter is adorable and really smart. The son, well . . ."

"What about the son?" Georgia asks, leaning forward on her shovel like she hasn't received a piece of gossip in decades. She's thirsting for it. "Is he a little jerk?"

"No," Mandy begins, deciding in the moment that Georgia can be trusted with this information. "But, it's the strangest thing—I actually know him. He used to come into the Quick Stop a couple times a week. Nice kid; I just don't understand why he pretended not to know me when Allison introduced us. I've gone along with the ruse because I'm not sure what the reason is, but I want him to know he can trust me."

Georgia considers this for a moment.

"And he's how old?"

"Seventeen, about to turn eighteen."

The woman shrugs. "The Bluff can be a strange place. Maybe he doesn't want anyone to know he's cheating on the commissary. It's a cute store, but sometimes kids just want a name brand pop or a candy bar, not this organic frou-frou stuff imported from other countries. He probably just likes to sneak to town and grab some snacks so he can feel like a normal teenager."

Similar thoughts have crossed Mandy's mind. It could be as simple as that. Remy just wants to feel normal once in a while and doesn't feel like explaining himself to his out-of-touch millionaire parents.

"You might be right. Also, I had a blast from the past with your friend. Amelia told me she knew my mother."

Georgia takes a step back, and the heel of her boot connects with one of Murphy's front paws. The dog yelps and Georgia scoops him up into her arms, cooing an apology into his small, floppy ears. When she's satisfied that the dog is okay, she gently sets him back into the soil, where he promptly trots off to the edge of the garden, where he lies in the grass with a huff.

"You don't talk much about your mother, so I hate to ask. I don't want you to talk about anything you're not comfortable with, but was she a friend of Amelia's?"

Mandy shakes her head.

"No, from the sound of it, they were just acquaintances. They were in the same bowling league. It must have been before the addiction took over; I remember seeing pictures of her in her bowling uniform, and she was beautiful. She looked so healthy."

Georgia's shoulders drop and she wears a sympathetic smile, gazing at Mandy.

"Do you have any pictures of your mother? I'd love to see her."

Occasionally, Mandy is asked about her past, and it requires an answer that isn't as easy as the more commonly asked questions. *Where are your parents? Do you have any siblings?* Those questions she can answer like they are second nature. Talking specifically about what she lost in the fire has proven to be more difficult.

"They were destroyed in the fire. Everything from my childhood was. If you'd like to see what she looks like, I'm sure you can pull her picture up on the prison website."

Georgia flinches.

"I didn't mean for that to sound as rude as it came out; I'd actually love to have pictures of her. I don't have very many memories from before she was addicted to drugs and alcohol, and it would be nice to see her when she was happy and healthy. I barely remember what she looked like back then."

"If this happened when you were ten, that means she's been clean and sober behind bars for twenty-six years. Have you considered visiting her?"

That's something Mandy has never wavered on. She has not once considered visiting her mother in prison. She didn't want to be confused or sympathetic; she's been content to live her life filled with rage and disappointment in her biological mother.

"We assume she's been clean and sober, but I watch enough TV to know they have plenty of options to get high in there. She's probably selling her body for some toilet hooch."

Georgia once again flinches, and Mandy regrets her choice of words.

"Sorry. I just have no desire to see that woman. She ruined my childhood, and she took my brother from me. Not that he was a great man, but she also took my dad. I don't have much to say to her."

"A lot of people change their lives in there. She's had decades to sit alone in her cell and think about every mistake she's ever made in her life. You may be pleasantly surprised."

"Georgia, I thank you so much for suggesting something you think may be a good idea. That's just you—you're a good woman with a good heart. Unfortunately, you didn't know my mother, so you can't possibly understand how sure I am that she hasn't changed."

Georgia nods in acceptance and changes the topic of conversation, much to Mandy's relief.

"Were you able to see your friend today? Wes, was it?"

Mandy smiles, despite herself.

"I did. I forgot how easy it is with Wes. We've picked up our friendship like no time at all has passed."

Georgia gives a genuine smile. Her eyes are filled with pride.

"That is just so good to hear. He sounds like an excellent young man."

The bass from an incoming vehicle steals their attention before realizing that it's coming from Braxton's truck. He goes a little too fast before cranking the wheel to pull into his driveway without using a blinker. Mandy mutters something under her breath about them being right about Illinois drivers. Georgia chuckles.

"Hello, ladies," he greets them after exiting his truck. He holds up one finger and jogs to his front door, fumbling for the key and finally unlocking it, much to the pleasure of little Max, who comes trotting out and lifts his leg the moment he's on the lawn.

"Sorry, it was a long shift, and I knew he'd be ready to go," Braxton explains, walking toward the ladies with Max at his heels.

Murphy bounds out from behind Georgia and straight to Max, where they exchange a few friendly growls before chasing each other around the yard.

"I met your ex-husband today," Braxton says, and Mandy's heart skips a beat. She knew it was a possibility when Braxton said he worked at the mill, but she hoped he was in a different department and would get lost in the sea of employees there, never to encounter that cheating, abusive bastard.

"How did you know who he was? Or was someone

referring to the piece of shit over in the boiler house and you made the connection?" Mandy asks.

"There was a mandatory safety meeting, and I saw Patrick Cramer on the list. I know your last name is Cramer, and I remember Georgia referring to him as Patrick, among a few other choice names, when she was telling me about you."

Georgia tuts. "I never called him anything that wasn't deserved."

"Hey, you're not going to get an argument from me. He's a real asshole," Mandy tells her. "Did he look horrible? Tell me he looked horrible."

Braxton's lips curl into a smile. "He looks like absolute death. Like he roams the streets screaming your name and wondering why he ever left you."

"That sounds about right," Mandy confirms. She likes Braxton. "Next time you see him, feel free to give him a good old-fashioned throat punch and tell him it's from me."

He holds a hand to his forehead in mock salute. "That's a promise."

Chapter 22

For the rest of the week, Mandy continues to get acclimated in her new role. She takes Frankie on nature hikes, trips to the park, and to the unincorporated library at the Bluff, where Mandy is impressed by the vast selection of books but disheartened that none of them show signs of being read. She works hard to push the jealousy down and let her growing fondness for Frankie flourish. What's not to love? She's adorable, polite, smart, and humble. Hanging out with her doesn't seem like a job at all.

By Thursday, Mandy's suspicions about Remy are quelled when he pulls her aside and explains himself, at last. Georgia had been right—he likes to escape the confines of the club when his parents are otherwise engaged so he can feel like a normal kid.

"Hell, sometimes I just sit in my car in the parking lot of the high school and pretend I go there. We've had this house my entire life and I still don't feel like a local," he told her, fidgeting with his cuticles as he spoke. "Being a regular at the Quick Stop was the closest I've ever come to feeling like one."

In a surprising moment of emotional maturity, he told Mandy that he understands how lucky he is for the life he has, but he also feels like a caged tiger and that it's possible for both things to be true.

Mandy assured him his secret is safe with her, and that she's been trying her best to refer to him as Remy, rather than Chandy. It's a strange feeling to greet someone by name for years, only to learn it's something different. So many of the confessions he'd made to her over the years, leaning on the cheap Formica countertop at the Quick Stop, are suddenly making so much sense. He'd said he wanted to travel far away for college but couldn't bear the thought of being too far away to help his little sister if she needed it. He loves his mother but resents her for being so submissive. She's surprised Remy described his father as a man he admires when they first discussed his family; that's the only comment that doesn't line up with what she's seeing.

Mandy screams internally for Allison to leave her husband each time she sees the light in her eyes dim as he enters the room. After everything Patrick put her through, she knows she's being a hypocrite for expecting Allison to pack up and leave, but it doesn't stop her from hoping it will happen.

At a quarter to five on Friday, Wes is in the foyer of the Hawthorne home, waiting to walk Mandy to her car, just as he has every day this week. They have taken a different route on their walk to the employee parking lot each day so Wes can show her the entirety of the club. "Well, as much as I can show you in one summer. There are tens of thousands of acres, so I don't think we could ever cover it all," he explained the day before.

Mandy has repeatedly assured him that he doesn't have to do this; she can explore on her own, and she can certainly handle the short walk to her car. Each time, he reminds her that they have nearly twenty years of catching up to do and that it does him good to have a familiar face around the club.

Today, they are taking a side road so he can show her a cul-de-sac dubbed "the Third Wives Club" because, simply enough, each of the husbands are on their third marriages. Not surprisingly, he explains that each of the wives are significantly younger and better looking than the husbands. As they walk side-by-side and Wes tells Mandy what he knows about the men, she daydreams about a rich older man propositioning her for a similar arrangement. After a short deliberation, she decides it wouldn't be worth it. She'd rather hold out for real love. Sure, it would be nice not to have to worry about bills, but having money has to get less impressive as time goes on. These women have designer bags, trips abroad, and jewelry worth enough money to feed a small country, but they don't get to feel butterflies when they see their husbands. They don't get to fall asleep smiling because they're so madly in love with the man lying next to them. They made deals with the devil and all the money in the world wouldn't be worth that agreement.

"Do you think any of them are really in love?" Mandy asks as they finish walking the loop and exit the cul-de-sac.

Without missing a beat, Wes answers, "Absolutely not. I've spent enough time with these people to answer that with certainty. A few of the marriages around here are still new enough that the wives still hold onto hope that the men they married aren't that bad, but the ones who have been together for a while are a different story. They know the monsters they married."

"Why don't they leave?" Mandy asks, regretting the question as soon as the words have left her lips. Again, she's being a hypocrite, in the truest sense of the word.

"I'm sure there are a lot of different answers to that question, but most of them have iron-clad prenups. They'll get nothing if they leave. These guys don't tend to choose second or third wives from affluent families. A handful of them are from other countries and were able to bring their mothers with them. They know how much they'd lose, so they stay."

"That is really sad," Mandy says, and she means it. She thinks of the feat she just completed herself. She interviewed and obtained a job making enough money to pay her bills and live comfortably, with no assistance from anyone else. Sure, they wouldn't be living like queens anymore, but these women could get a job like Mandy's and pay their bills without living with a miserable asshole who controls their every move. If they just got out on their own and gave it a try, they'd be surprised at what they could do without a man's help.

"Mandy, you've always been empathetic. I'm telling you this for your own good—you can't let their problems be your problems. I know how hard that is, but you have to treat this place like a job and nothing more. If you get too invested, you'll go crazy, and you'll also risk one of these guys finding out you're sniffing around and trying to help their wives. It won't end well. I promise you that."

She is perplexed by Wes's loyalty to this place, while knowing that most of the members are reprehensible people. He must be paid very well to look the other way.

While walking back to her car, she feels her phone vibrate inside her purse. She pulls it out to see a new email from Hawthorne, LLC. It's a paystub reflecting the direct deposit made for her first week of work. She frantically clicks over to her bank app and, sure enough, the largest weekly paycheck she's ever received is pending in her account.

"Do they not take taxes out of my check?" she asks.

"No, you're considered an independent contractor. I know it's tempting to spend it all, but you need to set aside a good chunk to pay taxes or you're gonna be real depressed next April when you go to file," Wes tells her.

This all feels too good to be true. She doesn't have any real responsibility when it comes to "watching" Remy, and her time with Frankie feels more like hanging out than performing actual job duties. It's a five-minute drive to her house, she's off work before dinner, and will rarely work weekends. Sure, Chandler is a bit of a prick, but at this hourly rate, she's happy to deal with it.

"Do you have plans this weekend? I'd love to cook you dinner if you're free," Mandy offers when they arrive at her car. Wes doesn't even take a moment to consider it before refusing.

"You may work banker's hours, but some of us have to stick around here on the weekends, Chubbs."

"Do the rich folk need someone to read their *Sunday Times* out loud to them or something?"

She cocks her head and shoots Wes a wry smile.

"No, but you wouldn't believe the amount of ass wiping I have to do in the evening hours," he replies with a wink. "See you Monday morning."

"Looking forward to it," she says and, against all odds, it's the truth.

Chapter 23

Mandy is only two hours into her first official weekend off, and it's already a luxury beyond expectations.

She placed an order with her favorite take-out restaurant on the way home and sprang for an extra side. While eating her meal at the kitchen table, she opened her laptop and made her car payment two weeks early. She transferred a hundred dollars into her savings account and then wrote out a grocery list for her weekend shopping trip. The one thing she didn't do was worry about receiving calls from the Quick Stop. Nobody bothered her for help manually entering a customer's loyalty rewards number, there weren't any delivery issues for her to handle, and she sure as hell didn't need to cater to Shorty's needs afterhours anymore. It's the weekend, and she's *off*.

"This is the life, Murphs," she says to her pug, who doesn't so much as lift his head from the post-dinner nap he's enjoying on the small dog bed in the corner of the kitchen.

For the first time in as long as she can remember, Mandy falls into her overstuffed couch and turns on a mindless reality show without an ounce of guilt. She smiles at the thought of going to bed tonight without money on her mind. She can't recall the last time her final waking thought wasn't about upcoming bills and the current balance of her checking account. She wonders what the rich worry about when they go to sleep.

Bored with an overdramatized episode of a show about New York City socialites, Mandy opens her laptop and focuses her attention on the screen.

First, she logs into a social media site to see if her friends, or rather acquaintances, have posted anything newsworthy. Two minutes of scrolling provides thirteen different arguments about the election, four shared warnings that if you don't post "I DO NOT GIVE THIS SITE RIGHTS TO MY PHOTOS" that pictures of your grandchildren will end up on the dark web, and a pregnancy announcement from a former classmate, with the news that they shall name their daughter Hunterleigh. *That's enough for today*, Mandy thinks as she logs off.

Her instinct is to reach for a bottle of wine since it's the weekend, but she's making a conscious effort not to engage in mindless drinking, as she has been doing since her divorce. Her parents were addicts, so it's in her DNA. That's reason enough to cut back. Reluctantly, she walks into the kitchen and grabs a sparkling flavored water from the fridge, the same can that Georgia gave her two months ago when she told Mandy that she looked dehydrated. "This will be fine," she whispers to herself, popping the top off the can. The first sip hits her tongue, and she sprints to the sink to spit it out. Murphy awakes from his nap and shoots her a judgmental glare. "What, do you want to try it? It's horrible."

Her eyes fall on the half bottle of wine she opened the night before. "Oh, what the hell?" she says to nobody, before reaching into the cupboard for a stemless glass.

Mandy retakes her seat on the couch and notices a new email notification on the bottom of her screen. Once she clicks on it, her heart skips a beat. It's from the Michigan Department of Corrections. An inmate has requested permission to communicate with her, and there is a link for the JPay site—Mandy will need to create an account and pay to purchase virtual "stamps" to respond.

Although she may never admit it out loud, it has been easier to pretend her mother is dead. Out of sight, out of mind. If she acknowledges that she is alive and well in a prison in lower Michigan, she will have to face her feelings about the person who took everything from her. Her childhood, her home, her family. Everything.

She stares at the screen for a few moments before rising to her feet, walking back into the kitchen, and pouring her untouched glass of wine down the drain. She pulls the cork out of the open bottle and empties it into the sink. Frantically, her eyes search the kitchen counters for anything else that needs to go. Retrieving an empty trash bag from under the sink, she doesn't even bother to open and empty the beer cans in the fridge, she simply throws them in the bag. A cheap bottle of champagne she purchased for the anniversary she and Patrick never got around to celebrating goes in the bag. Two mini bottles of Fireball from the freezer get thrown in. Before she can think better of it, she tightens the strings on the bag and struts out the side door and over to her city trash can. The bag lands inside with a thud, much louder than she expected, and her shoulders rise in anticipation of Georgia's concern. Sure enough, the light in the woman's entryway flips on.

"Are you burying bodies out here, young lady?"

Georgia is wearing a pink quilted nightgown with a

zipper down the front and her gray-white hair is wrapped up tight in curlers. Mandy can't help but smile, which is a stark contrast from the rage she has felt for the past ten minutes.

"I wouldn't tell you even if I was, Georgia. That would make you an accomplice," Mandy replies with a smirk.

"You can always tell me if we're getting rid of a body. I'm in my seventies with arthritis and a cabinet filled with Bengay; nobody is going to waste their time investigating me."

Mandy doesn't reply straight away; she simply looks at her neighbor in admiration. It's been an unlikely friendship, but one Mandy wouldn't trade for the world.

"I'm off tomorrow. If I pick up some burger meat at the grocery store, would you want to grill out for a late lunch?"

"Well, I guess that would be fine," Georgia replies, because it would kill her to act excited about anything. Mandy assumes it's her generation because her customers at the Quick Stop had the same permanently unimpressed demeanor, until they won a few dollars on a scratch-off. "Now go back inside and quit making all this ruckus so I can enjoy my program in peace."

"*Perry Mason*? Lawrence Welk? *Golden Girls*?"

Georgia huffs so loudly it makes Mandy chuckle. "I'll have you know, I'm watching *Forensic Files*."

Mandy lowers her jaw and gives a slow clap. "I'm impressed. I'll see you tomorrow, Georgia. Sorry about the noise."

She catches a brief grin on Georgia's face before she shuts her door, followed closely by the sound of her dead-bolt latching. Mandy laughs again. Most nights, she doesn't even remember to lock her doors at all.

Back inside, she throws a small bacon treat to Murphy

and reopens her laptop with renewed optimism—she's in control of her own actions. She will create an account and read the email her mother sent. Once the email is read, she will sleep on it before responding, so she's not letting her emotions take over.

First, she logs into Reddit, which is typically a stress reliever. She'll scroll for a few minutes before going back to her email. Mandy's relieved to see that she has a new message, knowing it must be from DANNYBOY06 because the only other time she's received a direct message on the site was last year when she commented on a post about grocery prices and some internet stranger took that as a sign to privately tell her she was too dumb to live.

Sure enough, a message from DANNYBOY06 came in less than an hour ago.

"How was your first week? Any sacrifices performed to maintain their youthful glow? Have any of the husbands offered you an audition to be their future ex-wife?"

Despite herself, Mandy laughs.

"Ha-Ha. No such excitement. Just a lot of fancy groceries, private tutors, and grass that is somehow already as green as a Christmas tree. Sorry to disappoint!"

He must be online because a response pops up in her inbox almost immediately.

"Keep your guard up."

It's slightly annoying that both Wes *and* this stranger on the internet have given her the same warning with next to zero context.

"Yeah, yeah. Guard is up. I actually thought about you earlier when my coworker pointed out a house on property that is supposedly owned by an actual scam artist. Or hacker. I'm not sure exactly what he does, but it's not legal and it's apparently made him a lot of money. His house is huge."

"Are you suggesting I use my particular set of skills to start scamming people so I can buy a place in Hawthorne?" DANNYBOY06 asks. Mandy wonders exactly what it is that he does with his skillset.

"We could go through with our Robin Hood plan," she replies. "Steal from the rich and give to the poor. Think of the good you could do in Delta County."

"Trust me, I think about it all the time. There are fifty families that live in the club, and they could be doing so much more to help the community, but that would mean leaving the gates and actually seeing what's going on in the community, which they mostly refuse to do. In their sheltered world, everyone has enough money for food and medical care, and their employees must go home and sleep on a bed of money, without a care in the world. They have no idea the struggle the rest of us face. If I ever decide to pull a heist on those assholes, I promise that I'll include you in on the plan."

Now Mandy is officially intrigued. This person has more knowledge of the Bluff than the average resident of Delta County.

She's also terrified by her gut reaction to his words. *Why should these families feel obligated to share their wealth with the people of this town just because they're rich? Why should they feel like they owe it to strangers just because they live in the same county?*

One week at the Bluff and she's already mentally defending them.

She remembers Luke's words, when he was fuming the morning of his late meat delivery to Chandler Hawthorne: "Just promise me, Mandy. Promise me you won't ever become one of them."

Chapter 24

If Mandy could take her happiness and bottle it up to sell, she'd name it "Grocery Shopping with Money." Walking up and down the aisles of Meijer while comfortably throwing name-brand ketchup and cereal in her cart is a kind of elation she didn't know existed. She now understands how so many people in this country compromise their morals for money—one paycheck and she's already forgotten all the horrible thoughts she had about the Hawthorne Bluff Club members just last week. They say money can't buy you happiness, but today Mandy says they are wrong.

Once she is done choosing two bags of pre-cut salad mix and a fancy poppyseed dressing, Mandy does something she's never allowed herself to do—she ventures into the fancy cheese aisle. The aisle normally reserved for middle-aged white women wearing designer peacoats and sunglasses indoors. Here she goes; she has officially made it.

Unfortunately, it only takes a minute or two for Mandy to realize that she has never heard of half of these cheeses and has no feasible plan for what she would even do with fancy cheese. She sees women in movies chopping them up in small pieces and serving them on wooden platters with olives and salami-style meats, but who would she possibly entertain in her home? Georgia? Braxton? She ultimately decides that paying nearly ten dollars for smoked gouda isn't the best way to spend her first paycheck from the Bluff. She does, however, spring for the organic, grass-fed ground beef and brioche buns for her planned lunch with Georgia.

While checking out, she proudly pulls out her debit card, rather than her credit card, and swipes without hesitation when the cashier gives her the total of nearly one hundred fifty dollars. She cannot remember a high like this. On her way out, rather than holding the receipt and analyzing every item to make sure she wasn't overcharged, she simply folds it in half and slips it into her purse. Total elation.

In fact, Mandy is so lost in her joy, she doesn't notice who she is about to encounter in a near-collision until it's too late.

Emily Myers. Single mother, two years younger than Mandy, fellow townie, stealer of husbands.

She swerves her cart to avoid Emily's at the last second. Both women are stunned, but Emily regains composure before Mandy can even form a coherent thought.

"Please get out of my way," Emily says, the words kind but the tone hostile.

"By all means, wouldn't want to inconvenience you," Mandy replies with her signature sarcasm.

"I talked to Dee, and she told me you're denying that you took Pat back. You might not be with him now, but don't you dare lie about him coming home that night. I'm not fucking stupid."

Well, she is fucking stupid because Patrick despises being called Pat, and Mandy has no idea what night she is referring to.

Normally a peacekeeper, today Mandy chooses violence. This woman does not deserve an ounce of her sympathy. She was sleeping with Mandy's husband four blocks from the house where she waited for him to come home from the "overtime hours" he was working several nights a week. Mandy's sole regret is that she didn't notice the lack of overtime pay on his direct deposits sooner.

"Emily, I understand it might help you sleep at night to imagine that the only reason he would ever leave you is to reunite with his estranged wife because of our history, but I'm here to tell you that I haven't seen that cheating bastard since the day he moved his belongings out and left me high and dry to pay our mortgage on my own. I'm so sorry to tell you that he grew bored of you so quickly, but if it's any consolation, a friend of mine saw him at the mill the other day and said he looked like shit, so maybe there's trouble in paradise already with whoever he left you for. Now, get the fuck out of my way, and while you're at it, keep my name out of your fucking mouth. So long as I'm breathing, I'll have nothing to do with that sorry excuse of a man ever again."

Although her delivery was impeccable and left poor Emily Myers in a stunned state of shock, Mandy's hands are shaking as she grips the cart handle and pushes her way out of the store. Replaying the conversation over again in her mind while she loads her groceries into the car, she finds herself smiling, which turns into hysterical laughter by the time she has returned her cart and settled into the driver's seat. After her upbringing, she sure tried her best not to end up in her thirties and divorced, publicly cussing out her husband's mistress in the middle of the grocery store, but alas, that's exactly where she ended up. She's just thankful she didn't have a baby on her hip while doing it.

The entire drive home, she racks her brain, trying to figure out who this mystery woman is and why Patrick would lie and say he was getting back with Mandy. She smiles at the possibility of it being one of Emily's own friends. Wouldn't that be karma working its magic a lot quicker than usual?

As Mandy pulls back into her driveway, she's greeted by the sight of Georgia outside cleaning her grill. Although she protested at her offer, Mandy's quite relieved because her own grill hasn't been used since last September, and she can't imagine the condition it's in or what kind of creepy crawlies might be living inside. Georgia also offered to make her famous German potato salad to go with the burgers, which didn't get an ounce of protesting from Mandy.

"How was it?" Georgia asks when Mandy exits her car.

"How was what?"

"Not worrying so much about the price of groceries," Georgia says with a wink.

"How did you know?" Mandy asks, popping the trunk and reaching in for the first few bags.

"Because I remember my first big paycheck and how it felt. Granted, I think a loaf of bread was fifty cents back then, but I sure got a nicer loaf than I was used to. My girl-friends and I went to the drive-in and got French fries and strawberry shakes, and I paid for all three of us. I'll never forget it."

The longing in Georgia's eyes nearly brings tears to Mandy's. Her thirty-six years are seeming to go by so quickly; she can't imagine how Georgia feels looking back on her life and all the little moments that have stuck with her all these years.

"I bought cereal in a box instead of a bag and I got the good peanut butter," Mandy tells her, reaching in the bag to retrieve the Jif and holding it in the air like it's a prize. "I don't think I'll ever forget this feeling and I'm glad you haven't either."

Georgia sits with her contented smile for a moment before waving Mandy away.

"Now, go put those groceries away and give me the burger meat so I can season it properly. I trust you with a lot of things, but that's not one of them."

She's the only woman who can repeatedly insult Mandy and receive a smile in return. Her judgmental nature is, against all odds, incredibly charming.

After handing Georgia the meat, buns, and fancy ketchup, Mandy props her side door open with her hip so Murphy can run outside.

Moments later, her fridge is nearly full, and so is her heart. She makes a solid promise to help out a family or two around Christmas this year. She's never had the extra money to help, but now that she has experienced this feeling, she knows it needs to be shared. Christmas should be a happy time for everyone, and she's spent more than a few years wondering why Santa didn't love her as much as the other kids at school. Maybe this year she can make it a little easier on kids like her. When she finds out which children need help, she'll do her research and buy them presents they'd love, unlike Chandler and Leslie Hawthorne and their strange dolls and oversized clothing. She will show those kids that she cares and that they matter.

The sizzling noise of the meat hitting the grill breaks her trance, and she realizes she's been inside a lot longer than she'd anticipated. Normally, she'd grab a cold beer to go with her burger, but today she retrieves a Coke Zero from the fridge and nods to herself. She's making changes. She's breaking the Smith curse.

By the time she's back outside, Georgia has brought Murphy into her own yard and set an outdoor table for two. Dining outside in April is a rarity and it's *just* warm enough today. The scent of grilled burgers sends a wave of optimism through Mandy's thoughts. She's about to have free nights and weekends all summer long. She will have enough money to grill out salmon and steaks if they feel like it. She'll set up her hammock in the backyard and check out a different mystery novel from the library every week. This is how life is meant to be lived, and she's finally joining in.

"Well, you survived your first week. Was it everything you hoped for?" Georgia asks while placing the buns on the top shelf of the grill. She's wearing a blue apron with white geese scattered throughout, reminiscent of the décor everyone's moms seemed to have in the nineties. Well, everyone's mom except for Mandy's. The thought jolts her upright—she forgot about the email. The request that remains at the top of her inbox. The first time her mother has attempted to reach out in years. "Are you okay, dear?" she asks when she realizes Mandy hasn't replied to her first question.

"Sorry, I just remembered something I forgot to do. It's not a big deal; I can handle it later. Yes, the job was easy, and the people weren't nearly as bad as I feared. I'm still going to keep my guard up, but I think all of us have created these urban legends about the Bluff people over the years because we fear the things we don't understand, you know?"

Georgia spins toward Mandy and places one hand on her hip, a spatula in the other.

"I can't disagree with you there, Mandy. But remember that these people are sometimes wolves in sheep's clothing. The reason a lot of them have so much money is because they're skilled at charming people into handing it over."

Mandy so badly wants to ask about why Georgia only said she worked in the kitchen and not for Jack and Tilly Hawthorne directly. What harm would there be in telling her now?

"Georgia, would you mind if I asked you a question about the fire?"

The look in Georgia's eyes tells Mandy she's been expecting this question, but that doesn't mean she's prepared to answer it. She silently nods.

"All of the stories I've heard refer to it as 'the fire,' but now that I've seen the layout of the club and where the two structures were located, I understand that it wasn't one fire that spread to the other building. They were too far apart. It was two separate fires."

After a beat, Georgia nods again. "So, what is your question?"

"What the hell happened? How did an employee cabin and a millionaire's mansion burn down on the same night?"

With a few smooth motions, Georgia slides her spatula under the buns and places one on each of the plastic plates on a small folding table set up next to the grill. She tops them with the burgers, turns off the grill, and scoops a dollop of potato salad on each of their plates. Mandy is watching the woman's every move, wondering if her questions went too far. Georgia pulls out the chair across from Mandy and sits.

"It doesn't matter what I think happened. Nobody will ever be able to prove it."

Mandy would expect to see sadness in Georgia's eyes when she talks about how justice will never be served, but instead her eyes are emotionless.

"You never went back to work after the fires. What was it like when you came back to clean out your belongings from your cabin? Was everyone just utterly devastated?"

This time, Georgia's lips curl into a smile but it's not a friendly one. It's the kind of smile a woman wears when she's holding herself back from crying or screaming.

"I didn't have any belongings left. They were destroyed in the fire, along with my best friend."

Chapter 25

It was Georgia's cabin. She lived there, with her best friend and another coworker and wasn't there because it was her night off. Mandy didn't have the heart to ask her where she was when the fire happened; she imagines the woman has been replaying it in her mind for the last twenty-six years. Was she at the movies? Enjoying a night of bowling? Finally venturing out on a date for the first time since her husband died? Whatever activity she was doing that night saved her life but also prevented her from saving the life of her best friend.

After washing her face and getting dressed for bed, Mandy sits at her kitchen table in a daze. She feels like she has more questions now than she did before the cookout.

It doesn't matter what happened. Nobody will be able to prove it.

Mandy did take a chance and ask Georgia what her best friend's name was, but she waved her off and said she'd talk about it another time when she was ready. She cannot imagine the pain this woman has lived through. After helping her with the dishes and wiping down the grill, Mandy bent down to pick up Murphy and thanked Georgia for cooking. When Mandy turned to leave, Georgia stopped her.

"Her name was Charlene, but we called her Char. She was the best human I'd ever known."

Mandy nodded. "I have no doubt she was very happy to have a friend like you."

The comment was met with a subtle glistening at the corner of Georgia's eyes before she turned to go inside.

Now, Mandy's mind is running wild with theories. Did the Hawthornes do something horrible that caused an employee to burn their house down? Did the other Hawthorne brother, Chandler Jr., catch them in the act and burn their cabin down in retaliation? How much did they pay the rest of the employees to keep their mouths shut about the fires? And, is there any truth to the theory that Jack and Tilly escaped, since their bodies were never found? Mandy pictures them now in their golden years, living on the ocean and sipping Mai Tais while they laugh about getting away with murder. Mandy can't imagine what motivated them to kill two employees and then light their own house on fire, but she can't rule out the theory.

She stares at the closed laptop sitting in the center of her small dining table. She questions whether she's in the right state of mind to read an email from her mother, but she accepts that she may never be in a state of mind to talk to Skylar Smith, so she may as well bite the bullet and see what the woman has to say.

Mandy goes through the process of setting up an account so she can view the email from her mother, cussing to herself every step of the way, particularly when she has to enter her debit card information to add funds in case she wants to reply. She also has the option to put money on a prisoner's books, allowing them to purchase snacks and toiletries from the commissary. She once again laughs at the irony of the Bluff Club calling their high-end grocery store the Commissary. She imagines it's quite a different experience shopping in the prison store. She doesn't have any intention of adding funds to her mom's account.

Once her login is created, Mandy gets the notification of one new email sent from the Women's Correctional Facility. The subject line is "FYI: Please Read," but when Mandy clicks on it, the sender's name is not Skylar Smith. It's a name she's never heard before. Maxine Dumas.

DEAR MANDY,

I KNOW YOU'RE PROBABLY WONDERING WHY YOU'RE RECEIVING AN EMAIL FROM A STRANGE WOMAN INSIDE THE WCF, BUT THERE IS SOMETHING YOU NEED TO KNOW. I STOLE YOUR CONTACT INFORMATION FROM YOUR MOTHER'S JOURNAL, AND SHE WOULD KILL ME IF SHE KNEW I WAS CONTACTING YOU.

SKYLAR IS NOT WELL. SHE HASN'T BEEN FEELING GOOD IN MONTHS, AND IT'S ONLY GETTING WORSE. NONE OF THE STAFF TAKES HER SERIOUSLY, BUT AFTER READING SOME BOOKS FROM THE LIBRARY TO TRY AND HELP, I THINK SOMETHING IS WRONG WITH HER LUNGS, MAYBE COPD OR LUNG CANCER. IF YOU WANT TO SEE YOUR MOTHER BEFORE IT'S TOO LATE, NOW IS THE TIME.

FOR WHAT IT'S WORTH, I UNDERSTAND HOW YOU FEEL. MY MOM WAS A REAL PIECE OF WORK, AND I NEVER FORGAVE HER FOR IT. BUT YOUR MOM ISN'T AS BAD AS YOU THINK. THERE'S SO MUCH MORE TO HER STORY THAT SHE NEVER TOLD YOU. PLEASE CONSIDER COMING TO SEE HER.

A CONCERNED FRIEND,

MAXINE

.   .   .

MANDY STARES at the screen for a few moments, attempting to process what she just read. What kind of monster does it make her when she hears her mother may be dying and feels nothing? She has pretended Skylar was dead for so long, she's not sure her actual death would even cause her to shed a tear.

Mandy can appreciate that there probably is more to her mom's life that she doesn't know about, but she cannot imagine it would be strong enough evidence to support all the horrible things she did. While her parents were never physically abusive, the neglect they showed their children ended up costing two people their lives. Four, if you count Skylar spending the rest of her life in prison and Mandy losing the rest of her childhood by being bounced between foster homes. That is damage that can't be reversed by whatever excuse she's going to spew.

Mandy will not be visiting her mother in prison.

She's not sure if she'll bother replying to Maxine or what she'd even say if she did, so she closes out the window on her browser and decides to once again sleep on it.

Traveling around the house with Murphy at her heels, Mandy closes all the curtains so that passersby can't have the same voyeuristic pleasure she enjoys on her night walks with her dog. She looks down at his sweet face and realizes they haven't been on a night walk all week. The oven clock says it's just past ten, and although her body is yearning for her warm bed and an episode or two of something on Netflix, she sighs and walks to the kitchen to slip on her shoes. Murphy begins hopping in circles when she retrieves his leash from the hook next to the door.

"Sorry I've been a bad mom, Murphs."

He sits still long enough for Mandy to clip the leash

onto the hook of his collar before leaping out the side door the minute she opens it. Mandy jogs to catch up with him, his leash pulled tight as he runs faster ahead of her. She gently yanks when she sees that her neighbor's light is on. She has yet to peer into Braxton's windows because when he's home, he's usually asleep with all the curtains drawn. She was once married to a mill worker; she gets it.

Tonight, a light is on in the living room at the front of the house. While he remembered to close all the curtains facing the street, he left one partially open on the side of the house, facing Mandy's. She stops in her tracks and squints through the opening to get a better look.

Braxton mentioned that he hadn't had enough time to get any art hung on the walls, and that's true. But what Mandy is seeing doesn't make much sense at all for a man who moved in nearly a month ago. His truck isn't out front, so she assumes he's working the night shift. She takes a chance by tiptoeing into his yard to get a closer look in the window. She looks to the left, which is the other half of his living room, and to the right, which opens up to a dining room and kitchen.

Not only is there no art or décor hung on the walls, but her neighbor's new house is completely empty. There's not so much as a packing box in sight. No groceries on the counter, no kitchen table, no rugs on the floor. The house looks as though he never moved in at all.

Chapter 26

Monday morning, Mandy is getting into her car for her five-mile commute when Braxton's truck pulls into his driveway. He wasn't home at all on Sunday, and Georgia messaged Mandy saying she wasn't feeling the best and would be resting for most of the day, so she hasn't had the chance to bring up her strange discovery.

After exiting his truck, Braxton waves hello as he searches his pockets for his front door key. Mandy returns his wave and yells, "Working overnights?"

"Yeah, I got transferred to Forty-Five Winder, and they're working us like rented mules," he shouts back. "How's the millionaire's club?"

"It's only been a week, but no animal sacrifices or secret society meetings yet. I'll keep you updated."

Braxton cracks a smile, but it stops before reaching his tired eyes.

"Get some rest," she shouts before getting into her car. *Just not on the couch, because you don't even have one*, she adds silently.

She saw the moving truck with her own eyes the

morning he arrived. She can't recall seeing what the movers were hauling, but they absolutely were unloading something, right? Did she even see movers, or just the moving truck backed into his driveway? She's not a conspiracy theorist, but seeing his empty house has her mind spinning. Could he have lost everything due to a gambling addiction? There's always the possibility that he's divorced, and his ex-wife got most of the furniture, so all he has left is a bedroom set until he can afford a couch and kitchen table. Maybe she and Georgia could share theories over a cup of tea tonight if she's feeling better.

When she arrives at the gates for the Bluff Club, Mandy's pulse quickens as Tanner peaks his head out of the guard's booth. She no longer sees the resemblance to Glen Powell, but maintains her opinion that he's uncomfortably handsome. More importantly, he's kind. Last week, there was a stark difference in demeanor between he and the other guard, and she found herself hoping it would be Tanner each time she arrived at the gate. The other guard asked for her employee ID each morning and treated her as if he'd never seen her before. Tanner, on the other hand, shouts "Morning, Mandy! How was your weekend?" as her car comes to a stop.

"It was pretty nice. I grilled out with my neighbor. What about yours?"

He considers this for a moment, as if he's not used to being asked about his day.

"You know what? It was also pretty nice. And every day we're a little closer to summer. Are you and little Miss Frankie doing anything exciting today?"

Miss Kelsey will be done tutoring Frankie around ten this morning and Allison suggested either a canoe ride, trip to the library, or both if they felt like it.

"Every day is an adventure with that little one. I just

hope I can keep up with whatever she has planned for us today," Mandy replies, and it's the truth. She's not sure what happened to the concept of nap time, but this girl goes full speed all afternoon without showing any need for rest. She's a ball of energy from the second Mandy arrives to the time Wes shows up to walk her to the car.

"If it's any consolation, you've seemed the best qualified yet to handle her energy."

Mandy's not sure why it's just now occurring to her that there were "keepers" before her. Frankie is seven, and Remy is seventeen; obviously she's not the first one to look after them.

"What were the others like?" Mandy asks, but her question is interrupted by a light tap on the horn by a vehicle she didn't even hear pulling up behind her. The driver, a man she was introduced to in the kitchen the week before, sticks his head out the window.

"You guys want to chitchat all day or can I get to work?"

Tanner holds up an apologetic hand, and Mandy blushes slightly. She waves her arm out the window and mouths *sorry* into the rearview mirror, hoping he sees it.

"We'll continue this chat next time. Have a great shift, Mandy," Tanner tells her, pressing a button on the remote in his hands to open the thick, wooden gate in front of her car.

"Looking forward to it," she responds, rolling her window up and beginning the scenic half-mile drive to park her car.

Her jaw unclenches and both shoulders drop when she spots Wes waiting for her. He's once again on a phone call, but the sight of him is enough to relax whatever tension she was holding in her body. When he sees her pull in, he ends his phone call and grabs two insulated disposable cups from the armrest of the bench in front of him.

"Caramel latte or vanilla chai?"

"Wow, they both sound delicious. Surprise me," she says, aiming her key fob to lock the car as she walks toward him.

"I'm glad you said that. I ordered two things I like so I wouldn't be disappointed by whichever you chose, but on the walk over here I decided I'd really like the chai," he tells her, handing over the latte.

"What a coincidence, I was hoping you'd give me the latte," she teases, raising her cup to cheers with his and taking a tentative sip. "Oh wow, this is delicious. What shop is it from?"

"The Bluff actually has its own coffee shop. It's called Serendipity, and they close during the off-season. A good amount of members are due to arrive this week, so today is their first day back in business. Anything you order there will be fantastic. The head barista went to some fancy espresso school in Italy . . . or maybe Spain. I can't remember. Either way, she knows her stuff."

"I can't believe all these businesses are sustained by fifty households. I had no idea how many amenities were inside the gates."

"Well, technically they are all owned by the Hawthorne family, so I don't think they are crying in their milkshakes over a slow sales day here and there. But to be honest, between the fifty households, their occasional guests, and the staff that live on-site, I think most of these places have enough customers to keep them busy."

Mandy wonders how comfortable the staff is with patronizing these businesses during their off hours. She can't imagine standing in line for a latte next to one of the members when it is glaringly obvious that she is the help.

"By the way, Allison is out of town today. She went to Colorado to see her mom for a few days. She left you a note."

"You've already been there this morning?" Mandy asks.

"Not yet today, but Mr. Hawthorne had a poker night with a few of the other arriving members, so I hung around to make sure they had everything they needed."

"Everything they needed . . . What does that mean, hookers and blow?" Mandy says with an uncomfortable laugh. Wes doesn't crack a smile. "You know what? None of my business," she adds. Chandler's wife is out of town, and his gaggle of overprivileged buddies has arrived for the season; it's obvious that he wasn't drinking tea and doing puzzles by the fire.

"Frankie spent the night at her friend Grace's house. Remy walked her back this morning, so she could start with Miss Kelsey at eight."

"Mr. Hawthorne, Miss Kelsey—do you ever just refer to them by their names? This place is so formal."

Wes shakes his head, but his tight-lipped smirk tells Mandy that he understands where she's coming from. It's all a little ridiculous.

"It's just easier to call them by their preferred names, even when they aren't around so you don't make a habit of being informal and let it slip in front of a member. There's a guy arriving this weekend, he has a PhD in microbiology, but if you don't refer to him as Doctor Waltrip, he'll chastise you in front of the entire room. He's insufferable."

"I admire you for blending in with these people so well. After the fucked-up childhood we had, you'd have every right to be hostile. But here you are, polite and complacent. I don't mean that as an insult; I'm genuinely impressed with how you handle yourself."

As they are walking toward the Hawthorne's house, Wes touches Mandy's hand, sending a shockwave through her body. She stops and faces him.

"You talk a lot about how horrible our childhoods were, and I understand your tragedy far outweighs anything I could imagine, but honestly, some of my best memories were in River Ridge. Sure, we didn't get dealt the best hands when it came to parents, but we made the most of it. I had so much fun with you and Jeff; I feel like most of my memories before the fire are happy ones. You two were like the siblings I never had."

She watches his eyes as he's speaking and she finally gets it. He *does* think of her as a sibling. That's why her love for him was never reciprocated—his love for her was a different kind of love altogether. She's his family. It guts her to think that she allowed Patrick Cramer to come between them. Life is full of regrets; the best she can do is make better decisions going forward.

"I'll try harder to remember the good," Mandy promises, and Wes squeezes her hand.

When they make it to the front door, Wes does his signature two taps before grabbing the doorknob, but it's locked. His auburn eyebrows come together in confusion before he tries again. Luckily, they hear footsteps quickly approaching and the door swings open.

Mandy and Wes are speechless when they are greeted by Frankie's tutor, Miss Kelsey. There are red splotches around her eyes and down her neck, and the top two buttons of her white shirt are undone. She doesn't make eye contact with them, simply pushes past them and runs down the path toward the employee parking. Wes calls after her but she doesn't slow down. When Mandy glances over to Wes to get his take, he's already halfway into the foyer, yelling for Frankie. Her muffled voice is barely audible, coming from the direction of her room. He ascends the stairs three at a time, Mandy closely behind him.

"What's going on, Frankie Franks?" he asks, kneeling in front of the young girl. She's sitting at a small table in the corner of her room that is primarily used for arts and crafts. Her eyes are also semi-swollen, and her bottom lip is quivering.

"Daddy says Miss Kelsey can't be my tutor anymore," she mutters, crossing her thin arms in front of her chest with a huff.

"What happened?" Mandy asks, taking a few steps toward the pair.

Frankie sucks in a few breaths and begins to cry again. Wes gives Mandy intense eye contact over the girl's shoulder and nods slowly, willing her to comply with whatever he's about to suggest.

"Hey Mandy, would you mind if Frankie and I talk alone for a minute? Maybe you could check with Chef Regina and see what she's planning for lunch. Monday lunches are always the best, right Frankie?"

She wipes under her eyes with the back of her hands and nods.

"Of course," Mandy responds, barely above a whisper. She backs out of Frankie's room, pulling the door behind her but leaving it open a crack.

She sucks in a breath when she turns to see Remy standing less than two feet away, in the hallway leading to his room.

"Do you want to talk about it?" she asks.

He shakes his head. His fists are at his sides, clenching and releasing at a rapid rate.

"Did your dad lose his temper or something?"

He laughs condescendingly. "I'm about to turn eighteen, and I won't have to deal with his shit anymore. If it weren't for Frankie and Mom, I'd move across the country."

He turns on his heels and Mandy calls after him. "If you want to talk about it, I'm here."

"Just keep your guard up, Mandy."

"You know, people keep saying this to me, but nobody will elaborate," she says, throwing her hands up.

After slowly shaking his head, he lifts a weak hand in acknowledgement but doesn't respond, only disappears into his room, slamming the door behind him. She hears the wheels on his computer chair gliding across the hard-wood floor, presumably to his desk. She only wishes he felt as comfortable confiding in her as he did when she was just a stranger managing the gas station.

Mandy creeps down the main stairwell, praying that Chandler Hawthorne isn't waiting at the bottom. She isn't sure what went down this morning, but she doesn't want to be involved in the encore. She just needs to get through the next eight hours without being noticed, then she can head home and leave this family to deal with their issues in private.

Luckily, he's nowhere to be seen when Mandy arrives in the foyer and walks to the back of the house and into the kitchen. Chef Regina is aggressively dicing vegetables on a butcher block on one of the two oversized kitchen islands.

"Good morning, Regina," Mandy says a little louder than she should because the woman doesn't seem to have noticed her yet, most likely not hearing her footsteps over the sound of the knife hitting the wood in front of her.

"Oh, I'm sorry Mandy. I didn't even hear you come in. What can I get you? Would you like a bagel or some coffee? I make a nice Americano."

Regina is on edge and treating Mandy like she's a

member of the club, not a member of the staff. Mandy smiles kindly.

"Do you want to talk?"

Regina is shaking her head before the words are done coming out of Mandy's mouth. "No, no. I have a lot of work to do. I've just had a strange morning. Will you tell Miss Frankie that we are going to have ham and cheese paninis today? It's in her top three favorite lunches, if she hasn't changed her mind since last week."

For the first time, Regina's lips curl into a slight smile. She really loves that kid.

"I'll let her know," Mandy says and excuses herself. She doesn't want to interrupt Wes and Frankie's conversation, so she heads to the bottom of the stairs to sit and wait it out.

As she's entering the foyer, Chandler comes stumbling out of the library, and Mandy can smell him before she even locks into his bloodshot eyes. It's after nine in the morning now and he's still drunk from his poker night.

"Oh, hi Mindy. I'm sure Frankie will be right down for you."

She doesn't bother correcting him as he staggers past her and down the hall toward the master bedroom. She cannot imagine what happened with Kelsey, but she has a horrible ache in the pit of her stomach. The ache grows as something nags at her thoughts. Something that Remy said before he stormed off and into his room.

Keep your guard up.

The same thing she's heard so often in the last two weeks, most often from DANNYBOY06.

She thinks of Remy and the hours he spends on that computer.

Surely it couldn't be possible that he's DANNYBOY06 . . . right?

Chapter 27

Mandy is not cut out for being a sleuth. The best she can do to solve this mystery is awkwardly question Remy about what it is he does on his computer all day. Since everyone is still recovering from whatever went down with Miss Kelsey and Chandler, she's not getting much out of him.

"I play video games," he grumbles while eating his ham and cheese panini at the kitchen counter.

"What kinds of games?" Mandy asks, doing her best to remain casual and failing miserably.

"Right now, I'm playing *Dayz* and sometimes I play *Call of Duty*. Why?"

He sets his sandwich down eyes Mandy suspiciously.

"I've spent the last week getting to know your little sister. I thought it would be nice to get to know you, as well."

She's sure he'd like to respond that she's already gotten to know him during their many chats at the Quick Stop, but he can't say that in a room with Frankie and Chef Regina, who is currently washing the dishes a few feet away.

Frankie is sitting on the bar stool next to her brother. The counter comes up to her chest, but she refused Mandy's offer to sit at the table with her so she could more easily reach her plate. She's been glued to Remy all morning since her chat with Wes.

"She'll be fine, just let her do her favorite things today," Wes had told Mandy, placing a gentle hand on her shoulder as he passed her on the stairwell after leaving Frankie's room.

"I let Frankie do her favorite things every day," Mandy responded, "but I'll make sure today is extra special."

"Thanks, Chubbs," he'd said before leaving out the front door, a look of utter defeat in his eyes.

Mandy ventures to guess this isn't the first time a staff member has had to comfort the Hawthorne children after their father behaved like an asshole. She has a tinge of guilt for assuming that children of privilege all had easy lives.

After finishing her sandwich and refusing Regina's offer to wash her plate and opting to put it in the dishwasher herself, she spots a Hawthorne Bluff Club social calendar on the side of the fridge. She finds today's date and sees that there's a Men's Club meeting (whatever that is), a Women's Spring Book Club gathering at the library, and a cookie decorating class for kids at two in the dining lodge.

"Hey Frankie, what do you think about going to this cookie decorating class? That could be fun," Mandy suggests.

Frankie considers it for a moment and asks, "Do we get to eat the cookies?"

"I would assume so," Mandy says, smiling when Frankie kicks her excited feet against the bar stool in response.

"Can Grace come?"

Mandy's not quite sure what the protocol is on including friends while she's in charge of Frankie, so she glances at Remy for any indication of how to answer that. He gives a subtle nod and returns to his sandwich.

"If it's okay with her parents, I don't see why not," Mandy tells Frankie, not sure who the girl's parents are or how she's going to get ahold of them.

Frankie claps her hands and scoots her half-empty plate to the left so she can focus on the coloring project she started while they waited for Chef Regina to finish making lunch. It's adorable watching the small girl attempt to color in a field of tulips when she can barely reach high enough to rest her elbows on the counter.

"I'm friends with Grace's keeper. I'll shoot her a text and have her come over with Grace around quarter to, so you all can walk to the class together. If that works for you," Regina offers. She's been short with her all morning, so Mandy is relieved at the kind gesture, which confirms her suspicions that Regina's mood has nothing to do with her. And, of course, Grace has a keeper. Mandy was foolish to think she'd be communicating with her actual parents in the middle of a weekday.

"That would be great," Mandy says to Regina and then turns her attention back to Frankie. "We might even have time to play in the park for a while after the class, if you'd like."

Frankie cheers again. The emotional events of this morning are a distant memory in the mind of a seven-year-old.

RIGHT ON TIME at a quarter to two, the doorbell rings and Frankie sprints down the stairs to answer it.

"Mandy, this is my best friend, Grace." Frankie grabs

the girl by both hands. She appears to be much more shy than Frankie, uncomfortable with the attention that comes with an introduction.

"Hi, Grace, it's so nice to meet you," Mandy says before turning her attention to the woman behind her. She appears to be a few years younger than Mandy, with high cheek bones and jet-black hair. Her eyes aren't unkind, but also not as warm as other members of the staff Mandy's met in the past week.

"I'm Jessica," she says, holding out a hand. Mandy can't help but notice how soft her skin is when she grasps her palm.

"Thanks for agreeing to join us. This will be my first group activity at the Bluff, so it will be nice to have someone who knows the ropes," Mandy tells her.

"Oh, it's my first season, too. Looks like we'll be learning together," Jessica says with a shrug.

The girls run ahead of Mandy and Jessica on the path to the dining lodge, which leaves the two women to make awkward small talk on the five-minute walk to the cookie decorating class.

"Chef Regina said you two are close; did you grow up together?" Mandy asks.

"Oh no, we just met on a travel gig a few years ago, so we try to take assignments together."

The confusion on Mandy's face makes Jessica laugh out loud. "I'm guessing you're not a travel gig girl then?"

"I'm going to shoot you real straight. I have no idea what the hell you're talking about."

Jessica tells Mandy all about the website for booking seasonal jobs where she met Chef Regina. You create an account, upload photos of yourself and a resume, and then apply for seasonal jobs all around the country, and even overseas. It's great for single men and women without kids

—they can see new places, get paid for it, and make new friends along the way. It's an entire subculture Mandy didn't know existed. A girl she went to high school with posted on social media about being a traveling nurse, but it never occurred to Mandy that there were traveling nannies or personal chefs.

"So, Regina and I will be here in Michigan until mid-November, and then we're heading to Colorado to work at a ski resort until April."

What a life, Mandy thinks.

"How did you find out about the job?" Jessica asks as they near the entrance for the dining lodge.

"I grew up here and saw it on a local job listing site. The members don't have the best reputation among us who live downtown, but the hours and pay are great, so I sucked it up and accepted the position, and here we are."

Jessica pauses after nodding in acknowledgement. Mandy gets the impression that she wants to say more, to give her opinion of the members, but thinks better of it. They just met; it will take time to build trust and decide who you can and can't confide in. Mandy hopes Jessica learns that she's on the good side. The side she can trust.

Once they open the door to the dining lodge, Frankie and Grace sprint toward the two women teaching the class and hug their legs. Both women, wearing chef's aprons and baseball hats with the Hawthorne logo, return the love by bending down to hug the girls and ask how their winters were. It's evident that Mandy and Jessica don't need to know much about the class; the girls are right at home with the staff.

There's a long table set up with a dozen place settings and every color of icing and sprinkles you could imagine. Unfrosted sugar cookies are set in front of each spot with printed pictures for inspiration. Over the next ten minutes, several more children (and their keepers) join the class. The children each take a seat, with the keepers seated at an empty table behind them.

"Would you mind keeping an eye on Grace so I can go outside and make a quick phone call?" Jessica asks, gesturing to the cell phone in her hand.

"Of course," Mandy replies. She's positioned directly behind the two girls, who are positively giddy while pointing to their piping bags and assorted frostings. One of the employees teaching the class begins to speak while the other walks slowly behind the children to assist where needed. Mandy can't imagine the excitement she would have had in a class like this at Frankie's age.

She stands, leaning against the back wall to get a better view of the cookies the girls are decorating. She's lost in thought, focusing on the joy radiating from Frankie each time she turns her head to face her friend and display what she's made. She doesn't notice the woman who has arrived next to her until she speaks.

"Which one are you in charge of?"

Mandy clutches her chest and then laughs at herself for being caught off guard. The woman is wearing a kitchen uniform and a hairnet, with wispy gray tendrils escaping around the nape of her neck.

"I'm Mandy; I work for the Hawthornes. I'm in charge of Frankie and Remy, but usually focus my attention on the one who's too young to drive," she responds, forcing her voice up a few octaves to convey her friendly nature.

"Oof, and how is that going?"

Mandy is caught off guard again, but this time by the woman's candor. She feels the tension escape from her body, replaced with hope that she has found a kindred spirit. She knows she can speak freely with Wes, but she also knows he's been drinking the Hawthorne Kool-Aid long enough that he won't speak ill of the members, even to his childhood best friend.

"Well, the kids are lovely. Allison doesn't seem so bad," Mandy answers, leaving out the obvious member of the family who isn't so lovely.

"The first wives never are. It's the second and thirds you need to look out for. Allison is a good lady."

"I'm sorry, I didn't catch your name," Mandy says, turning to the woman and holding out her hand. She smiles when the woman takes it in both of hers, the signature handshake of Hawthorne members and employees. She must admit, it is a friendly gesture.

"I'm Dorothy, but you can call me Dot. This is my fortieth and final year with the club; I retire in December."

"Forty years? Wow, that's amazing. I bet you're going to enjoy a well-deserved retirement," Mandy says, patting her arm and then pulling it back because the woman looks mildly uncomfortable with the gesture.

She gives Mandy a tight smile that loosens slightly when she mentions the time she'll get to spend with her grandchildren. Mandy knows what to do next.

"Grandchildren? Do you have any pictures?"

Dot looks both ways before pulling an oversized flip phone from the front pocket of her apron. It takes her a few moments to access the photo album, but she eventually finds a few grainy photos of her two grandchildren. She oohs and ahhs at the appropriate times and feels Dot warm up to her more with every declaration of how precious her grandchildren are and how much they're going to love having her around more often. Mandy pauses when she catches the woman staring at her, her forehead wrinkling as if she's trying to figure out a math equation.

"I'm sorry, dear. It's just that you remind me so much

of someone, and I just can't put my finger on who it is. Are there any celebrities you've been told you look like?"

Mandy wracks her brain; she's not sure she's ever been told she resembles a celebrity.

"Not that I can think of," she responds.

They watch the children for a few more moments before Mandy dares to ask a question about the patriarch of the Hawthorne family.

"So, Chandler . . ."

The edge of Dot's mouth curls up slightly, but it's a devious smile.

"I'm on my third generation of members now, and I've learned a lot by watching. For forty years, I've watched men of privilege take whatever it is that they want with little to no consequences. There's never been any use complaining about it because nothing's going to be done inside these gates. They pay me a decent wage, good benefits, and I'm home with my cats every night. I keep my mouth shut and collect my check."

Mandy can't imagine the things this woman has witnessed, but she also can't imagine staying quiet all these years. She's not sure she could watch someone being taken advantage of and not speak up. Then she remembers Miss Kelsey's appearance that morning. She can't get the vision of her unbuttoned shirt out of her head.

"Are the men worse now than they were when you first got here?"

Dot locks eyes with Mandy and lowers her voice even further.

"The men who founded this club worked their hind ends off to make something of themselves. The problem is, once they achieved the success, they got bored with everything they got on the way up—the cars, the wives, the kids, bored with them all. They felt they deserved an upgrade

187

because of everything they worked so hard for. They were horrible men, but they were reasonably discreet. Rumors of mistresses were just that, rumors. But the new generation?" She tsks and shakes her head. "They're loud with it. It's like they're daring their wives to say something. When I cater the Men's Club lunches, they're bragging about cheating on their taxes or screwing their employees out of overtime. They talk about sexual conquests like I'm not even there. It's enough to make you sick."

None of this is surprising to Mandy, but it is interesting to hear the difference between generations and how much worse it's gotten over the years.

"Have you ever had the overwhelming urge to fight back, or have you always complied and stayed quiet?"

Dot's lips twitch slightly.

"Oh, we've gotten our licks in here and there, but nothing that's kept them down for too long."

"Sounds like you could write a book," Mandy tells her, not knowing how else to respond to the information.

"Honey, if it weren't for the NDA, I would. I'd take them all down. I'd leave it on my deathbed, but the bastards would probably go after my family. The best I can do is let the girls like you know what to look out for until I retire in a few months."

"They had you sign an NDA?" Mandy asks.

"We all did. They just bury it in your new hire paperwork. You were probably so blinded by the hourly wage they were offering that you didn't pay attention to what you were signing. They cover their asses, trust me."

Although Mandy was undoubtedly blinded by the offer of thirty dollars per hour and the possibility of overtime, she's observant enough to know she didn't sign an NDA. Or at least, she doesn't think she did . . . There was the official employment offer, an informational sheet on hours and work environment, a W-9 form, and her direct deposit information. She's watched enough salacious reality TV to know what these rich people normally include in an NDA, and there's no way that language wouldn't have caught her attention. She doesn't want to argue with Dot, a woman who has worked inside these gates for forty years, so she simply shrugs.

Jessica returns from her phone call and apologizes for taking so long. Mandy doesn't mind; it's not like it put her out to make sure two butts were staying in their seats instead of one. Mandy introduces her to her new friend, Dot, and they exchange pleasantries. Dot's eyebrows raise slightly when Jessica tells her that she works for the Burrow family, which means the husband is probably one of the men she was just telling Mandy about.

The instructors blow a whistle to get everyone's attention before inviting all the "keepers and parents" to join their "littles" in decorating a cookie, but the knowing smiles on every keeper's face means they know how ridiculous it is to assume any of them are club parents. Mandy and Jessica excuse themselves, and Dot motions to the kitchen, telling them she's got to get back to work anyway.

As Mandy turns to leave, Dot snaps her fingers and says, "I've got it." Mandy turns back around and tilts her head.

"Got what?"

"It came to me . . . who you remind me of. Are you related to a Skylar Smith?"

The usual flush of embarrassment washes over her. If someone knew her mother, chances are that they knew her as an addict who may or may not have killed half her family with an errant cigarette butt.

"She was my mother. Is . . . she *is* my mother. We don't exactly talk anymore. How did you know her?"

Dot chuckles like there's an inside joke there, but Mandy doesn't catch on.

"She started the same year I did, 1984. We were in orientation together. She's a really special lady; we had a lot of laughs."

"Oh, I think you may be confusing her with someone else. My mother never worked at the Hawthorne Bluff Club; I can assure you of that. The only job she had when I was growing up was scamming the government out of a check every month."

There isn't a hint of doubt in Dot's expression. She's certain of her story.

"Sweetheart, you might want to ask her the next time you talk, but she absolutely worked here. If I remember correctly, she was here for two seasons and then quit when she got pregnant with your brother."

Jeff was two years older than Mandy and born in 1986, so that timeline would make sense. How in the world did Mandy's own mother work for the club without her knowing about it?

"I have to ask; was she an addict when you knew her?"

"An addict?" Dot asks, placing a hand over her chest while she laughs. "Your mother was as straight as they come. Unfortunately, we lost touch after she left because life happens, but no, she most certainly was not an addict."

"Dot, I hate to be the one to tell you this, but life wasn't too kind to my mother after you lost touch. She did become an addict—alcohol, prescription drugs, and occasionally the hard stuff. There was a fire when I was ten that killed my brother and my dad. My mom has been in prison ever since."

Dot looks like Mandy slapped her across the face. She's slowly shaking her head back and forth, willing it to be a lie.

"It was actually the same year as the fires here, which I'm sure you remember."

Dot nods. "Of course."

The older woman pulls a handkerchief from her pocket and dabs the skin beneath her eyes. "I'm very sorry for your loss, Mandy. I had no idea. I was busy raising children at that time and didn't hear the news. I just can't reconcile the Skylar I knew with the one you're describing."

Mandy shrugs and Dot smiles sympathetically before turning to leave, still wearing a look of bewilderment in her eyes from the news.

This time, Mandy is the one to stop Dot after they part.

"Wait a minute; I might know one of your other former coworkers. Do you remember Georgia Afton?"

Mandy's not always the best at detecting when people are being dishonest, but there's not a doubt in her mind that Dot is lying through her teeth when she straightens slightly and says, "Sorry dear, I don't think I recall anyone by that name."

Seconds later, Dot has disappeared into the kitchen, the double doors swinging closed behind her.

Chapter 28

For years, Mandy's entire body has been screaming for something extraordinary to happen. Now, *nothing* is ordinary, and her head is spinning.

Chandler Hawthorne is a certified asshole, and it seems that's the status quo for men in this club. Wes may be the only man in these gates she can trust. Well, Wes *and* Tanner, the hunky security guard.

Remy may or may not be DANNYBOY06, but the more Mandy thinks about it, the more sense it makes. When DANNYBOY06 said he could "hack" into the system at the club to get her an interview, it probably wouldn't have taken any hacking at all. The disparaging comments he made about the members of the Bluff would make perfect sense coming from the disgruntled teenage son of the club's president.

Most importantly, Mandy just learned that her own mother may have worked at the Bluff before she was born. She has very few memories of her mom before the addiction took hold, so it would be nice to hear stories from Dot, but she also has a lot of hesitation speaking to her after she so obviously lied about remembering Georgia.

Mandy's heart skips a beat when she remembers Georgia's instructions not to let anyone besides Amelia know that she's back in town. She replays her conversation with Dot, trying to recall if she mentioned how she knows Georgia. She never said she was her neighbor; she's sure of it. If Dot asks her, Mandy will just say that Georgia is a woman she used to work with at the mall years ago and mentioned that she used to be an employee at the Bluff.

How is she supposed to last another hour until her shift ends, pretending her thoughts aren't being pulled in a million different directions? Luckily, the girls ask Jessica and Mandy if they can play at the park after they are done decorating cookies.

"Sure, let me just see if they have a container to put your cookies in, and then we can head over there," Mandy says.

One of the kitchen employees who taught the class swats a dismissive hand in Mandy's direction.

"Oh, you don't have to worry about that. We package the cookies up that each child decorated, and then we deliver them to the household. They should be on the front porch by the time you get done at the park."

Mandy thanks the woman, but mentally she's adding it to the never-ending list of things that are just easier if you're rich. She also volunteered to help with the cleanup, and both employees looked shocked before responding that it's their job, but they appreciated the offer.

On their walk to the park, Mandy lowers her voice as she asks Jessica if she's noticed the cameras installed on all the streetlamps.

Jessica looks above, clocking each of the cameras, and shrugs. "The wealthy like to feel safe. I don't think it's that weird. The resort I worked at in Aspen last winter had cameras everywhere. So long as they aren't recording me in the bathroom, I couldn't care less."

Mandy wonders if she's overreacting. She chooses not to discuss it further with Jessica, but she is surprised by the woman's nonchalant response to the presence of dozens of cameras in one of the safest towns in America.

"Daddy!"

The women look ahead to see Grace running toward a man entering the Nightingale Supper Club across the street from the park. Mandy watches him swallow his irritation and replace it with forced excitement to see his daughter.

"Gracie, I thought you girls were taking some sort of ballet class this afternoon."

He doesn't bend down to hug her, simply pats her on the back a few times when her twig-like arms wrap around his left leg. Grace laughs like her father is purposely being silly by naming the wrong class, not the more obvious option that he just didn't know or care to remember.

"Daddy, we decorated cookies for spring. I made a bunny, and Frankie made a puppy, and we both made flowers. We can eat them for dinner."

He reaches down to unlatch her arms from around his leg and dusts imaginary dirt from his pants.

"Sweetheart, I won't be home for dinner tonight, but I bet you and Mommy can eat every one of those cookies and take pictures for me. Now be a good girl and go play so Daddy isn't late for his meeting."

Grace's dad shoots daggers at Jessica, and it takes her a few seconds to understand that she should not have let the girl approach him while she's on the clock as her keeper. It's her job to make sure the kids aren't seen or heard between the hours of nine and five, Monday through

Friday. She mumbles a quick apology before scooping Grace into her arms and distracting her with questions about the squirrels and chipmunks that are scampering across the artificial grass at the entrance to the park. The girl looks back at her father momentarily before falling for the rouse and switching her focus to the wildlife. Frankie glances back at Mandy and shrugs. Allison was right; her daughter is wise beyond her years.

Mandy watches several other men entering the supper club, disappearing inside the darkened entryway each time the door opens. She checks her watch—nearly four o'clock. The Men's Club meeting she saw on the calendar is about to begin.

The foursome makes it to the park, and the women sit on a bench while the two girls hustle over to the slide, their soft voices erupting in laughter several times before they reach their destination. Mandy situates herself so she can keep an eye on the entrance to the Nightingale. She stiffens when Chandler Hawthorne rounds the corner and comes into view. He's obviously showered since their encounter in the foyer of his home, when the smell of alcohol was radiating from his pores.

"Hey, Hawthorne! Can I bend your ear for a second?"

Another man Mandy's never seen before quickens his pace to catch up to the club's president.

"What's up, Stew?"

The man pulls a sheet of paper out of the manilla folder in his hands and points at something on the page. Chandler glances at the information, snaps the folder shut, and his eyes dart around, scanning their surroundings. They land on Mandy and the hair on the back of her neck stands on end. He whispers to Stew, without taking his eyes off Mandy. Stew matches his gaze and nods. He holds the door open for Chandler and they disappear into the dark club.

"Chandler Hawthorne, Stew Maynard, and Brock Burrows, who is Grace's father. Don't ever be in a room alone with any of them," Jessica mutters.

Mandy turns toward her, begging for more information, but Jessica shakes her head- she's said all she's going to on the matter.

For the next hour, they watch the girls play and give them their full attention each time they plead for the women to "watch me do this trick," or "tell us who goes faster down the slide." Shortly before five, they inform the girls it's time to go. Mandy and Jessica share a look that says, "and it's time for us to clock out and go home."

Mandy and Frankie say their goodbyes when they arrive at the driveway to the Hawthorne's home. Jessica isn't overly talkative, and Mandy's not sure they'd even have anything in common other than their nannying jobs, but she will admit that spending the afternoon with her and Grace was a welcome change.

As she's walking into the house, Mandy receives a text from Allison. Chandler won't be home until after dinner, but she can leave Frankie home with Remy for a few hours.

Remy is sitting at the kitchen table with his phone propped up, a YouTube video playing loudly on the screen. He's eating a bowl of cereal so he must have received the memo that his parents won't be home for dinner.

"Hi, Frankie girl," Chef Regina shouts when she sees her enter the kitchen. "I'm just cleaning up to go home, but I fixed you a special plate and left it in the fridge for you. I bet your brother will help you heat it up. Right, Remy?"

Remy grunts with no attempt to unlock his eyes from the screen in front of him. Whatever video he's watching ends about ten seconds later, and he realizes he has no idea what was just said to him.

"Right, Remy? Even though you chose to eat a bowl of cereal that has more sugar than a bag of Skittles, you'll help your sweet sister heat up her nutritious dinner?"

Frankie beams, which is met with an eye roll from Remy.

"Yeah, yeah. I'll make sure she's fed."

"And you're both okay with me leaving? Your dad shouldn't be long," Mandy says.

It catches her off guard when all three of them erupt in laughter. Regina doesn't even try to hide it in front of the children. It's obviously an inside joke Mandy isn't privy to.

"Daddy has Men's Club. He won't be home until it's very, very dark out," Frankie explains to Mandy. Having that knowledge at seven years old is sadly a familiar feeling for Mandy.

"I'm going to leave my cell number on this piece of paper," Mandy says. "If either of you need anything, I'm a five-minute drive away. You can call or text me anytime."

"I don't know how to text yet," Frankie says.

"Well, you just get your brother, and he can send me a message. Deal?"

Frankie shakes her hand, signifying the deal, and Mandy nearly melts from the cuteness. "Deal."

"What are you going to do tonight, Remy? Maybe spend some time on Reddit?" She tries to throw him off guard as she's putting on her shoes to leave.

"Reddit? That's a random suggestion. Did you just Google what today's youth is up to these days or something?"

As if Mandy needs another mystery in her life, she's surprisingly convinced he's telling the truth. Back to square one.

Chapter 29

Wes is waiting on the front porch when Mandy exits the Hawthorne's, ending the call he's on as she appears outside.

"Hey, Chubbs, how was your day?"

Something in her breaks, like a dam finally giving way and allowing the water to rush through. She used to tell everything to Wes, and now she has an arsenal of secrets and suspicions and concerns that he knows nothing of. She needs a friend to talk to.

"My day was okay, but a little strange. Is there any chance you'd have some time to talk, or are you permanently on-call these days?"

He pulls his phone back out of his pocket and checks the time, contemplating her offer.

"How about a drink at the Rail? It's Monday; they shouldn't be too busy. We can grab a table in the corner."

Mandy smiles, relieved. "That would be perfect. I'll call my neighbor on the way and have her let my dog out. Do you want to ride with me, and I'll drop you back off after we're done?"

This time, he doesn't need a minute to contemplate. "Nah, I'll bring my truck. I've got some errands to run in town anyway."

"Oh, you mean there's something you could need that's not available inside these gates?" She winks, still feeling the need to convey she's joking about this place he seems to love so much.

"I'll meet you there. If you get there before me, I'll take a Stella Artois."

She begins to pull a face in response to his high-brow taste in beer when he rolls his eyes and turns to walk toward Easy Street. "I'm just grabbing something from my cabin. I'll see you there."

It surprises Mandy how alone she feels walking to her car since Wes has accompanied her every time she's left the Bluff. It does, however, give her the opportunity to take in her surroundings and appreciate the sounds of the birds chirping overhead and the scampering squirrels that bound across the path in front of her. This place really is magical.

When she gets to the employee parking lot, she once again sees Georgia's old friend, Amelia Crain.

"Amelia," Mandy shouts, jogging to catch up with the woman before she enters her vehicle.

She's not imagining it; Amelia is forcing a smile after momentarily grimacing at the sight of Mandy.

"Hey, I met one of your coworkers today at the dining lodge. Her name is Dot. She said the strangest thing to me. She told me that my mom used to work here."

At her age, you'd think Amelia would have the skills to at least attempt a believable lie, but the woman responds with such forced casualty, it's nearly laughable.

"Oh, you know what, now that you mention it, that must have been where I knew her from. My memory just isn't what it used to be."

The corners of her mouth twitch slightly.

"So, were you also in bowling league with her then?" Mandy asks.

"Oh yes, a few of us were also in bowling league. We had to blow off a little steam after a long week of work, you know? Now if you don't mind, I'm going to head home and eat the chicken soup I put in the crockpot this morning. Have a great night, Mandy."

WES ARRIVES NEARLY fifteen minutes after Mandy orders his Stella and a Diet Coke for herself and finds a tall bar table in the corner. He was right; the place is nearly empty, with four guests sitting at the bar and only one other table occupied.

"Sorry if your fancy beer isn't ice cold; I didn't realize you'd take so long," she says as he takes his coat off and hangs it across the back of his chair.

"If you took a sip, you'd realize it's delicious and you're just being a hater," he says, offering the bottle to her. She shakes her head and holds up her Diet Coke, which she had the bartender pour into a rocks glass with a cocktail straw to avoid any conversation about why she's not drinking.

"So, what's on your mind?" he asks. His elbows are on the table, and he's focused entirely on Mandy. She can't imagine her ex-husband ever giving her the same courtesy. He'd normally nod and throw in a "that's crazy" every few moments in response to her stories after a long day at work, while not bothering to stop scrolling on his phone while she spoke.

"We haven't been close in years, but you still know me well enough to know I hold a PhD in minding my damn business and pretending everything's okay."

Wes chuckles. "Yes, ma'am."

"Here's the thing—a lot of things have happened in the last week that don't make any damn sense. I need you to hear me when I say that some sort of fuckery is going on in that club. I know the men of the Bluff have a history of being liars and cheats, so that's not news to me, but there are just a lot of things that aren't adding up."

"Such as?"

"Did you know my mom worked at the club?"

Much to Mandy's surprise, Wes *doesn't* seem surprised.

"I didn't find that out until just a few years ago, but yes. I do know she worked in the kitchen for a couple years."

"And why wouldn't she have told us that, Wes? Why would working at the Bluff be a family secret?"

He shrugs and takes a drink of his overpriced beer.

"I don't know, Chubbs. Do you know every job she ever had before she was a mother? I mean, you were ten when the fire happened. You probably didn't have a lot of conversations about her work history. You were a kid."

Next, Mandy tells him about the strange email she received from her mother's fellow inmate. He takes a moment to digest this information, chewing on his bottom lip while he contemplates.

"Well, are you going to go see her?"

"You know I don't follow all that therapy nonsense, but those self-help books might be onto something when they say it's important to have closure. I've been thinking maybe I should go."

He places a hand over hers on the table. "I think that would mean a lot to Skylar. It's easy to forget that she also lost everything, even if some of it was her own fault. She's had a long time to sit in there and think about what she's done."

Mandy hates feeling sympathy for her mother. She

made the decisions. She neglected her children. She is the reason her father and brother are dead. Why should she feel an ounce of sympathy for this woman who is now a stranger?

"There's more," Mandy says and takes a deep breath before rapid fire confessing everything that's been bothering her.

She begins with her sweet neighbor Georgia, another woman in her life who omitted the fact that she used to work at the Bluff. She tells him about her Reddit friend, DANNYBOY06, and the conversations they've had. She replays the events of the night she was walking Murphy and peered into Braxton's window to find a house void of furniture or moving boxes. She details her run-ins with Patrick's mistress, Emily, and his sister, Dee. Wes smiles at the last story because he remembers how afraid Mandy was of Dee in high school. She talks about the unease she felt when they saw Miss Kelsey leaving the Hawthorne house and how upset the kids were. Although she doesn't name names, she mentions that she met a tenured employee who spoke of the generations of morally corrupt men at the club. Finally, she tells him about witnessing the men arriving for their club meeting that afternoon and the cold stare she received from Chandler.

She stops herself from telling him about Remy, aka Chandy, and their prior meetings at the Quick Stop. She isn't sure why she feels the need to protect that information after all she'd already told him, but she does. There's a reason Remy doesn't want people knowing about his visits, and she's going to respect that.

To Wes's credit, even if he doesn't agree with Mandy's suspicions, he's giving her the benefit of his full attention while she details all the things that have been on her mind.

"I'm really sorry for dumping all of that on you," she says, honestly.

"Don't ever be sorry. I'm the one who is sorry; I've been so preoccupied with work that I haven't even noticed that something was on your mind. There was a time I knew you so well, I could spot your anxiety from a mile away. I can't imagine how heavy this all has been to carry."

She wants to hug him from relief, but they are in the middle of a bar on a Monday, so she restrains herself. It feels so good to let it all out; she didn't realize how much tension she had from keeping these suspicions inside.

"Well, as far as Patrick goes, I think you're onto something about your theory. Why would he lie and say he was going back to you? Because he thought she'd accept it and move on. I think it's very likely he's shacking up with one of her friends."

"Shacking up? What are you, ninety?"

"Moving on," he continues with a smile. "Your neighbor—you said her name is Georgia, right?"

Mandy nods.

"Okay, well there is probably a reason she doesn't like talking about her time at the Bluff. It ended with two fires and four deaths, one of which was a close friend. It's probably a dark time for her. Did she talk about how close she was with Jack and Tilly Hawthorne? Even if she hated her employers, surely it was traumatic to lose them both on the same night."

Mandy sets down her drink and claps her hands together, startling Wes.

"I forgot to tell you that part—I only learned she worked directly for Jack and Tilly from my little Reddit friend! She hasn't mentioned it once. She only told me she worked in the kitchen."

"Mandy," he begins, with a smile that transports her

back to high school, "I know you, and I know the way your brain works. You think it's a possibility that your neighbor had something to do with these fires, don't you?"

She can't lie to him. It's been dancing around at the back of her mind since she found out Georgia's last day was the day of the fires.

"Why else would she not want people to know she's back in town? And why did she leave town to begin with, if she wasn't running from something?"

"Why haven't you driven by our old neighborhood in twenty years?"

"How do you know I haven't?"

Wes gives her a look that only he can.

"Okay, you're right. I haven't. It just hurts too much," she admits.

"And you don't think Georgia felt the same way after the fires?"

Mandy shrugs and sips on her drink. Maybe he has a point.

"As for your other neighbor . . . I admit that it's strange his living room and kitchen are empty, but if my cabin didn't come furnished, I can't tell you it would look much different. I think you're right to assume he may be divorced. Give him time, he'll have the place looking like home. It wouldn't kill you to see if he needs any help."

She shrugs once more. She came to Wes for help, and yet she's annoyed that he's offering it. He's always led with common sense and rationality, most likely as a coping mechanism. She's not sure why she thought he'd buy into her suspicions and theories, but he's doing nothing but making her feel like she's been overthinking them all.

"And the men of the Hawthorne Bluff Club? What say you?"

This time, Wes's lips form a tight line and his brows

furrow so deeply, they nearly touch. "There is obviously so much I'm not at liberty to discuss, so please trust me when I say I get it. This isn't something that you need to feel like you should investigate or theorize—these men are horrible. They cheat, they lie, they do whatever they need to do to keep their pockets lined and their asses out of prison. It's reprehensible. And whoever told you that it's been going on for decades is right—Chandler's dad, Chandler Jr., was the worst of the worst. Whatever you're imagining, you're right. I can only promise you this—everyone has their limit, and I've come close to mine. I need you to trust me when I say that there's a plan."

"Wes, that's so ominous. A plan?"

He takes both of his hands in hers. "I'd never let anything bad happen to you. Do you trust me?"

That's the easiest question she could be asked by the man who has saved her more than once.

"Of course."

Chapter 30

The days following her meeting with Wes are relatively uneventful. She feels lighter for having unloaded her mental pile on him; yet more tense than ever about what's going on behind the scenes at the Bluff. The plot thickens when Allison arrives home from her "trip" on Wednesday morning and Mandy swears she sees bruising around her right eye, barely visible beneath the caked-on foundation, which is also uncharacteristic of her. Allison is a natural beauty and normally only throws on a few dabs of blush and a swipe or two of mascara before leaving the house.

Although Mandy hasn't replied to her mother's prison friend, she did make the decision late last night that she should make the trip to visit her. If it's true that her mother's health is failing, Mandy fears she'd never forgive herself or be able to move on without an attempt at closure.

Chandler has been noticeably absent around the house, which has been nice. Allison explained Miss Kelsey's departure as "family issues she needs to tend to," so Mandy has been handling Frankie's lesson plans for the time being. Allison walks into the room as Mandy is observing Frankie fill out her math worksheet and attempts a smile that doesn't quite reach her eyes. Mandy isn't sure what's going on between Allison and Chandler, but it doesn't take a genius to know there's trouble in paradise.

"Mrs. Hawthorne, I hate to ask this so soon after being hired, but do you think it would be possible for me to leave a few hours early on Friday? I need to drive downstate and check on a friend, and I was hoping to arrive before dark."

Although Allison seems caught off guard by the request, she quickly nods.

"Well, of course. Friendship is so important. If you just want to come and do Frankie's lesson plan with her at nine, you should be able to get out of here and on the road by eleven. Is your car dependable enough for the trip? Is there anything I can do to help?"

Much like any kindness shown to her by a motherly figure, Mandy is caught off guard by the gesture.

"No ma'am, my car should be just fine, but I really appreciate the offer, and thank you for being flexible. If you'd like me to stay late and make up the hours next week, I'd be happy to do that."

"It's no problem at all," she answers sweetly.

It's settled. Mandy will drive downstate on Friday, find a decently priced hotel near the prison, and then arrive first thing Saturday for visiting hours. She can only hope she's on her mother's list of approved visitors.

There's rain in the forecast for the rest of the afternoon, so she and Frankie watch cartoons on YouTube, color a few pictures, and put together a Bluey puzzle that takes every bit of two hours. Before Mandy knows it, it's time to go home.

"Mandy," Frankie says as she's walking her to the front door.

"Yes, my dear?" Mandy responds, smiling when she realizes she's sounding more like Georgia every day.

"You are one of my best friends. I have two, you and Grace. Wes is kind of my best friend, but he's a boy, so he doesn't get to be in the top two."

It takes everything Mandy has not to break down. She wants to tell Frankie that Wes was *her* best friend when she was her age, but their history isn't something they've broadcasted around the club, so she opts instead to bend down and hug the girl.

"How lucky you are to already have two best friends," she whispers.

She pulls away to see the girl's tiny, rose-colored lips turn up into a smirk as she nods in agreement. Spending her days with this precious girl is feeling like anything but work.

The beeps and hums of construction vehicles fill the air when Mandy exits the house. She's surprised to witness any new development; the club already has every amenity the members could want, and she's been told countless times that the member homes are forever capped at fifty, a tenet that was ironclad in the original club rules.

Wes comes jogging from the path to the dining lodge, in the general vicinity of the noise.

"Sorry I'm late," he says, slightly out of breath.

"I've told you a hundred times, I'm a big girl, I can walk to my car alone. I mean, I always appreciate the company, but if you've got somewhere to be, I get it."

Wes gestures to the woods behind him, where Mandy can barely make out the shape of several pieces of construction equipment.

"I'm supervising the installation of the new pickle ball courts, and we ran into a few issues. My cousin Rex is actually laying the foundation; you remember him, right?"

How could she forget Cousin Rex? His family was on the lower end of middle class, which meant they were filthy rich in the eyes of the River Ridge Estates Mobile Home Park residents. His parents were incredibly kind, but Wes's parents shunned them for being "highfalutin" and thinking "their shit don't stink," so Mandy, Wes, and Jeffrey didn't get to hang out with Rex and his sister as much as they would have liked to. It's fascinating to observe how insecurities manifest themselves differently in every adult, but it was entirely too complex of a concept for them to wrap their childhood minds around.

"Of course, I remember Rex. How kind of him to help the overprivileged with their pickle balling," Mandy says with a laugh as Wes shoots her a scolding look. "What? If they didn't want us to laugh, they shouldn't have given the sport such a ridiculous name."

"Chubbs, I fear you're continuing to make fun of anything you're afraid to try. When the courts are finished, I'll personally give you a lesson, and you can tell me if you hate it. But if you love it, you have to drink a Stella when you're done."

She gives an exaggerated eye roll. "Fine."

"How was work?" he asks as they begin their walk to the parking lot.

"It rained most of the day, so Frankie and I stayed in the house, but we had a good time. Also, I made up my mind about visiting Mom. I'm going to go on Friday. Allison said I could take the rest of the day off after Frankie's lesson plans, so I'm going to head down and find a hotel close to the prison so I can be first in line for visitation Saturday morning."

It catches Mandy off guard when Wes wraps his arm around her shoulders, but she welcomes the gesture. "I'm proud of you."

"You know what? I'm proud of me, too. I appreciate the nudge you gave me."

"Will you let her know I'm doing okay?" Wes asks.

"Of course, I will."

Wes always was her mother's favorite, but Mandy has always chalked that up to him being the responsible one who made sure they were fed when she and Mandy's dad were off doing god-knows-what.

"I am, however, going to have to tell her about that tattoo," Mandy adds, gesturing to his back.

Adorably, his face reddens.

"You saw my tattoo?"

"When you bent over to pick up Frankie on my first day. I was too overwhelmed with everything to give you shit about it that day, but here we are," she says with a cunning smirk. "Some sort of tribal thing it appears, yeah? Even though you moved to the Bluff, you didn't escape the god-awful trend of every twenty-something frat boy getting one, now did you?"

"Yeah, yeah. Just give Skylar my best and drive carefully, Chubbs. That little girl has grown attached to you."

MANDY IS surprised to see Georgia exiting Braxton's front door as she pulls into her driveway. Georgia waves enthusiastically when she spots Mandy's car, pointing to her left arm, under which Braxton's dog, Max, is snugly secured. Mandy can't help but smile.

"Do I need to call 9-1-1 and report a dognapping?" Mandy yells as she gets out of the car.

"I was helping Braxton with some things earlier and he got called into work. I asked if I could borrow Max for a playdate," Georgia yells back, holding the tiny dog in the air as if Mandy didn't notice him before. "Murphy is going to be so excited."

"You didn't ask me if I was willing to attend this play-date," Mandy teases.

"This is between us and Murphs. Now, unlock the door so we can play," Georgia replies, hustling across the lawn with Max bouncing in her arms.

"What were you helping Braxton with?" Mandy asks as she unlocks the door. Murphy is in the kitchen waiting and squeaks out a high-pitched yap when he sees Max. Georgia sets the dog down and they take off, chasing each other in circles around the living room. Georgia claps her hands together and smiles like someone watching their grandchildren open gifts on Christmas morning.

"He had a new couch delivered today and wanted me to tell him which color throw pillows to order online, in case he has female company. Do you know that man has been living the last month without a couch? No wonder he hasn't had any female visitors."

So, I'm not crazy, Mandy thinks.

"How do you know he hasn't? You don't spy on your neighbors, do you, Georgia?"

She gives the woman a wry smile and raises her eyebrows slightly. Georgia bats a dismissive hand through the air and takes a seat on the couch, watching the dogs take turns pinning each other on the carpet and grunting.

"Hey, I'm actually glad you're here. What would you think of watching Murphy overnight on Friday?"

Georgia pulls a plush hotdog toy from the basket next to the couch and waves it between the two dogs, with Murphy hopping up to grab it first.

"I've known you for over a year and you've never been gone overnight. Please tell me you're doing something fun."

"No such luck; I'm going to visit my mom in prison."

Georgia stops playing tug of war with Murphy and turns her attention to Mandy.

"Oh wow, Mandy. What made you decide to do that?"

Mandy hasn't decided if it was her talk with Wes or the thought of her mom dying before she could say goodbye, but late last night the decision became clear to her. She needed to go.

"I guess I'm getting a little less stubborn in my old age," Mandy replies.

"Oh yes, the advanced age of thirty-six. I can't imagine," Georgia says in a playful tone. "But of course, I'll watch Murphy. It would be my pleasure."

"Thanks, Georgia. I'm looking forward to asking her the questions I've had on my mind all these years. I think it'll be good for us both. Oh, and I just found out she briefly worked at the Bluff. It was before your time and before I was born, but she apparently worked in the kitchen for a couple of years. I'm not sure why she never talked about it."

Georgia is quiet, staring forward at the two dogs who are now lying on the carpet, panting with their tongues out.

"It was before the years you worked there, so you wouldn't have worked with her . . . right?"

"Dear, I'm not sure you even told me what your mother's name is."

"Skylar. Skylar Smith."

"And what was her maiden name?"

"Well, her maiden name was Penny, but she would have already been married to my dad when she worked there. Apparently, she quit when she got pregnant with my older brother in 1986."

"Hmm, doesn't sound familiar. I'm sure she just didn't

talk about her past jobs with you because you were a child, dear."

"That's exactly what Wes said."

"Well, it sounds like you'll have the opportunity to ask her all about it this weekend and then you can come back and tell us what she says."

Chapter 31

Mandy can't remember the last time her heart has beaten so fast and hard that she felt it may pound right out of her chest. She convinced herself during her drive downstate that she was prepared for this reunion. She woke up at the Best Western this morning, showered, ate a lukewarm breakfast in the lobby, and convinced herself she was a strong and capable woman who could glide through the process of seeing her mother today without issue.

Now, she sits in her idling car in the parking lot of the prison, staring at the brick wall and wondering how she ever thought she could handle this. It hits her so quickly, she doesn't see it coming.

Anger.

Anger that she's alone, as she often is in this life.

Anger that her brother isn't here to do this with her.

Anger that everyone else seems to have a family except for her.

Anger that she's about to sit two feet away from the woman who is responsible for it all.

Despite everything Mandy's been through, she's not an

angry person. She's passive. She keeps to herself. She is rational. This morning, she feels like someone else's emotions have invaded her entire being. It's foreign and she hates it.

The only way she's going to talk herself into going through with this is to focus on something good, no matter how small. She needs something to look forward to when it's over. Her mind drifts to the Bluff, and she quickly derails the thought because that will only cause her stress. She's got it. Tim Horton's.

Tim Horton's is a fast-food chain that she's only had twice in her life, but the coffee was so good and the bagels so fresh, she still thinks about it. She knows there are several of them downstate. She swipes to open her phone and search for the nearest location. Sure enough, there is one thirty miles north and only two miles off her route home. That's it; if she can get through this meeting, she's going to treat herself to a plain bagel with melted butter and a coffee with two creamers. Then, she's going to drive north over the Mackinac Bridge and enjoy the beautiful view of the lake, all the way home to her warm bed and trusted companion, Murphy.

She's got this.

Mandy doesn't allow herself to overthink it anymore; she simply gets out of the car and makes a beeline for the front door. She checks in, gives them her ID, waits in the lobby to be called back, fills out the required forms, and before she knows it, she's sitting in a chair waiting for the guards to bring in Skylar Smith.

She considers bending forward to put her head between her knees, as she's been advised to do in the past while feeling lightheaded, but she fights it. She closes her eyes and counts as she inhales. One, two, three. Exhale. One, two, three. She repeats this process until the sound of the thick metal door unlocking jars her eyes back open.

A stocky middle-aged man in a prison guard uniform escorts Skylar into the room and sits her down on a blue plastic chair across from Mandy. There is a thick plastic wall and table separating them, but it's cleaner than they show in the movies, and Mandy can see her mother perfectly.

She's often imagined how her mother has aged, and her expectations were not great. A drunk and a drug addict who chain-smoked during Mandy's entire childhood; time surely had not been kind to the woman. As she sits in the chair and raises her gaze to meet Mandy's, she gasps at the sight.

Against all odds, her mother is beautiful. Her hair, although graying at the roots, looks healthy and clean. Her skin is clear and even toned, and her focused eyes are a beautiful emerald. She appears this way in the split-second memories that fade in Mandy's mind as soon as they appear—the brief moments of pure joy in her childhood, before her mother became a slave to her addictions.

The guard unlocks Skylar's cuffs, and she immediately brings both hands to her mouth, stifling a sob.

Mandy's bottom lip is shaking so dramatically, it's causing her teeth to clatter.

"My baby," Skylar whispers.

Mandy nods, over and over, willing herself to hold back the tears. This woman does not deserve her tears. She finds herself rocking back and forth, her hands placed underneath her body in the chair to hold them still.

"Thank you for coming," Skylar says. "What made you change your mind, after all these years?"

"I heard you weren't well. I'd never forgive myself if I didn't come."

Skylar's head cocks slightly, wondering how she knew about her health issues. Her eyes raise above Mandy's head, in deep thought, before nodding, a silent confirmation that she knows exactly who contacted her daughter on her behalf.

"It's not that bad," Skylar says, but she begins a coughing fit before the words have left her mouth. "Okay, it's a little bad."

"What do the doctors say?" Mandy asks, perhaps a bit foolishly.

"I'm a lifer, baby. They aren't in any hurry to fix me."

Her casual use of the name baby sends a shock through Mandy's system.

Hand mommy her lighter, baby.

You and Jeffrey can have whatever you want for breakfast, baby.

Mommy loves you even when you think she don't, baby.

"Can you tell me about your life, Mandy? Are you married? Do I have grandchildren?"

Mandy reminds herself that her mother is dying. She doesn't have much time left, and to deny her this knowledge would be cruel. Unlike her mother, she doesn't have it in her to be cruel.

"I married my high school sweetheart, but we got divorced last year. Don't feel bad for me; it was a good thing. We never had any kids, but I do have a little dog named Murphy. I own my own home downtown. Well, I won't own it outright for about twenty-five more years, but I make the payments on time, and it feels like home."

Tears form in the corners of Skylar's eyes, seconds before they spill out and down her cheeks. She takes her time wiping them away. "That's great, baby."

"How bad is it in here?" Mandy asks, doubtful she'll get an honest answer.

Skylar waves a hand, dismissing the notion that prison

is a bad place to be. "It's nothing like you see in the movies. Most of the women on my cell block are around my age, and we're all too old and tired to cause any trouble. Of course, I'd rather be on the outside, but I hear about prisons all the time that are far worse than this. I'm lucky, in a way."

"Do you miss them?" Mandy asks, not needing to specify who she's referring to.

Skylar cocks her head back, as if her daughter just slapped her across the face. "Do I miss them? Mandy, I miss all three of you. Every morning and every night, you're my first and last thought every single day. I replay every mistake I made that cost me my entire family. I'd give anything, *anything*, to go back and make better choices."

Mandy locks eyes with Skylar as she asks her next question, doing her best to detect deception in her answer. "Mom, why didn't you tell me you worked at the Bluff?"

Skylar's eyes grow wide. "How did you know that?"

"Because I work there now, and I met two women who said they worked with you there before Jeff and I were born."

"You work there? What do you do? How long have you worked there?"

Her mother is manic; this is the behavior she remembers clearly from her childhood years.

"Two weeks. I'm a keeper, which just means I'm a glorified nanny. I work for Chandler and Allison Hawthorne; he's the grandson of the club's founder."

Skylar slaps her hand on the table so loudly, Mandy nearly falls out of her chair.

"Mandy Smith, you get out of there. Never go back. Don't ever go into that man's house again. You have to believe me—do not go back to that job," she says, her voice growing louder with every word. Her hands are shaking. She slaps the table again. "Mandy, do you hear me? Do you hear what I'm saying?"

Her voice has grown so loud, Mandy is sure the people occupying the other visitation rooms can hear every word. A guard bursts into the room, grabbing Skylar by her bicep and pulling her to her feet. As he leads her out of the room, she's still screaming.

"You have *no idea* what that family is capable of, Mandy!"

As she's drug down the hall, Mandy can hear her pleading with the guard.

"You have to tell her she can't go back. Please, please tell her. She can't go back to that place. That's my baby. Don't let them hurt my baby."

Chapter 32

Mandy doesn't stop at Tim Horton's. Other than filling up her tank a few hours from home, Mandy doesn't stop at all. She drives straight home in silence, staring forward at the light rain splashing her windshield and replays every word. She blinks and she's home.

She apologizes for being rude when she walks over to Georgia's to retrieve Murphy, but tells the woman she's feeling under the weather and just needs some rest.

For the rest of the weekend, she only leaves her bed if she or Murphy need to eat or use the restroom. She doesn't watch TV; she doesn't scroll the internet. She just lies under a pile of blankets and stares at the ceiling during the times that sleep doesn't come easily.

Much to her credit, Georgia doesn't push the issue. She texts once, a briefly worded message that no doubt took her ten minutes to type on her ancient phone. She asks if there's anything she can do to help, and Mandy politely declines her offer.

For the last twenty-six years, Mandy has not given two shits about how her mom is feeling, but Monday morning she feels like she is betraying the woman who birthed her by getting dressed to go back to work. She's returning to the Bluff, the one thing her mother begged her not to do.

"SOMEONE SHIT IN YOUR CHEERIOS?" the security guard asks with a wink as Mandy pulls her car up to the gate. It's not her favorite guard, Tanner, but rather a more abrasive, immature man several years older than her. She's only encountered him two or three times, but from their limited interactions she assumes he's the jerk who made Luke late for his meat delivery.

"Just tired, that's all," Mandy responds, putting her employee ID back in its place in her wallet. She didn't realize she was displaying her emotions so obviously on her face.

He waves her through, and she musters up whatever enthusiasm she can in preparation for her morning with Frankie. She deserves a happy, stable adult to look over her.

"Hey, you didn't return my text," Wes says, greeting her with a Styrofoam cup as she shuts her car door behind her.

"I was sick all weekend, I'm just now feeling better," Mandy replies. "I'm sorry."

The truth is, she knew if she began a conversation with Wes this weekend, she'd dump everything on him, and she wasn't yet ready to do that.

"Did you go see Skylar?"

Mandy nods, taking a sip of her latte, which is somehow even better than last week's.

"Sobriety has treated her well; she looked beautiful. She coughed so hard, I thought she may hack up a lung, but she looked otherwise a lot better than I expected,"

Mandy answers, avoiding the mention of Skylar's frantic warning.

"Did you get the chance to ask her about working here?" Wes asks as they begin their walk to the Hawthorne's.

"I was so shocked to see her, I think it just slipped my mind. I'll have to ask her next time."

She takes another sip of the hot liquid, ridding her mouth of the taste of the words. She hates lying to anyone, but Wes most of all. She needs to figure out why her mother is so terrified of her working at the club. She's heard all the horror stories by now about the misogyny and greediness, but her reaction was more intense than some "boys will be boys" behavior.

Shortly before they arrive at Chandler and Allison's house, Wes tells Mandy that he needs to go check on the construction crew and they part ways.

"I'll be back at five to walk with you," he calls out to her as he walks away.

This morning feels different as she walks into the house. All her senses are alerted to possible danger around her, Skylar's words echoing in her mind.

"Mandy," Frankie cries out when she turns the corner, coming from the library. She hurries across the foyer to wrap her arms around Mandy's legs. "I missed you. I haven't seen you in days and days."

Mandy smooths the curls running down the girl's neck.

"It was only the weekend, silly."

"Maybe you should come on the weekends, too."

Mandy smiles, thinking of the overtime that would come with those hours.

"How was your friend?" Allison asks, entering from the kitchen. Her face has returned to its perfect porcelain complexion, with no hints of bruising around her eye or anywhere else.

"My friend?" Mandy asks, realizing her mistake immediately. "Oh, my friend! Yes, she is sick but was in good spirits. Thank you for asking. And thank you again for giving me those hours off. I think you accidentally paid me for them, though; my direct deposit was for the full forty hours."

"Oh, don't worry about it. Just a little something to thank you for being so great with Frankie and helping with her lesson plans since Miss Kelsey left."

"Is Miss Kelsey coming back?" Frankie asks, turning her attention to her mother.

"I'm afraid not, sweetheart. She went back to live with her family and help them out."

Allison's lies are effortless when speaking to her daughter.

"That's okay. I'm just happy Mandy is here to do my work with me," Frankie says in response.

"What a mature, smart little woman you are," her mother tells her. "We *are* extremely lucky to have Mandy here."

For the next few hours, Mandy and Frankie fly through her lesson plans for the day and arrive fifteen minutes early for lunch in the kitchen. Frankie asks Chef Regina if she can help, and she patiently allows Frankie to stand on a stepstool and stir the homemade soup on the stove. Just as Regina is finishing the cornbread muffins to accompany the soup, the doorbell rings.

"I'll get it," Mandy says, abandoning her seat at the table, where she was reviewing the answers on Frankie's math worksheet.

She's surprised to see little Grace and her nanny,

Jessica, on the front porch when she opens the door. Jessica is holding a plate of brownies, wrapped in decorative plastic and tied with a red ribbon on top.

"We made extra brownies and thought you might like some," Jessica says, handing the plate to Mandy.

"Frankie!" the little girl cries, flying past Mandy and running into the house.

"Hey, you don't just enter someone's house without asking," Jessica calls after her, but Grace doesn't seem to notice. She mouths *I'm sorry* to Mandy, who simply shrugs.

"Kids, right?" Mandy says, backing up and motioning for Jessica to come in.

When they enter the kitchen, Mandy is certain she sees a look pass between Jessica and her friend, Chef Regina. It's over just as soon as it begins, but it's confirmation of a secret they share. Regina nods quickly before bending over to pull the cornbread out of the oven.

"Who is hungry?" she asks, with both girls shouting in response. "Lucky for you both, I have enough soup to go around. Frankie, where is your brother?"

All three women laugh when Frankie screams at the top of her lungs for Remy, instead of going upstairs.

"Damn, chill, I'm coming," he yells, his voice muffled through the closed door of his bedroom.

Mandy eyes the plate that Jessica brought in, which easily contains over a dozen brownies. She opens the pantry and retrieves a small Ziploc bag.

"Would you mind watching Frankie for five minutes? Wes loves brownies and I think he's still stuck at the pickleball construction site, so I'm going to surprise him with a couple. Don't worry, you'll get full credit. He knows I can't bake," she says to Jessica.

"Of course. Tell him we say hello," she responds.

Mandy carefully tucks two brownies in the bag after

wrapping them in a sheet of paper towel. She slips her shoes on by the front door, and within minutes she's made it to the future home of the Hawthorne pickleball courts. It may be a small gesture, but she's been looking for some way to repay Wes for the coffee and daily walks to and from her car.

"Hey Mandy, long time no see," yells Rex, Wes's cousin. He hops down from the tractor-like piece of equipment he was driving and gives her an awkward side-hug.

"Hi, Rex. I heard you were heading up this project. Looks like you're doing well for yourself."

He pats his slightly rounded stomach and answers, "Can't complain," as if Mandy complimented him for being well-fed.

"Are you here to see my good-for-nothing cousin?" he asks.

Before Mandy can answer, Wes ends his conversation with one of Rex's crew members and jogs in Mandy's direction. "Hey, Chubbs, everything okay?"

"Yes, everything is great. I just wanted to bring you some brownies," she says, holding out the bag. "Still your favorite?"

"Of course they are. Thank you so much."

As soon as Wes takes the bag from her, he places a hand behind her back and leads her away from the job site and back toward the Hawthorne's. She gets the strangest feeling that he doesn't want her there; it's a feeling she's never had before with Wes.

"Are you worried Rex is going to hit on me or something? I'm a big girl, Wes."

He lets out an uncomfortable laugh. "I just don't want you to get hurt. Chandler would kill me if he had to pay your workman's comp."

Mandy glances back one last time before disappearing

onto the wooded path back to the house. What she sees sends a chill down her spine. Rex and his three employees have all stopped working and are standing shoulder to shoulder, staring directly at her. Wes notices her reaction and shouts to the crew. "Come on guys, back to work. The pretty lady is leaving. Nothing to see here."

He winks at Mandy and shrugs like *what can you do, right?*

But Mandy hasn't heard a word he said because she's staring at his skin, which is now exposed as he pulls his t-shirt up to wipe the sweat from his face. The tattoo she saw earlier wraps around his side and travels down below his jeans and out of view. It's a beautiful pattern, although it's not tribal like she originally thought. It's beautiful script style wording with trees surrounding the letters, much like the trees that surround them now.

She can't see the tattoo in its entirety, but what she *can* see are three initials: A. F. R.

Her mind is rapid fire listing anything important to Wes with those initials. Not her, not his parents, not his own initials.

It hits her like a slap in the face.

Allison.

Frankie.

Remy.

Against all odds, he doesn't register where her eyes have fallen. He mistakenly thinks she's looking at the brownies in his hand.

"What, you want me to eat one now? You're so impatient," he says with a smile, opening the bag in his hand and retrieving the biggest one. He takes a bite and throws his head back in exaggerated pleasure. "These are the best brownies I've ever had in my life, Mandy. You have outdone yourself. Now, go enjoy the rest of your day."

She's entirely too distracted to tell him she's not the one who made them. She forces a smile and turns to walk back to the Hawthorne home, more confused than ever about who she can trust.

Chapter 33

After lunch, the sun comes out for the first time in what feels like a week, and Frankie asks Mandy if they can go down to the river and collect rocks.

"I don't see why not," she says. Allison left the house hours ago, and she hasn't seen Chandler around. When laying out the ground rules and expectations for the job, Mandy was told she can take Frankie anywhere she'd like, as long as it's inside the gates. The river is only a quarter mile down a paved path in the woods on the other side of the house.

Frankie is in an especially chatty mood this afternoon, which gives Mandy extra time to think while the young girl rambles about Taylor Swift's new album, Grace's new trampoline, and the American Girl doll she wants for her birthday. Mandy replays the scene at the construction site over in her mind.

"Don't you think?" Frankie says, stopping to gauge Mandy's response.

She has no idea what the girl was saying while she was

lost in thought. "Yes," Mandy answers, hoping it's the correct one.

"But, 1989 was a good album, too. It's Grace's favorite."

Mandy exhales. It's just more talk of Taylor Swift. She never thought she'd hear a seven-year-old have enough knowledge to reference a specific album, but this girl has been exposed to a lot more culture than most kids her age. When Mandy was seven, she could tell you that she loved New Kids on the Block and that the hunkiest one was Jordan, but that's where her knowledge of the subject ended.

When they get to the river's edge, Mandy stops to admire its beauty. Much to her pleasure, Frankie does the same. Wes was right about this kid—there's still hope for her to turn out okay.

"Can we take our shoes off and go in up to our ankles?"

Mandy checks the temperature on her phone. It's sixty-seven degrees out and not a cloud in the sky.

"Oh, what the heck?" she says, shrugging, and Frankie squeaks out a little celebratory cheer before dropping back onto her butt to start untying her shoes.

Mandy can't remember the last time she did something so carefree. The girls walk back and forth across the smooth rocks on the river's bottom, careful not to lose their balance. Frankie's eyes are trained down, as to not miss any "cool rocks" to collect, while Mandy's gaze inventories their surroundings.

She gasps. "Frankie, look," she tells the girl, pointing to the sky.

"An eagle!"

"That's right," Mandy answers. "You're a pretty smart cookie."

Mandy watches the creature glide through the air, its impressive wingspan floating overhead without a single flutter. She understands why eagles are often described as majestic; it's the word that keeps coming to mind as she watches the bird in flight.

Their eyes follow the eagle for a few more minutes, and then they spend the better part of an hour collecting rocks, which Mandy is placing in the pockets of her khakis because they didn't think to bring a bag or bucket. For the eighth time, Frankie finds a rock that she describes as "the most beautiful one she's ever seen." Each time she wipes it on her shirt and examines its edges, before handing it to Mandy and reminding her to be careful. Mandy's heart melts a little more with each one.

The five o'clock hour has snuck up on her again, as she reluctantly tells Frankie they need to head back to the house. To her surprise, Frankie doesn't argue; she simply sits back down to shake her toes dry the best she can, puts her socks and shoes back on, and gets to her feet, looking at Mandy to start the journey home. She is an incredibly special child.

Allison still isn't home when they arrive, but Remy is in the kitchen doing homework and says he can keep an eye on Frankie until his mom gets home.

"Is there anything I can help you with before I go?" Mandy asks, ashamed that she doesn't spend much time with Remy.

He gives her a mischievous smile. "You any good at AP Algebra?"

"Remy, I'm fighting for my life with these second-grade math equations. I might have to politely sit this one out."

For the first time since she started the job, she gets a genuine laugh out of him.

. . .

MANDY IS NEARLY home when she feels something sharp poking into her leg. She reaches in her pocket to find one of Frankie's "favorite" rocks from their little expedition. She can just picture the girl having a meltdown when she lines up all the rocks they found today to show her mom and is missing the one she was most excited about. Without thinking twice, Mandy pulls a U-turn and heads back to the club.

Oddly, there is nobody at the entrance when she arrives, so she leans inside the window of the guard's booth and presses the large green button to open the gate. Maybe these guys take dinner breaks, too.

For a split second, she considers parking directly at the Hawthorne's, since she's just running in quickly to give Frankie the rock, but doesn't want to ruffle any feathers so she compromises by parking in one of the visitor's spots at the dining lodge, as she did the day of her job interview.

It's odd being at the club after five. She thought she would experience the hustle and bustle of everyone returning to the club after work and then laughs at herself for being so foolish. These men don't have regular jobs in town, and most of the women don't have to work at all. There is no five o'clock traffic. The only sign of life is the clanging of pots and pans coming from inside the dining lodge, where the staff is preparing for the six o'clock dinner seating.

Mandy walks on the path from the dining lodge to the Hawthorne's, stopping briefly by the water to admire the mansion that sits vacant; the one Wes told her is supposedly owned by a master computer hacker who rarely shows up at the club. She can't imagine having a house like that and barely using it. What a waste.

Just as she turns to leave, movement from the corner of her eye steals her attention, and a small animal begins running in her direction from the yard of the hacker's mansion.

As he gets closer, the labored snorts give away the breed before her eyes come to focus enough to see the pug. It's another brown dog with a black snout, like Murphy and Max. Mandy never imagined this town had so many pugs; she wonders if she should do a pug meetup at the dog park in town.

As it gets closer, Mandy bends down to pet the dog and is taken aback. This dog *is* Max. She recognizes the small black patch on the back of his head that looks like a diamond and his Green Bay Packers collar. He obviously recognizes Mandy as well; he's frantically licking her hand and squealing with excitement. What the hell would Braxton's dog be doing inside the gates of the Hawthorne Bluff Club?

The dog spins back toward the mansion's back lawn and, against Mandy's better judgment, she follows him. He trots a few feet ahead of her, without a care in the world.

"What is happening?" she whispers to herself.

When she arrives at the back of the house, Max enters through the sliding patio door, which is wide open.

"Hello?" she asks.

No answer.

She tentatively places a foot inside the house, onto the tiled floor of the kitchen.

"Hello?"

Nothing.

"Max, there you are." A deep, male voice sounds from a room just off the kitchen. When he rounds the corner, Mandy sucks in a breath.

It's Braxton, her neighbor. But he's not dressed like

Braxton. He's wearing linen pants, a button-down shirt, and loafers that look like they cost more than her mortgage payment. Max, oblivious to the drama at hand, prances back over to Mandy and sits at her feet.

"What the fuck is happening?"

Footsteps sound from the open door to Mandy's left, presumably leading to the basement.

Seconds later, Georgia arrives at the top of the steps.

"What . . ." Mandy whispers, a hand clutched to her chest.

"Mandy . . . Mandy, I need you to take a deep breath. This is happening a little sooner than we expected, but that's okay. Sit down and I'll tell you everything."

Chapter 34

October 30th, 1998
  Devil's Night

IT USUALLY DOESN'T TAKE this long for the numbness to kick in, but Skylar's tolerance has increased at a steady pace in recent years. By the seventh Jack and Coke, she begins to forget. That's the sweet spot.

Her husband, Mark, is across the bar, dressed as Hulk Hogan and hustling some poor college kid on the pool table. Skylar's current focus is the man next to her named Gary, who she strongly suspects will continue to pay for her drinks so long as she doesn't stop leaning into him and grabbing his bicep in a fit of laughter each time he tells a joke that isn't funny. His attention is split between Skylar—dressed as Monica Lewinsky in a blazer, skirt, and black wig—and the man on the other side of him, who is leaned forward on his elbows with a cigarette hanging from the corner of his mouth over a can of Busch Light. Skylar leans closer, not only to remind Gary she's still there, but also to catch a few words before the man's story is over. The music in this place is shitty *and* loud—not a great combination.

She leans over just enough to hear the name she's been avoiding for the last twelve years. The name that makes her entire body tense up with fear and absolute disgust. Hawthorne.

She doesn't want to hear that stupid name ever again in life, but in this town it's a little hard to avoid. That godforsaken family is the topic of conversation with every has-been and never-was that live around here.

"Oh yeah, he and his old lady built a brand-new mansion, even bigger than the last. They just moved in. A buddy of mine hauled their furniture from one house to the other. He said the couch was a brand name he couldn't even pronounce. That's how rich these mother fuckers are. They got shit we ain't even heard of."

Skylar's mind is racing. Chandler Hawthorne moved? How nice of him to escape the house of horrors. The home where he abused god-knows-how-many women. Maybe he built a nicer dungeon in this one. His son is in his twenties now, and she's heard rumors that he's just as bad as his father. He can move all he wants, but Skylar will never escape the house that torments her in her sleep. If she drinks enough and has something a little extra at the end of the night, it normally numbs her into a dreamless sleep for a few hours. Her head aches in the morning, but at least that mother fucker isn't invading her nightmares.

"Yeah, I guess he built it over on the other side of the property, close to where the employees live. I'm sure the guy just wants easier access to all the nannies and house-keepers he's sticking it to, ya know?"

Skylar tunes out the rest of the man's words; she can't stand to hear them. She orders another drink and slams it in record time, staring straight ahead at the frosted Miller Lite mirror behind the bar. She doesn't bother confirming with Gary that he'll pay for her final round; she simply grabs her purse and the pack of cigarettes in front of her and leaves the bar. Gary's so buzzed and lost in the other man's story, he doesn't even notice she's gone until her car has left the parking lot. If her husband, Mark, saw her leave, he doesn't bother chasing after her.

She knows she's too drunk to drive, but she's too mad to care.

She finds herself focusing too hard on the center line, and her car drifts repeatedly over it before she slaps herself in the face to focus. She just got her license back; the last thing she needs is another DUI.

Within minutes, she's at the gates of the Hawthorne Bluff Club, a place she swore she'd never return to. She parks her car outside the closed gate and peers into the guard's shack. It's unoccupied. Tonight is the club's annual Halloween party, so all the members who remain in town are already inside the gates; no need for a guard.

Leaving the car door wide open and her key in the ignition, she stumbles her way to the gate and squeezes her petite frame through an opening between the posts. Her black high heels sink into the gravel as she walks toward the dining hall, so she clumsily reaches for them, one at a time, and throws them into the woods beside her. The rocks dig into the bottom of her tights, but she's just drunk enough for the pain to be tolerable.

Skylar marches down past the dining lodge undetected. The lights are on, and Prince is blaring from the speakers. She can see ample movement inside, but she's too intoxicated to focus on the dancing figures to identify them, so she continues her journey toward Easy Street. If she can make it to the employee housing, she can figure out where

Chandler Hawthorne Jr.'s new mansion is, according to Mr. Busch Light's description.

She tries not to think about all the horrible things she experienced and witnessed behind these gates. It's too much to bear. If she thinks about how there's not a damn person who has stopped these men from their reign of terror behind these gates, she'll go even crazier than she already is. She simply focuses on her mission—to ruin Chandler Hawthorne's happiness and, if she's lucky, his life.

As she turns the corner onto Easy Street, the bottoms of her feet begin to bleed from the gravel, but she powers through. A couple of the employee cabins have their lights on, which surprises Skylar because she assumed it would be all hands on deck for the party. She makes it to the end of Easy Street, and there it is, a brand-new mansion in the distance. Right on the lake. She fumes when she sees how close it is to the employee housing. That drunk at Stinky's Tavern was right—Chandler wanted to be closer to his victims. The ones whose lives he threatens, after he traumatizes them.

The house seems quiet, with the couple likely at the Halloween party, but Skylar does her best to stay quiet, nonetheless.

She reaches into the front of her bra and retrieves a lighter. Without giving it a second thought, she simply begins to ignite whatever she can find.

Click. A pile of leaves piled against the corner of the house.

Click. Potted mums next to the front door.

Click. A decorative scarecrow on the front porch.

She stumbles to the shed on the far side of the house and finds it unlocked. The first thing she sees when she swings the door open is a gas can.

"Jackpot," she whispers.

She pours it over each of her small fires and jumps back, surprised each time the flames multiply. Satisfied, she throws the gas can into the fire and turns around to reverse her path back to the car.

When she makes it to the rear of the dining lodge, Chandler Hawthorne III, the newest prick in the line of insufferable assholes, is standing out back talking to another member. They are both dressed like mobsters. *Fitting*, she thinks. He stares straight at her, and she lifts both hands, waving her middle fingers, before laughing hysterically and increasing her speed to a clumsy jog, the soles of her feet so damaged she can't bear to think about how they'll feel tomorrow.

A half mile down the road behind her, a fire rages.

But the home doesn't belong to Chandler Hawthorne, Jr.

Skylar didn't hear the beginning of the man's story at the bar.

The home belongs to Jack Hawthorne and his wife, Tilly.

Although the residents of town like to lump him in with the rest of the men in his bloodline, Jack isn't like them at all. He is kind, he is generous, he's a fair employer, and he is a caring and loyal husband to Tilly.

Tonight, while trying to avenge all the horrible things Chandler Jr. did to Skylar and her coworkers, she burned down the house of Jack and Tilly; the only Hawthornes worth saving.

Chapter 35

October 30th, 1998
  Devil's Night

"NEVER QUESTION the Lord's timing, Tilly," Jack says as they watch in wonder. One of Chandler's old employees, who was also most likely one of his victims, is drunkenly pouring gasoline around Jack's brand-new home, which is now erupting in flames. Jack and Tilly are standing in the woods, less than fifty yards away, watching as the woman stops to re-adjust her wig several times while committing arson.

"That young lady walked onto our property like God personally sent her as a punishment. What in the world did we do to deserve it?" Tilly asks, setting down her suitcase because it's beginning to make her wrist ache.

"Sweetheart, that girl is drunker than a skunk and appears to be filled with rage. I'm no detective, but I'd venture a guess that she thinks it's my brother's new home.

Let's just stay another minute and make sure she makes it out okay. The women will wait; they know we're coming."

For the next five minutes, that's exactly what they do. She's throwing a little kink in their plans, but they devise a new one in hushed whispers while they watch her set their dream home ablaze.

"Well, the plan was to make Chandler and Leslie think their goons kidnapped us to keep us quiet, so it's not very far-fetched to think they'd also light the place on fire. I'm a little ashamed we didn't think of it first," Jack muses.

When Skylar Smith throws the empty gasoline can into the fire and nearly trips over her own feet leaving the property, the Hawthornes follow at a safe distance. They watch her pick up the pace as she makes her way down Easy Street, and breathe a sigh of relief as she turns the corner to head toward the club's exit. She'll need to pass by the Halloween party at the lodge, but that crowd will be too intoxicated to notice her in the dark.

Once she's safely out of sight, Jack and Tilly place their suitcases in the back of Charlene's car and quietly enter the first employee cabin on the right. The door swings open, revealing the smiling face of his favorite employee.

"Oh, thank God," Charlene says, opening the door wider to reveal three more employees, rising to their feet at the sight of Jack and Tilly. "You're so late; what happened? Is that smoke I smell? Did you guys light the place on fire?"

"Never mind that; we've got a change of plans, ladies," Tilly explains, willing her voice to hold steady. "We don't have much time, so listen up."

Each of them nod, and stand in silence, waiting for their instructions. Jack and Tilly are like family to these women, and they'd do anything for them.

"Amelia," Jack begins, pointing to his favorite pastry chef. "The only change from the original plan is that you saw the two men in black suits pour gasoline around our property and light it on fire. Those need to be the first words you tell Chandler when you call the dining lodge."

"Dot, you'll stick close with Amelia while she's recounting what happened and tell Chandler that you swear you saw the men throw two bodies in the trunk of their car before they took off," Tilly instructs. "The most important part is that you go along with whatever he tells you to say to the police. Make him think you're on his side. The cops are for appearance only; they're all in his pocket. There will be no investigation, I assure you. If you don't tell the police what Chandler wants you to say, it will be very dangerous for you and your family. Remember that."

"Jane, stay here in your cabin and call the guard's booth, letting them know you smell flames. If nobody answers, call the dining lodge. You didn't see what happened and you didn't hear anything," Jack tells her. She nods.

"Charlene, do you have your bags packed?" Tilly asks. "And your boys?"

"I packed them each a few changes of clothes and their favorite toys, along with their birth certificates and some medicine, just in case. It's all in the trunk of my car with my bags," Charlene answers. "My parents think I'm taking them on a trip to Wisconsin to see one of my high school friends."

The flames are now growing large enough to be seen over the trees. They don't have much time.

"Okay, we'll take your car and pick up the boys on our way to the airport. Jane, in about an hour we need you to complain that the smoke is bothering you and you're going to stay in town for the night. Charlene, I know it's going to be uncomfortable, but you've got to ride on the floor of the backseat so nobody sees you leave. Jane, here's fifty dollars to stay at the Value Host after you drop Charlene off with us," Tilly tells her, handing her a folded fifty. "Here's another twenty to grab food in case you're hungry."

"We need you remaining girls to remember that you're not going to hear from us for months. Stay strong. Chandler's going to be too busy covering up our supposed kidnapping by telling the world that we're dead, I assure you. He shouldn't be giving you any trouble," Jack assures them. "We're leaving you each with a few hundred dollars in cash. As soon as we're settled in with our new identities, we'll start making small deposits into your accounts, as to not raise any suspicions. Once you have enough to leave, do it."

"We've told you a million times, Jack. We don't want your money. We just want to help you both get out of here and take Charlene with you so she can give her boys the life they deserve. May they never have to learn who their father really was," Amelia says, a tear forming in the corner of her eye. She watches Jack flinch slightly at her last words. "Jack, we know you're nothing like your brother and we also know you and Tilly will help Charlene raise these kids right."

"If things go south, we may have to stay in hiding longer than expected. But one day we'll send a message, so remember our new identities," Tilly says, pulling five passports from her purse, still crisp from the counterfeit printing operation. "Danny and Bobby will now be Tanner and Braxton Cole, and Charlene will be their mother, Cathy. As for us, arriving in Myrtle Beach with their daughter and grandsons, you're looking at South Carolina's newest retirees, George and Georgia Afton."

Chapter 36

Present Day

"YOU'RE . . . TILLY HAWTHORNE?" Mandy manages to say. Her mouth is as dry as cotton, and her head is beginning to pound.

"I know it's a lot to take in, Mandy. We never meant for you to find out this way," says the woman she's known as Georgia since the day they met.

"My mom burned your house down."

"Your mother burned our house down because she thought it belonged to a monster. For decades, we never told a soul about what we saw that night. The women in the cabin assumed we did it to our own home. Skylar has no idea that we were there in the woods."

"But . . . they found two bodies in the cabin fire. Two employees. Who were they, if Charlene and Jane escaped with you?" she asks.

Georgia takes a few steps across the room toward Braxton and takes his hand in hers. "After we left to go pick up Charlene's sons, who you know as Braxton and Tanner," she begins and Mandy gasps. *Tanner, the handsome security guard?* "Amelia and Dot did what they were supposed to do; they ran back to their cabin and called to alert my brother-in-law, Chandler. When the chef who answered the phone at the dining lodge couldn't locate him, they ran down to the lodge themselves. He was nowhere to be found, so they grabbed a few of his associates and let them know there was a fire. By the time they got back, Charlene's and Jane's cabin was also up in flames. Their bodies were recovered hours later, after the fire department put it out. For years, we didn't know what happened."

Mandy's eyes dart between Georgia and Braxton, waiting for an explanation.

"George and Georgia, as we were taught to call them, raised my brother and me in South Carolina. We had normal lives; they made sure we were raised with love and compassion. I was twelve when Mom died, and my brother was only seven, so he barely has any solid memories of her. When we were old enough to learn the true story of our mom and how she was assaulted by her employer and threatened into silence for years, we dedicated our lives to making him pay for what he had done."

Mandy furrows her brows. "But what happened with your mom and the other employee? Please don't tell me Skylar started that fire, too."

"No," Georgia says, shaking her head. "She did get another DUI that night on her way home and spent the night in jail, but she didn't have anything to do with that fire. She actually knew Charlene; they were friends. We finally found out what happened four years later, when we, George and I, paid Chandler and Leslie a visit in Florida.

It's amazing what people will confess when their lives are on the line."

Mandy's eyes grow wide. "Chandler's wife was involved, too?"

Georgia nods, a look of disgust on her face. "I'll never understand how a woman could choose not to protect another woman when given the chance, but Leslie was the worst of the worst. She knew what Chandler was doing to those poor women, and she allowed it to happen. She lit the match that started the fire in Charlene's cabin; she was there, watching it burn. I always wondered if people like Jack and me would be capable of taking a life, but allowing Chandler and Leslie to die behind the wheel of that Cadillac was the easiest thing we'd ever done. They were horrible humans and this world is a better place without them. I know this is going to hurt, Mandy, but they are the reason your childhood home burned down. Their son, who you now work for, saw your mother leaving the club that night. A month later, they destroyed your family as punishment and let your mom take the fall. Skylar probably believes it *was* her cigarette that started the fire."

Mandy leans sideways, bracing herself on the counter to her right. The room is spinning. Her brother and dad, gone in an instant, taken as payback for her mother's drunken, dirty deed. She was supposed to die in that fire. They all were.

"That's why we made sure Wes accompanied you to the job interview. We had to make sure Chandler didn't recognize you. It's been twenty-six years since he's seen your mother, but you do look a lot like her. Luckily, that prick was too self-involved to even notice," Braxton explains.

"Wes? Wes knows about this?" Mandy asks, incredulously.

Georgia and Braxton share a look and then glance toward the basement door.

"I think it's time you know everything. Follow me," Georgia instructs, walking down the stairs. Braxton motions for Mandy to follow her.

As she descends the stairs, it feels like her body is on autopilot. This must be a dream.

When she gets to the bottom stair, the sight that greets her nearly takes the breath right out of her lungs.

The people staring back at her seem just as surprised by her presence as she is by theirs.

There's a large, round table in the center of the room with a flat-screen TV next to it, playing the local news.

Whether she's known them for years or just met them this week, every face sitting at the table is familiar to her.

Wes.

Jessica, Grace's nanny.

Tanner, the security guard.

Amelia, Georgia's "old coworker."

Dot, the kitchen employee who said she'd never heard of Georgia.

Regina, the Hawthorne's chef.

Allison Hawthorne, wife to Chandler III.

Wes looks too stunned to speak when he sees Mandy. His eyes are simultaneously saddened and alarmed. He stands up and runs a hand through his golden hair before looking at Georgia and Braxton, who both shrug in defeat.

"Well, fuck," he says, collapsing back in his seat.

Chapter 37

"Ladies and gentlemen, our little Max McGee blew our cover," Braxton announces, reaching down to pick up his dog, who is oblivious to the chaos he caused by leading Mandy to this house.

"But that's okay; we always planned to clue Mandy in on everything. It's just happening a little sooner than we expected. She's up to speed on who Georgia and I really are and how Chandler confessed to killing my mother and Jane, and lighting Mandy's family home on fire."

None of this seems real. It's not possible. Mandy is experiencing what feels like the most extreme case of vertigo imaginable. Maybe she's dead and this is the afterlife.

"We don't have much time; the news is on at six. Why don't you each briefly tell Mandy how you got involved in the resistance?"

Georgia laughs. "You make it seem so organized. We are just a group with a common goal."

Amelia speaks up first. "George and Georgia sent money to Dot and me over the years, but we had no idea that George had passed away and that Georgia was back in town. We've stayed on the staff here to keep an eye on the younger girls and keep the enemies close. Chandler and his cronies are under the impression we're loyal to them because we've kept our mouths shut. We can't go to the police; they're on the payroll. We've been waiting for someone to come along and end it all, so once we heard what the plan was, we were all in. We miss Charlene and Jane every single day. We don't want these types of men to be in charge anymore; not of any organization, but this club is a start. Until last week, we had no idea your mother was here the night of the fires. She may have gotten the wrong house, but her intentions were right. She's our hero."

Dot nods in agreement.

Georgia speaks up, directing her attention to Mandy. "My sweet Jack, or George as he was known for the last two decades, passed away in his sleep two years ago. When he left this world, I decided to finish our mission on my own. We stopped his brother from ever hurting someone else again, but his nephew Chandler III was still in charge and that sickened me. The women, the lies, the abuse, the manipulation; it's worse than anyone could even begin to imagine. I needed to get close to you to see how much your mother had told you, how much she remembered. When the house next to you came up for sale, I couldn't believe my luck. I quickly found out you didn't know anything about the fires, but when I witnessed the abuse you suffered at the hands of Patrick, I couldn't leave. I owed it to your mother to stay until I knew you were safe from him. When Braxton was ready to enact the final phase of our plan, our neighbor Tom died, so I contacted his children about buying the house on the other side of you. The universe doesn't send such perfect gifts very often, so when it does you have to act. We never planned for you to get a job here; that threw us all for a loop."

Everyone in the room seems to turn their heads toward Tanner, the security guard, at the same time. Heat travels up his neck and reddens his cheeks.

"Hi, Mandy. By now, you know I'm Charlene's son and Braxton's brother. But I'm also an experienced IT professional that dabbles in a little bit of what you refer to as *hacking* on the side. You also may know me as DANNY-BOY06. Danny was my birthname."

Mandy gasps. Tanner wears a look of pride, while everyone else seems annoyed.

"It was so dangerous for him to speak with you at all, let alone encourage you to apply for a job and falsify Georgia's work records when you asked. He could have blown this entire thing," Braxton says. "I could have killed him, but I needed him to stick around and manipulate the camera footage here and there and keep tabs on what was happening at the club."

"Well, now you know my involvement," Tanner says, taking a mock-bow. "The only thing I regret is telling you that I couldn't hack into bank accounts. It pained me to downplay my skillset for the sake of not blowing my cover."

With this, everyone around the table rolls their eyes in unison. Tanner throws his hands up. "You people don't appreciate me nearly enough. This is not child's play."

Next, Jessica raises her hand in Mandy's direction. "Jane was my mother. I've spent my entire life trying to make sense of her death. When I was in college, Tanner contacted me and told me everything. Once we got to know each other, he knew he could trust me with the plan. My wife, Regina, can tell you how she got involved."

Regina smiles, holding up her left hand, which is now

donning a steel wedding band, one that she never wears to work in the Hawthorne's kitchen.

"Chandler Hawthorne and his business partner Stew Maynard took my father for every dime he had. He was too ashamed to tell my mother what happened, so he took his own life. I've been vowing revenge every day since. Meeting Jessica for the first time our little group got together was the best thing that's ever happened to me."

"I've been trying to get a divorce for years," Allison Hawthorne begins, a tinge of sadness in her voice. "He's threatened me, he's carried out a few of those threats, he's promised he'll have my parents killed and leave me penniless; the list goes on. I've been trying to take my children and leave for years. One morning, Regina came to work early and caught Chandler slapping me across the face. She took a chance by assuming I'd join in on the plan. By lunchtime, I was all in."

Wes leans forward and grabs Allison's hand. That's all the confirmation Mandy needs.

"How long?" Mandy asks, nodding toward Wes.

"How long have I loved Wes? Since the day I met him." She wipes a stray tear from her cheek.

"Your tattoo. . .they are your kids, aren't they?" Mandy asks Wes.

His hand quickly travels to his side and Allison tuts. "I told you someone would see it," she says, barely loud enough for anyone to hear.

"I knew the plan would be in place and the kids would be free soon, so I didn't see any harm in displaying my love for my *family* with a permanent reminder," he says sweetly, once again squeezing Allison's hand.

"All of you keep referencing this plan and telling me when you knew you were *in*, but I still don't know what the hell you're talking about. What is this big secret plan?"

Tanner speaks up first.

"First, planted listening devices inside The Nightingale, where they hold their meetings. Next, I gained access to their investment accounts and the club's financial—"

He's interrupted by Georgia's gasp as the opening scenes of the evening news on TV6 begin. "This is it," she says, grabbing the remote and turning the volume all the way up.

Mandy sucks in a breath when she sees the face of Chandler Hawthorne III, along with two other men from the club, one she recognizes as little Grace's father and the other as Stew, the man Chandler was speaking to outside the supper club while Mandy was at the park. You could hear a pin drop in the crowded basement den as the female anchor begins to speak. Everyone is staring at the TV. Jessica and Regina's hands are clasped together, and Allison has already begun to cry, with Wes slowly running his hand up and down her back.

"Tonight's top story is coming out of Delta County, where the President of the prestigious and notoriously private Hawthorne Bluff Club, along with two of the club's executive officers, are accused of embezzling millions of dollars from the organization's bank account, as well as emptying the accounts of several club members who invested their retirement savings with the men. Chandler Hawthorne III, the grandson of the club's founder, along with Brock Burrows and the club's treasurer, Stewart Maynard, are wanted on several charges, including embezzlement, tax evasion, and falsifying records. TV6 can confirm that all three men also face sexual assault allegations that were filed late last night by over a dozen current and former employees of the Hawthorne Bluff Club. Local authorities fear the men have fled the area, and possibly the country, as each of their families have now reported them missing, along with numerous personal items, including their passports and unconfirmed amounts of cash, which was kept in the families' safes. Delta County Airport records show that a private plane was chartered out of Escanaba early this morning, but authorities are not yet releasing details of the passengers on that flight. If you have seen any of these men, or have knowledge of their whereabouts, you are asked to call the Michigan State Police or Crimestoppers at the number below."

When the news program concludes, the room erupts in cheers.

For once, Mandy doesn't need to overthink or try to read the situation. She knows the authorities will spend a lot of time searching for three men they'll never find alive. Against all odds, the plan worked.

Epilogue

1 Year Later

MANDY PULLS UP to the gates of the old Hawthorne Bluff Club and smiles when she sees the club's new sign, freshly printed and hung over the entrance: THE DELTA COUNTY COMMUNITY CLUB.

One of the new guards is working this morning, and she laughs to herself while the flustered man waves his hands, trying to capture the attention of a busload of screaming elementary school students so he can give them the rundown. She noticed the trip on the club's schedule yesterday—they are going on a hike through the south woods on the far side of the lake and touring the new nature center—the first group to do so after its official dedication last week. Mandy doesn't need his permission to pass through. The gates remain open during operating hours now.

The club is free for anyone who qualifies as low income, and family memberships are available at a reasonable fee for those who can afford it. Most county residents come for the walking trails and excellent fishing spots, but the new pickleball and tennis courts have attracted enough attention that the club is considering adding additional courts. Allison Hawthorne has proved to be an excelled President; she holds monthly community meetings and listens to the concerns of every resident who chooses to speak during them.

A few of the members immediately sold their houses after the scandal, which made them easily identifiable as the men who only stayed above the law because Chandler Hawthorne III *was* the law. Now that the men were being held accountable for their crimes, they didn't bother to stick around. Rumor is, most of them relocated to countries without extradition laws, in fear of Chandler and his two accomplices selling them out for a plea deal when they're caught.

The residents who stayed are surprisingly happy about the changes to the club's fundamental values and the inclusion of "outsiders" inside the gates. The restaurants, stores, bowling alley, and movie theater were reconfigured as employee-owned businesses, with all profits split evenly among the workers. Business has never been better.

Although the remainder of Chandler's assets were seized by the federal government, they didn't have much to take. They believe all three men emptied their accounts before fleeing the country. Allison was granted possession of the family home, but willingly turned over the deeds to both of their vacation homes located in warmer climates. She doesn't need or want them—she plans to remain in Michigan year-round. No longer worried about the threats Chandler has directed at her family, she purchased the home right next door to hers for her parents to live.

Mandy checks her watch. Just enough time to swing

into *Serendipity* to grab a latte before she's due at Allison's home. Although Remy went off to Northern Michigan University last fall and Mandy's only responsible for Frankie now, Allison insisted on continuing to pay her at the same rate. Frankie also has a new homeschooling teacher—Chef Regina, who has admitted she was never trained as a chef at all, but rather holds a degree in early childhood education. When Tanner falsified her resume to get her hired, she was annoyed with him for choosing a chef background. "Fake it 'til you make it," she told Mandy over dinner one night, recalling all the videos she watched online to prepare for her role. "I could barely make a grilled cheese when I got hired."

As Mandy's walking from her parked car to the coffee shop, she spots Tanner coming out of the Nightingale, where he teaches cybersecurity and scam awareness classes to the community members twice a month before the supper club opens for regular business hours. Mandy sat in on one a few weeks back, smiling when she saw Eunice Spencer, the elderly woman she prevented from falling for the grandparent gift card scam down at the Quick Stop. She was sitting in the front row and taking detailed notes. Tanner is doing a great service for this community, especially the older generation. He's used his skills for a lot of good in this world, and although they joked about it in their chats, he really is the Robin Hood of Delta County. The victims of the three men who disappeared that night are now financially comfortable, but various charities in the area have also received sizeable anonymous donations throughout the year, and Mandy is certain that Tanner is behind them. She's never asked him directly, because there are some secrets she's just better off not knowing.

"Hey, Mandy," he calls out when he sees her. She still remembers the first day they met, when she thought he resembled Glen Powell. She may not see it anymore, but he still makes her cheeks flush every time he says her name.

"Hey, Tanner, how did your class go today?"

He smiles as they stop in front of the coffee shop. "I never considered that storing things in the cloud was an overly difficult concept until I tried explaining it to a room of octogenarians at eight in the morning."

"You deserve a medal," Mandy says with a laugh, but she really means it. After the news broadcast ended that night one year ago, she turned to Tanner and asked, "Tell me the other two deserved it?"

Tanner's eyes grew dark for the first time since they met, and he said, "Mandy, if you knew the extent of what these men have done, you wouldn't rest until you knew they got what was coming for them."

That's all the confirmation she'd needed.

"Hey, I was wondering," Tanner begins, breaking eye contact with Mandy and kicking a small pebble on the sidewalk in front of him. "Would you maybe want to grab dinner, just you and me?"

Finally, she feels the rush that she's heard so many other women describe—the one that starts at the top of her head and travels all the way to her toes, causing rippling goosebumps in its wake.

"I'd love that," she replies, for once not worrying if she sounds too eager.

"Great, you pick the restaurant. Anywhere you want to go."

Mandy smiles. It doesn't matter, as long as it's with him.

When she enters the coffee shop, Georgia is seated at a corner table with Amelia and Dot. They've started a book club and, although their meeting this morning was supposed to be about discussing the latest John Marrs thriller, it appears they are knee-deep in gossip and have yet to even take their paperbacks out of their bags.

"Mandy," Georgia squeals when she sees her old neighbor. "Did you call the movers?"

"Yes, Georgia," she tells her for the third time this week. She knows the woman is just excited for Mandy to move to the club, so she's trying to have patience.

Braxton and Tanner bought the house next to theirs for the woman who raised them. After some prodding from them both, Mandy has agreed to move in and look after Georgia (not that she requires much looking after at all). Her one stipulation is that all three of their houses in town (two of which were purchased just to keep tabs on her) will become long-term rentals at an affordable rate so they can help three families in town who have been priced out of renting homes due to out-of-town investors. Everyone agreed, so long as Mandy is willing to be the landlord, and if she promises never to let anyone dig up Georgia's precious garden. The woman was incredibly adamant about that. Braxton has even reminded her a few times, which Mandy finds odd.

Mandy can't believe that after everything that's happened, she's going to be living at the Bluff and overseeing three rental properties. Never in her wildest dreams was this life a possibility.

Georgia stands to get herself a refill from the self-serve drip coffee station when Mandy pulls her aside.

"My mom's lawyer called me this morning. Not only has she suddenly been receiving undivided attention from the medical staff and put on a new medication, but they got word yesterday that her case is officially being reopened because the DA received new information. Would you happen to know anything about that?"

Georgia shrugs. "I'm just a harmless old lady; I can't

see how I'd know anything about an innocent woman possibly getting some justice after being imprisoned for a crime she didn't commit."

Mandy shakes her head. Unbelievable. Georgia sits back down with her friends while Mandy orders her latte. On her way out, she says goodbye to Dot and Amelia and turns to Georgia. "I'm only leaving so I'm not late for work. I'll deal with you later."

Georgia smiles.

Mandy's not sure how Georgia made it happen, but against all odds, her mother has renewed hope. Learning more about her mother's history at the club and Georgia's admission that Chandler Hawthorne had something to do with the death of her family caused Mandy to reach out and begin to repair her relationship with Skylar. It's not perfect, but she has begun to understand why her mom turned to drugs and alcohol to numb the pain of what happened to her while working for the club. When asked if there was a possibility that Chandler was the real father of her brother, Jeffrey—causing her to quit the club when she found out she was pregnant—her mother sobbed and admitted that she wasn't sure. The greatest gift she's given Skylar was to let her know that she did *not* kill Jack and Tilly Hawthorne in the fire, and that fire did *not* spread to the employee cabin that killed Jane and Charlene; a guilt she's been carrying with her for nearly thirty years.

Mandy pulls into her new parking spot, directly in Allison's driveway, with two minutes to spare. She smiles when she sees Allison sitting on the newly installed porch swing, staring into the distance with a cup of coffee resting on the blanket in her lap.

"Morning, Allison. Sorry I'm cutting it close; I ran into Georgia at Serendipity."

Allison scoots over and pats the spot next to her on the

swing. Mandy sets her bag on the porch and joins her, stealing a sip of the latte that's just now cool enough to try.

"Mandy, you don't ever have to be sorry. Regina is in there with Frankie doing math, anyway. I'm not even sure why you still come at nine."

"Because you pay me to come at nine," Mandy reminds her.

"How about I continue to pay you for eight hours, but you come at eleven, when Frankie is ready for her lunch?"

"Why are you so good to me?" Mandy asks.

She has somehow become friends with the woman she never dreamed she'd have common ground with. She spent most of her life in love with Wes, but sometime in the last year she learned to see that love exactly as he did: as family. She could not be happier for the love he found with Allison; a love that no longer had to be kept under wraps.

Allison takes a deep breath. "Mandy, you've been told most of what went on inside these gates, but I'm not foolish enough to think it only happened here. Georgia told me how horrible your ex-husband was, and that's just one story in a million. For years, us women have just shut up and taken it. Took the hand we were dealt because we didn't think we deserved more. That night, the night of the fires, they shouldn't have had to flee with Jack. They did nothing wrong. I'm not sure how Chandler got wind of the plan, but there's no doubt in my mind that's why he killed them both. In his mind, women should have never fought back; they should just sit back and take it. After what happened last year, we decided enough was enough and we stayed. We stayed without them and took over. The club is now a happy place, one where nobody ever has to feel afraid. For years, we felt the need to run. We don't have to run anymore."

"Do you ever regret it?" Mandy asks.

"Not for a minute."

Allison has never come out and told her that Wes and his cousin Rex buried the three men underneath the pickle ball courts, or that she's responsible for any of the anonymous tips about those men being spotted abroad, alive and well, but Mandy has enough sense not to ask. She has spent an entire year coming to terms with everything she learned in the basement that night. She still has so many questions, questions she has created answers for because she can't bring herself to ask.

Apparently, the other members of the Bluff really did think Braxton's and Tanner's house was owned by a successful scam artist, but most of them were running their own scams within the corporate world, so they kept their mouths shut and minded their own business. Braxton was just a child when he would visit his mother at work, so nobody recognized him when he'd show his face periodically inside the gates. She wonders how Tanner got into the house at night, but between most members being gone half the year and Tanner himself in charge of the security footage, she can assume it wasn't as hard as one would think.

She also wonders how Wes got involved, how much Allison's kids know, and how exactly Georgia and her husband staged the car accident that killed Chandler Jr. and his wife, but none of these questions matter now because she's actually enjoying being blissfully unaware for once. Her thoughts did begin to race when she received a call from her former sister-in-law, Dee, in January, letting her know that their mother had passed, and they couldn't get ahold of Patrick. When Mandy asked how long it had been since she heard from her brother, Dee said it was last year when he texted to let them know he had met someone and was moving out of town immediately. When Mandy relayed the story to Wes, she could swear he was fighting back a smile when he shrugged his shoulders.

Speak of the devil, Wes jogs up the path to the house and climbs the front stairs, saying good morning and kissing Allison's forehead before taking a seat in the wicker chair next to the porch swing.

Again, all the signs she missed are dancing through her mind, taunting her for being so foolish. Remy gushing at the Quick Stop about how much he respects his father yet shaming his mother for being submissive. Remy's resentment toward Chandler. Frankie's attachment to Wes. His undeniable bond with the kids.

"I still can't believe you have children, Wes. You're such a good dad," Mandy says. He also raised a very good actor, as Mandy later found out that Remy knew just about everything, the entire time. One afternoon a few months back, Wes and Mandy had a long talk about his oldest child over lunch:

"We were so mad when we found out Remy was coming to see you at the gas station. We had gone on a fishing trip, and I told him everything about my childhood —how we were best friends, and I saved you from the fire. I told him about your mom and what she did. I don't know what got into me, but I just spilled my guts and told him everything. He's my son; he deserved to know. Well, curiosity got the best of him, and he tracked you down the minute he got his driver's license. We actually didn't find out about it until after you started working here."

Mandy watches Wes swipe a few crumbs off Allison's lap from the muffin she consumed before they arrived. He's always been a standup guy, and now he has a woman who will never have to wonder what it's like to be loved and cared for every minute of the day.

"It sounds like my mom may be getting a new trial. Can you believe it – after all these years?"

"I always had a feeling that someone outside the trailer had set the fire, but I was twelve and nobody would have listened to me, even if I had proof. I know I was half asleep, but I have these memories that come in flashes, voices outside my window and squealing tires. I wanted to tell you so many times, but I didn't want to cause any more stress in your life than you already had. Years later, when I met Georgia and she told me what she knew, it all made sense. I was on board to make that asshole pay for what he'd done."

"But, by that point, Chandler and his wife had already died in Florida," Mandy points out.

"I'm not talking about him; I'm talking about his son. He's the one who identified your mom, and I wouldn't be surprised if he's the one who lit the fire. From what Allison and Georgia told me, his dad didn't like to get his hands dirty when he didn't have to. He was already on my radar and once I found out he was abusing Allison, among other women, I became hyper-focused on taking him down. That's why I refused to leave the property; I had to stay as close to Allison and the kids as possible so I could keep an eye on them until the danger was removed from their lives."

Mandy directs her gaze forward at the partial view of the lake, obstructed a little more each day as the trees and flowers bloom around the property. She feels slightly nauseated before an unexpected wave of peace washes over her. She's surrounded by people who care about her, people who stood up to injustice, even when it was the hardest thing they'd ever done.

She remembers all the nights she walked Murphy up and down the sidewalks downtown, peering in the windows of strangers and creating little stories for them all, theories of what their lives must be like. She'll never make that mistake again, thinking she knows someone's story based on what she sees from the outside.

All the events of the past year have taught her that the hardest battles are often fought quietly, behind the scenes. The most important thing to remember is when it seems that all hope is lost; that's when you need to keep fighting.

"In revenge and in love, woman is more barbarous than man."
-Frederick Nietzsche

Acknowledgments

Dear reader, whether this is your first book of mine or you've been around for years — there aren't words for how grateful I am that you're here. I'm still convinced there's some sort of mix up and there's no possible way this is my life. Thank you for allowing me to continue to tell stories for a living. I'll never take it for granted.

For my friends, family, and the love of my life: thank you all for being patient, supportive, and honest.

My books are infinitely better thanks to the following people: Carly, Erika, Brandon, and Raven. You four are so good at what you do; I'm just lucky to know you.

To the bookstores, libraries, and gift shops who carry my books: you're helping me prove that self-published authors do belong on bookshelves and I'll forever be grateful for your support.

Whether it's Goodreads, social media, or wherever you purchase and review your books — I cannot thank you enough for your kind words. Soliciting reviews is my least favorite part of this job and you all have been kind enough to help me spread the word by posting yours.

If you have any questions or would just like to reach out, my email is info@jlhyde.com or you can shoot me a DM on Instagram, Facebook, or TikTok!

Thank you for reading; I'll be back in the summer of 2025 with my 10th novel. It's a story I can't wait to tell.

Printed in Great Britain
by Amazon

60204882R00160